G. H. KARSHNER

Symphony in Blood and Rust

First edition

ISBN: 979-8-9999083-0-8

This book was professionally typeset on Reedsy.
Find out more at reedsy.com

To Chris, Elijah, Isabelle, Maxwell

Definition of Marga:
1: Hinduism: one of several ways of approaching salvation — compare bhakti-marga 2: Eight-fold path
—Merriam-Webster

"Marga is someone who you might always need in your life, , if she cares for you she will take care of you and put you before her even though sometimes it hurts her. ... She wants perfection so much it can break her, your job is to be there to collect the pieces."

—Urban Dictionary

Contents

"Because I know that time is always time
    And place is always and only place
    And what is actual is actual only for one time
    And only for one place...
    Consequently I rejoice, having to construct something
    Upon which to rejoice..."
    —T. S. Eliot, *Ash Wednesday*

1

Solutions

Forgive me for starting in Cleveland, but everything has to start somewhere. Whether here or there, it's always some place, even if that's a non-place—the kind of generic space whose architectural design could be reproduced from a rubber stamp. Airports are generally non-places, unless it's Singapore Airport, which is *really* someplace. As a rule, shopping malls are also non-places. But in the heart of downtown Cleveland, lost in time and space, there sits a singular someplace called The Old Arcade: a grand Victorian cast-iron and glass structure built in 1890 as the first indoor mall in America.

The roof of the Old Arcade is one giant skylight made of thousands of panes of glass that allow a cloud-filtered gray illumination throughout the open atrium down to the ground floor. Balcony railings are the original brass attached to ornamental cast iron posts and the spaces between are filled with wrought iron filigree now covered in gold paint. Corridor walls are clad with white marble slabs that have been painted over, stripped, covered in wood panels and re-exposed numerous times, depending on the fashion trends of interior decorators over the decades. On the three lower floors, there are some swanky hotel rooms as well as commercial spaces where one can get a cup of coffee or a haircut and browse an art gallery.

On the fourth floor, there are offices where people go only if they have a specific need. One of these upper offices has a starburst-textured glass window with gold lettering that spells out the name of a company: "SRT Solutions." Behind that door, the owner, Amity Halifax, 26, sifts and sorts through rows and columns of data points she has extracted from the dark web. Amity created SRT Solutions right after she finished her PhD dissertation in quantum psychology and theoretical physics. How she defines "solutions" is her secret, as is the source of her funding.

None of Amity's friends or family knows exactly what her business is. Still, they are all too sheepish to ask the obvious questions—after all, Amity is a member of MENSA, and responds to most silly questions with a musical little laugh and a beautiful smile that reveals perfect, white teeth. We recently got engaged to be married, so Amity checked that item off her to-do list.

I suppose I am an average man, tolerable in most every way, with an average amount of healthy curiosity—unlikely to interest a woman with an intellect like Amity's, except for the fact that I am also a composer, which puts me into that mysterious category of creative genius: someone whose talents cannot be measured with an IQ test. Unlike Amity's brilliance which is like solid gold bars—weighed, measured, and perfectly molded; hallmarked, neatly stacked, and sorted; highly polished, reflective, and radiant; their worth variable, but objectively valuable—my treasure is like a pirate's sea chest spilling over with ducats, doubloons, and a boodle of precious doodads, not weighed out like a commodity showing the purity of the pour or the uniformity of the mold, but reflecting instead the creative brilliance that artists' inspired hands have shaped over the centuries: festooned with jewels, overflowing with strings of pearls, bracelets and earrings with glittering rubies and emeralds, and buckets full of diamonds. My worth is objectively incalculable.

I enter without knocking.

"What are you working on?" I ask. Amity laughs, smiles, and accepts my kiss without rising from her chair. (I want to know. I want to brag about the amazing work my beautiful fiancée is engaged in.) I run my fingers through her soft blonde hair and massage the nape of her neck. "Seriously. What are you working on?" "A project," she answers, "a boring project." I am not willing to accept that pat answer today. Since our engagement, I have developed a sense that I am entitled to a deeper level of trust and disclosure. "I really *am* interested in what you are doing, you know, and I *do* have the capacity to understand. There's nowhere you could go that I couldn't follow."

Amity seems annoyed and stares at me intensely, then smiles, pulls out a summary margin legal pad full of numbers and diagrams, and launches into a professorial monologue. Without any context, it is impossible for me to follow with any utility. I can only remember certain words because of their peculiar musicality: "anisotropic spin," "leading edge flutter," and "ionic pocket." Amity ends with a smug smile which, it seems to me, has a sadistic quality. "Any questions?" she asks. "Yes," I say. "What precisely?" "Too many to be precise," I say, which serves as an effective conversation stopper. Amity abruptly transitions to cheerful chit-chat about dinner plans.

"Tonight, pick me up at 7:15 and then I'll tell you where we are going," she says. "Wear the navy blue suit, white shirt, and the new tie I gave you." I understand this to mean that she has bought a new dress, probably aquamarine to accent her eyes, and she needs my outfit to complement hers. I know better than to question; her ideas are always better than mine—on these fashion kinds of things. I also know that if I follow her instructions, we will look wonderful to whomever can afford to eat at the restaurant she will choose.

Amity's computer plays two tones, an F-sharp and a B-flat, and her monitor screen turns gray displaying only one word: *Incoming.* "I'm a little fatigued," she says while putting on her headset, "Would you mind picking up a caffè mocha for me at Arabica?" I nod. It's time for me to disappear.

When I walk into the hall and lean over the railing, I can smell the fresh roasted coffee from the second floor, then I realize that I don't have any money, and I've left my phone in the little anteroom next to Amity's office. I turn the knob slowly so as not to disturb her, and catch only her side of the call.

"Well, naturally. A certain amount of electrical mass reduction will produce those optical effects. Right, what you called, 'warble.' And the light rolls through the spectrum to blue until it's charged, *then* it transitions to white. No. It's unlikely that the photon shedding can be eliminated without putting frequency in-phase which would double the energy requirement and might weaken the leading edge on acceleration. *Or*, it might actually cloak it. Yeah, invisibility, wouldn't that be great? Definitely need practical *and* drop-shift testing. Next week? Oh sure. Subcontract for ICI? Got it. Wonderful! I'm looking forward to finally meeting the team. See you then. Bye-bye."

B-flat. F-sharp.

Amity takes off her headset and turns to find me standing here.

She's wearing a big smile, but not the 'I'm-so-happy-to-see-you' kind of smile, more like an 'I-just-landed-a-big-contract' businessy sort of smile. Obviously she has forgotten that she sent me out for a caffè mocha-style wild goose. And I'm not going to remind her.

"I have a little cleaning up to do here. Why don't you go home and get ready?"

"I think you have a good idea, Amity."

"Always do!" Smile. Kiss. Turn away. "See you at..."

"Seven fifteen," I finish.

* * *

Dinner is at the newly reopened and retro Top of the Town on the 38th floor of Erie View Tower. I have spent too many conversations with friends ragging on about the limitations of this city, but at this moment, looking out over the sparkling lights of late night office workers, Shoreway travelers, and family dining rooms, I have to admit—Cleveland has its charm. But then again, it's only fall; I can't guarantee I'll feel so positive come winter.

I skip the sauerkraut balls and go straight for the Caesar salad and filet mignon. Amity has *coquille Saint Jacques* and asparagus. For wine we split the difference and get a Blush Cabernet. By the end of dinner I am feeling a little groggy and excuse myself to splash some cold water on my face in the men's room. When I return, the waiter is clearing dishes and I wait a few steps behind him. A middle-aged man, a salesman type with too many single malt scotches under his belt, has cruised up to the table to take advantage of my absence and hit on Amity. He's not very creative though. Looking out the window he says to my fiancée, "Look at all those lights. How many do you suppose there are?" Amity answers, "Why don't you count them?" The cruiser is still sober enough to know he hasn't a chance, and returns to the bar. At this moment I am awed by Amity's presence and feel proud to be with her.

The waiter returns with some tiny cakes on pretty little dishes artistically splashed with black currant syrup, a sprig of mint, and a coin-shaped slice of Swiss chocolate embossed with its brand name: *Suchard.* The wine has loosened me up a bit, and made me forget about my money troubles, and how high this fantasy meal must be racking up Amity's bill.

With the city lights twinkling in my peripheral vision, I stare at Amity, and try to drink in the beauty of this woman and this moment. For an instant I see her as she looked when we were teens, and that feeling of "being in love" slowly radiates from a warm place in my chest. Unfortunately, this sensation quickly dissipates when I remember that—according to Doctor of Psychology Amity Halifax—"The feeling of being in love is just a phenomenon called *limerance*, and limerance consists of one part attraction and three parts fear, and is therefore, necessarily transitory."

But arguably, necessary.

When we finish with dessert and coffee, the waiter presents the bill. Amity scans it for errors and lays a black American Express credit card on the little tip tray. The waiter, who has obviously never seen one, raises his eyebrows as he walks it over to show the *maître d'*.

"He thinks those are only for high rollers."

"I guess that's me," Amity says. "Are you ready to roll? Oh, by the way, I have to go out of town next week, so please water the plants."

"Wait. Where are you going?"

"New York," she says. "Not the City, farther upstate, a place called Iron Mountain."

"Sounds ominous. What's the occasion?"

"Just some training. I landed a nice little contract for International Computation Industries."

"What have they to do with psychology?" (When we're in public I speak with a serious and formal tone—Amity likes that.)

"Nothing, well nothing directly. It's a project involving theoretical physics. Remember my dual degree?"

Something seems off. There is a hiccup in time and we stare at each other—immobile and silent, my eyes seeking and hers blocking. It's like there's a glitch in her software and I'm waiting for the cursor to start blinking again. There is something she's not telling me and it makes me very uncomfortable. As Uncle Dan once said, "You don't have to tell your wife everything you do, but you shouldn't do anything that you couldn't tell your wife." I wonder what it is that Amity can't tell me. In her silence, Amity thinks she is reading my mind.

"Oh Jonathan, my brilliant and handsome man. I'll only be gone for two or three weeks." Then she reaches across the table and places her hand on mine.

I wonder if all good marriages revolve around such odd pathos.

2

Arrives Marga

Arrives Marga—new red hair and smiles:

"Been a long time. Always been crazy mad about you. May I come in?"

"*Entrez vous,*" I say, and wave her in with a diplomatic flourish.

"Do you always open your door to strangers?" she asks.

"Depends on how strange. Besides, I recognized your scratching."

In our college dorm, Marga Delaunay lived down the hall from me and she never knocked. If my door were locked, she would scratch on the wood from top to bottom with her cherry-red epoxied fingernails that she kept sharpened to dagger-like points. Marga said our student neighbors were nosy and she could see the light in the peep holes dim from their shadowed eyes when she walked down the corridor. She never knocked because she didn't want those busybodies to make up rumors that we were lovers—which we weren't—but the rumors *did* go around which annoyed her which delighted me. Marga was unflappable, and I found her efforts to control a flap to be entertaining. Only once did I see her almost lose her composure.

It was at Severance Hall after the debut of my *Sinfonietta for Strings in G*, the final requirement for my MFA in composition from the Cleveland Institute of Music. Marga was there with her father, Lance, whom she calls, "The absent-minded brain surgeon." He really is a brain surgeon, but only absent-minded when forced by social conventions into boring conversations that involve any topic other than carving up brains. Small talk sends him straight to the bathroom where he keeps several issues of the *New England Journal of Medicine* and a dog-eared copy of that classic book by neurologist Oliver Sacks: *The Man Who Mistook His Wife for a Hat.*

Lance likes me—I think because I'm genuinely interested in the things people love, and so I ask him lots of questions about his work, then listen attentively for the love. I suspect he also views me as a potential son-in-law, or maybe a lab assistant. But it was after my concert, while Amity was still waiting in line for the ladies' room, that Lance came with Marga to the Green Room to congratulate me and he tweaked Marga by inadvertently calling her by her real name. Her face went ghost-white, then tomato-red, while her eyes revealed that she was closely observing her own reactions so that she would never have those reactions again. (Mercifully, a waiter broke her trance with a glass of *Liebfraumilch*.) There is nothing unusual about Marga's real name—which is probably why she hates it. But I have never mentioned that name since then, and it now hangs above us and unites us like unspoken confidential knowledge shared by two secret agents.

This morning, Marga stands with her hands behind her turning the doorknob while she slowly backs up, quietly closing the door to my studio apartment and engaging the deadbolt— never once taking her eyes off of mine. Her look is one of guilt and seduction, but I have learned not to take this seriously. Marga is a performance artist and a master of looks. Outside it is sunny but cold and Marga is wearing a heavy, oatmeal-colored, cable-knit, Irish fisherman's sweater over a jade green angora sweater over a cream-colored cotton turtleneck, and loose, ripped jeans over black tights and she looks...

"Can I take off these clothes," she asks while in the process, "and snuggle with you on that bed?"

"We're just friends. Remember?" I ask, but she's already stripped down to the turtleneck and tights and climbed under the blanket. She pats the mattress next to her and says, "Hurry."

It's Saturday at 10 AM and I'm not tired, but I obey and cozy up next to her. She smells faintly of autumn leaves and automotive grease, and one long green pine needle stands out against the redness of her hair. I gently remove it and place it on the nightstand as a souvenir. I rub her back and feel the smoothness of her skin through the thin cotton of the turtleneck. Marga bolts around to face me with a serious look.

"Antoine, I really like you and I value our relationship too much to get physically involved with you. Every romance I've ever had, has ended disastrously. Can we just cuddle and sleep and still be friends?"

"What do you think? Can we share a bed and just sleep?"

"I think it will be hard, but let's."

"Just one thing, Marga."

"What's that?"

"I don't mind you giving me a new name, as long as it's not the name of one of your European boyfriends."

"Yes Trotwood," she says with a smirk and exhales into a deep sleep.

Breathing in her industrial yet female bouquet, I feel a peaceful, almost meditative calm, and out of fear of breaking it, I do not move.

3

Dunch

Some hours later when the wind blows, I hear acorns thwacking on the roofs and hoods of cars in the parking lot below. When I struggle to extricate my dead sleeping arm from under her pillow, Marga awakens, smiling.

"What's for lunch?"

"It's five in the afternoon."

"Really?" she asks, rustling her hair and pulling it back through her fingers which tightens her face and makes her look more awake, "So, what's for dunch?"

"I usually just eat at the diner," I say. "I don't have much here beyond coffee, but you're welcome to whatever you can find in the fridge or the cupboard."

So Marga makes a lot of noise moving around empty containers and dishes and generally acts as if it were her own apartment. She checks a half bag of flour and announces: "Good—no bugs." Then takes out the olive oil and some sweet Japanese plum wine—a gift I'd kept unopened because of its beautiful, white porcelain bottle painted with sakura blossoms. She adds some of the oil and wine to the flour and works it into long snake-like rolls of dough, coils them, presses the coils into disks, and fries them in the cast iron skillet. When they are golden brown, she rubs the tops with more plum wine, sprinkles them with white sugar from little packets she's found in the junk drawer, and uses the broiler to make them crisp. We sit on the secondhand Queen Anne love-seat and eat from a low coffee table in my sunny yellow kitchen. With the strong Ethiopian coffee from the flip drip espresso pot I picked up at Goodwill, it ranks as one of the best dunches I've ever eaten.

"Now that you've had a nap and a good snack, will you be off again?" I ask.

"You make it sound like I came here just to sleep."

"Didn't you?" Marga pauses to cross her legs and her skin glows through the shiny tights.

"I wasn't sure that I *would* sleep today, or eat, or that you would even be home, or alone," Marga says while examining the bottom of the coffee saucer, "Wedgwood. Generous. By the way, where is she, your mathematician?"

"Amity is away on business for 'Icy', International Computation Industries. Three weeks in Iron Mountain."

"She won't come back you know," Marga says matter-of-factly.

"Yeah she will. In three weeks."

"Maybe. But one of these days, she won't come back. Icy keeps that mountain stocked not only with food and office supplies, but also with healthy, fertile *Übermenschen* and *Übermädchen* of a certain type—*her* type—to repopulate the planet after the feces hit the fan. They're probably matching her up with a company man as we speak."

"Marga, I do believe you're jealous."

"Jealous? If I wanted to own you, I would have done it by

now."

I laugh, but it's nervous laughter because I know she's right. Anyone who hangs around Marga for more than a few minutes wants to stay around her for a long time. Some women (and men) get jealous because she attracts so much attention—even though she tries not to. I have sometimes thought that her ever-changing styles might be a ploy to deflect attention by making herself a moving target, but in fact, she is attractive *because* she is so unpredictable. We wait for her to speak, never knowing what she will say next; we watch how she moves because each movement seems choreographed; we make note of her dress because we know she is setting trends for the next generation of clothing designers.

With another woman, a totally different one, I might question her mental stability, but with Marga, the *non sequiturs* are logical—not proceeding linearly like a syllogism, but logical in multiple dimensions—and sometimes one needs to wait patiently over several visits to see the genius of her mind developed. And when, in protecting her boundaries she hurts our feelings, especially when she hurts our feelings, we want to stay with her until she applies her social healing balm and accepts us once again. As the hipsters say in their abstract and non-committal language of androgyny, "We have a special relationship."

Marga slides the coffee table away and stands up. "Leave those," I say referring to the cups and saucers. Her eyes express the slightest annoyance that lets me know she wasn't even considering washing the dishes. I am still sitting, watching—a performance has begun. She moves closer, takes my head in her hands and slides her fingers into my disheveled black coif. "Your hair is so much softer than it looks," she says in a liquid voice just above a whisper. Pressing my head against her bosom she says, "I'm so glad you're here for me, Jonathan." Then she caresses my cheek and cradles it against her breast as if I were her child. Her smell is intoxicating and I feel euphoric. I put my arms around her and feel the curves of her waist and hips. She slowly takes hold of my arms and says in that still soft voice, "Feel good?"

"Um hmm, very."

"Then we'd better stop," she says and quickly disengages from my embrace.

"Right. What was I thinking?" I say, "And what am I supposed to do with this feeling?" "Use it," she says, "I want you to write some music. For my next performance. And it has to be beautiful, and optimistic, and as loving of life as a dawn chorus of robins, cardinals, and thrushes. I'm tired of darkness. I want something bright."

I take a deep breath, wipe my face with my hands and rub my eyes which are dry from too much sleep. I struggle to recall the sounds of bird songs and make mental notes of rhythms, cadences, and timbres. When I look up, Marga is dressed and putting on her purple Doc Marten boots.

"I have to go," she says. "Tonight Lance and I are hob nobbing with the nabobs. I'm really looking forward to hearing your new, bright composition."

Her words deconstruct in my mind:

"Looking forward to hearing...Looking to hearing...Look here...Hear hear...Bright."

Maybe I'll write an opera, or a choral piece.

4

Assignment

Marga's request, rather, her assignment, is a welcome challenge. I've wanted to write a piece for voice ever since I heard *The Super*, Laurence Gilderman's opera about the life of a Manhattan janitor. Gilderman's piece is a singular work of genius. There is a section in that opera where he has the chorus sing whale songs to represent the groaning of radiator steam pipes. But I will need a quicker tempo and less submarine chord progressions to capture the mood of morning birds.

Funny, Marga wanting something cheerful and bright. She always seemed to be fascinated by the dark stuff. I guess every college student has some ghosts that need to be exorcised. Perhaps she's beyond that now. Purged herself with a year abroad in Berlin. Wants to start a new direction. That's understandable. I do too. But it's so much easier to move an orchestra audience with sad music. Critics throughout history have preferred the *Pathétique* to the *Playful Pizzicato*. And the listening public typically conflates sadness with depth. If only they knew how difficult it is to write serious music that expresses joy. Mozart did it, but that just proves my point. Rock and roll is the music of *joie de vivre*, but how deep can you go with *Louie Louie* and *La Bamba*? Rock is also the music of angst, but angst is just a wrestling match between emptiness and reason.

My writer friend Enzo says that the theme of most serious literature is loss. That's the way of the world I guess—the way of all flesh. Anyone who really understands the terminal quality of life will find *that* reality raining on every parade that he or she organizes. That's why I never venture too deeply into philosophy. But understanding mortality is not enough; one needs to accept the ultimate fate and then put that knowledge aside and be grateful for every blazing moment of life right up to the end—like Meursault's blissful anticipation of the onlookers' "howls of execration" as he is led to the guillotine. And even *he,* up to that point, was too damn numb with fear of death to appreciate his life.

So here I am, sitting in Mocha Moe's Campus Cafe, straining to hear bird calls through my earbuds over the sounds of a latte steamer, and poorly transposing those aural shapes into a music notebook. I'm sure there is an app that can do the transcription for me, but I don't want to get it *exact*—after all, this isn't pro-grammatic music, and I'm not writing a Renaissance madrigal. This is metaphysical. I want to interpret the joy inherent in nature, to get to the source of the birds' *mood.* I should probably wake up earlier and hear the real thing. If Amity were in town, I would suggest that we take a weekend in the country so I could hear the birds. But Amity is in Iron Mountain and working weekends.

Is it me, or is the crowd is this coffee shop getting younger every day?

5

Missed Connection

My phone was in airplane mode and I missed Amity's call. Since her new incarnation as a corporate executive, I'm beginning to think I'm missing her altogether. We met formally a decade ago at her Sweet 16 party, and all through high school we were on the same page. In college, we chose different majors; we were on different pages of the same book: we still shared that portion of our identities that was "student." But now that we have graduated, we are each becoming someone new. We are creating the ones we are becoming. We are choosing to become people we never were, and I hardly recognize myself, let alone Amity. I long for some familiarity, and there is less and less each day. That's probably why I recently felt the urge to get engaged—I want to stop the clock and hold on to what we've got.

It's still her voice, her face, but I don't recognize the score anymore. It's as if someone took the music that was Amity—classical, orderly, harmonious—and rewrote it for popular consumption: Mozart's 40th Symphony set to a synthesized dance beat, then tonally dialed down and rolled out in lo-fi for an upscale hipster cocktail lounge. I punch in voicemail and the message begins.

"Is this the phone of the soon-to-be-famous composer, Jonathan Brendel? Hi Jonathan! *C'est moi*, Amity. You must be *so* busy writing a new masterpiece. It must be super! I can't wait to hear it. Just don't expect me to know the allegros from the allegrettos. You know, music never really was my *forte*, but I do love anything *you* do."

(Does she even know what I do? The saccharine message continues.)

"We're *so* busy here with all the training, but it really is super! Everyone is *so* nice. There's a guy named Edmund and his initials are E.T. and we all kid him about being an alien. He said, 'Well, I may be turning a little *gray*.' He's *so* funny! I think you'll really like him. He's just super! When I finish here, they're sending us to Texas for more training. Rumor has it that everyone in my cohort will be promoted after the next round. I'm *so* jazzed! I may have to stay here a few more days, or a week even—we are just *so* busy. Oh, I can't call during the week because there is no reception inside Iron Mountain, it's like a giant Faraday cage, but I'll call you again next week when they let us out to have dinner in town. So, have fun, but not too much fun! Love you! Bye-e."

Bye-e. Bye-e. I suppose by now she has checked "Call Jonathan" off her to-do list.

And "*Super!*" Wherever did she pick up that ejaculation? My throat tightens like it did the first time I smoked a cigarette, and my stomach grumbles with a hunger between loneliness and grief. In a few weeks I'll probably get invited to a cocktail party for up-and-coming ICI executives and their significant others. And there will be a big athletic Scandinavian with graying temples who will look me squarely in the eyes and use his squash-racquet grip to try to crush the bones in my right hand. And he'll say, "Well, Jonny Brendel. What a pleasure; Amity has told me so much about you."

I get a sickening vision of the two of them, out on a 12-hour pass from Iron Mountain, sitting in an Italian restaurant in Kingston, New York sharing a bottle of Chianti over a red-glass votive candle from the Dollar Store—the whole ridiculous, jealous fantasy swimming in a miasma of garlic butter and *linguine alla vongole.* But in his eyes I read what ET is thinking: "What's a sharp girl like Amity doing with a loser like you? Composer, my balls! What are you really Jonny, a waiter? I bet you don't even have an IRA account." Instead he asks,

"Are you a member of MENSA too?"

"No."

"Pity that."

* * *

It's ten o'clock and Mocha Moe's Campus Cafe is closing. I've been here for three hours and haven't seen anyone I know, and nobody has recognized me. There was a time in undergrad when I held court in this place. The music students, the dancers, the theater majors, and even the painters-slash-performance artists from Cleveland State and the Cleveland Institute of Art all came here and all knew me. Even a lousy stage piece looked good if it had my music to shape it. And I happen to know there are a couple of choreographers who aced their final performance projects simply by having their dancers react to my aural inspiration. I knew what they were doing. And I drove their movements where I wanted them to go. But that was over two years ago. Now I'm almost 26. Now I'm competing with my former professors for commissions and grant money. Now I feel old.

"Yes I know you're closing. Yes please take this cup. Yes it is finished."

$$* * *$$

I had hoped to walk around the lagoon at the Museum of Art and see the autumn colors reflected on the water, but I stayed too long in Mocha Moe's and the only reflections are of LED street lights: steely and cold. I am alone, and the mood is all wrong. In the car I reach for the seat belt, push myself up to adjust my coat, and the heel of my shoe punches through the rusted floor.

6

Prelude to the Evening of a Wolf

When I get home I check my mailbox and find a single postcard
from Amity. She writes: "Having a 'super' time!" (Yes, she
put 'super' in quotes.) "Wish Iron Mountain were closer to you!
Ciao! Amity." (And she drew a smiley face.) I flip the card over.
It is a commercial promotional item with a view looking down a
wooded road at two huge shining steel vault doors installed in
the side of a mountain whose top is out of frame. Three words
are printed in hazard yellow beneath the picture: "Security,
Dependability, Permanency."

I sniff and say out loud, "What about *Liberté, Égalité, Frater-
nité?*"

And even *I* don't know what I mean.

I trudge up the flight of stairs to my apartment feeling as
though I were wearing ankle weights and shackles. There is a
note written on the inside of an empty cigarette pack jammed
into the crack between my door and the door frame. The note
reads, "Jack, I'm here, where are you?" It's from my friend
Jimmy Strong; nobody else calls me Jack. Once inside, I drop my
laptop backpack next to the bed and fling the postcard toward the

22

coffee table. It slices through space, banks, hits the wall beside a framed photograph of Amity, and falls behind the radiator. Just below the heater's cast iron ribs, the smiley face looks out toward my bed. There is a knock at the door.

"Open up, Jack! It's the police. We know you're in there."

I open the door to find Jimmy leaning against the wall smoking a cigarette. He is dressed in an extreme slim-fit suit with a skinny black tie and two-tone shoes. The jacket has been tailored to end just above his hips in a style called the "Ike" jacket, similar to what General Eisenhower wore in WWII. His hair is combed straight back with a slight pompadour up front. With a different pair of shoes, he could pass for the singing toreador in Bizet's *Carmen*.

"Cool it knucklehead. My neighbors might believe you, especially with how you dress."

Jimmy is a retro-rockabilly singer/songwriter I met in a notation class. He audited the class to learn just enough to write down his songs so that he could register them for copyrights. Most Saturday nights he's at Phallacy Nightclub in Lakewood, either performing or picking up groupies. Tonight he's walking into my apartment at quarter past eleven, checking every room and detail.

"Where is she Jack?"

"Who?" Jimmy points to the framed picture of Amity above the radiator.

"That hot blonde you keep hidden away. Is she bound and gagged in the closet?"

"Jimmy, the judge who released you from reform school should be impeached."

"Ha ha! You know it's true, admit it, you like that shady gray stuff."

"C'mon man—the way you look at women requires a notarized consent form."

"So where is she?"

"Away on business for the next two or three weeks. How did you get in without buzzing?"

"I came in the back way, through the laundry room. All these buildings are open."

"So what brings you here, no gigs?"

"Nah, nothing happening at Phallacy. I'm trying to stay sober. Thought we could grab a cup of coffee."

They say that if you get a drunken horse thief to stop drinking, you will have a sober horse thief. Jimmy is a pathological extrovert who tends to drink too much. He calls me when he wants to stay sober. Memories of past coffees with Jimmy flash through my mind: like the time he stole a gallon jar of pink pickled eggs from a deli counter and delivered them to the pizza shop across the street, or when we walked into IHOP at two in the morning and he belted out a few bars of his song *Born on Booze* at a volume worthy of *The Lion King* on Broadway. I try to think of a safe place we might go, maybe The Egg Palace: a vanilla shell of a greasy spoon that after midnight fills up with flamboyant drag queens, newbie punk rockers, and Goth vampires dressed in Vantablack hoping to suck all the light out of the crowd for their inverted pleasure.

Maybe some other night.

I tell Jimmy that it has been a weird day, that I've had too much coffee already, and that it's kind of late to start again. He takes Amity's picture off the wall while I am talking and traces the outline of her lips with his index finger. He adopts a tone of faux serious concern. "I understand," he says looking sadly at the picture, "When the one you love is away, you feel incomplete.

Am I right, Jackie boy? Hey, we can just stay here and talk about your feelings. Maybe warm up some milk, and later do some needlepoint." I give him a look. Jimmy beams with a restrained laugh, shrugs his shoulders, then caps it with a mawkish, "Hey, I'm here for you baby."

I am about to surrender to cruising Cleveland till dawn with this insatiable wolf when a long scratching sound comes from the door. Even Jimmy is startled and asks me *sotto voce*, "They allow tigers in this building?"

I know who it is, but I'm surprised that she would drop by again so soon. After all, before this morning, I hadn't seen nor spoken with her since her visit to the green room. In fact, counting this morning, this is exactly the second time I've seen her in two years. I reach for the door knob, and Jimmy shakes his head 'no' as if he's really expecting a large jungle cat. I roll my eyes and open the door wide. Marga is instantly bathed in incandescent light that makes her cocktail dress shimmer. It's a style I saw once in a dentist's copy of *Vogue*: knee length, pleated, emerald-green satin, with an off-the-shoulder boat neck and a matching sash across the front. Her red hair is done up in Marilyn Monroe glamour curls. Her shoes are ecru-colored heels that match the small clutch bag she holds in front of her. Except for the high-gloss lipstick and eyeliner like a Pharaoh, she wears the face of a demure debutante. She is about to speak when she notices Jimmy standing behind me. Instead she just exhales a disappointed, "Oh."

I look and Jimmy is staring wide-eyed, absorbing the image of Marga in full-effect, and all he says is, "Red!" I try to make introductions, but Marga says everyone knows Jimmy. When Jimmy asks, "Do I know *you*?" Marga answers, "No. You don't."

Marga begins to apologize for interrupting something and

Jimmy motions for her to come in. "I was just leaving; gotta see a man about a gig or a dog or something." Out in the hallway he lets out a loud "Yeow!" like James Brown and spins on one foot in a BTS style K-Pop move imitating Michael Jackson. When he stops spinning he pulls the picture of Amity out of his jacket and kisses it. (The knucklehead stole Amity's picture!) "Jimmy, give that back," I yell in a forceful whisper. "No man, I'm doing you a favor." I give chase. As he moonwalks backwards down the corridor, Jimmy starts singing a line from *Mack the Knife:* "Well the line forms on the right, dear, now that *Jack* is, back in town." He runs down the stairs to the street, and I can hear him singing and laughing for about two blocks. Now as I walk down the corridor back to my place, I see the lights in the peep holes of my neighbors' doors dim from their shadowed eyes as they watch me pass by.

When I return to my studio apartment, Marga is still standing at the foot of my bed with clutch purse in hand. "Is this a bad time?" she asks. "Time? What is time?" I answer. Marga shakes her head and shrugs. "He's quite the rapscallion, isn't he?" she asks. "Jimmy? He's alright. He's a miscreant, but he has a certain charm. How did you get in without ringing the buzzer?"

"I came in the back way, through the laundry room." (Of course. Who needs keys?)

"How are the nabobs?" I ask.

"Same as always: dull and boring."

"Are you hungry?"

"No. We had dinner at Severance Hall. Lance is a 'Signature Supporter' which means he gets invited to every fundraiser. His woman friend is visiting from Boston. Can I stay here tonight?"

"Sure. You can have the bed; I'll get my sleeping bag and camp on the floor."

"No, I don't want to inconvenience you. You sleep on the bed. I'm not tired, so I'll just sit on the love-seat in the kitchen and read for a while. I flirted with a waiter and he gave me some packets of chamomile tea; would you like some?"

I am still thinking about Jimmy stealing my photograph of Amity; now I think about Amity in her nuclear bomb-shelter hotel room inside a mountain; now I think about Amity and ET sharing a couch in the hotel lobby, shoulders touching, reviewing their project notes. And now, *right now*, an Emerald Princess is sipping chamomile tea from a Wedgwood cup in my kitchen. My brain begins to fizz.

I feel pressure between my temples and so lie down, fully dressed, on top of the bedspread. From that angle, I can see Marga in the kitchen: the green of her dress, the red of her hair and lipstick, the lemon yellow wall paint behind her—colors so rich in their saturation that I can't be sure that this scene isn't a lucid dream. She takes a small paperback from her purse, probably the only thing she has in there besides her phone. It's a German book, a Bertolt Brecht play: *Mutter Courage und ihre Kinder*. Amity's smiley face stares at me from the postcard under the radiator. When I awake, the sun is shining, the door is ajar, and Marga is gone.

7

Amity's Return with Roses

Aside from the surprise visits from Marga and Jimmy, and the percussive sounds of acorns and buckeyes hammering micro dents into parked cars, there's been little entertainment here in the three weeks since Amity left. I haven't done any composing and almost forgot about the piece Marga asked me to write for her. One day at a time, I've successfully put off working on it, and only remember when I wake up early enough to catch the birds' singing. Today is one of those days. I hardly slept last night and was already awake for the dawn chorus when the alarm rang. Amity is coming back today on Amtrak and is supposed to call me when she's nearing the station so I can pick her up. I expected her early this morning, but it's already nine and she hasn't called. My text goes out without reply and my calls go to voicemail. There must be some delay.

My imagination takes dark flight. I remember that after one nasty rail disaster, Jimmy, with macabre humor, referred to the railroad as *Slamtrack*. I shake my head to shuck off the images of derailed cars falling off a rickety wooden trestle bridge into Pennsylvania's Grand Canyon. *Balderdash!* is the appropriate

19th century word to dismiss my steam-punk fantasy. Only the audio is believable: timbers snapping, scraping of steel against steel, Doppler effect stretching the screams of innocent victims as they fall, the rumble of tons of iron battering the river banks below.

No matter what John Cage might have said, not all sounds are music.

I start to get worried, so I call Amity's mother, I-cannot-tell-a-lie Lisa, who tells me that her daughter is sleeping. "The train arrived early and she didn't want to wake you, so she went to breakfast with some of her co-workers and I guess they had a few mimosas or Bloody Marys and so then they called for an Uber car," (somebody is knocking on my door) "and now Amity is sleeping it off and she will probably call you when she wakes up, is that OK?" Sure why not.

I toss the phone on the bed and answer the door. It's the widow Mrs. Finnegan, the landlord's rep. She's wearing her official uniform—a dusty black suit from the old days when she did clerical work in a carpet store.

"I'm here for the rent, Mr. Brendel. It's late."

"Right. I'm waiting for a check to clear the bank. Shouldn't be more than a few days."

"You're already a few days late. Rent is due on the first of every month, Mr. Brendel, not the fifteenth."

"Yes I know. I'm working on a new commission right now." She's not impressed.

"Oh, are you now. What's it called?"

"Uh, *Performance Mix*." She squints. "But that's just a working title. I'm thinking about renaming it *Finnegan's Mix*." She rolls her eyes.

"Well, with a name like that, it had best be good."

"Thank you for your patience Mrs. Finnegan."

"Patience is one thing, but to pay your bills, you've got to work."

Work.

I submitted applications for a National Endowment grant and a teaching fellowship, but those payoffs—if they come—are a long way out. Rent is due, and I'm damn near broke. I went online to post as a piano tutor, and browsed the Craig's List entries in that category. My competition includes soloists and accompanists from the orchestra, conservatory professors, and graduate performance majors working on PhDs. Right now, I'd settle for a piano playing gig in a honky-tonk if there were such a place in this town. In the meantime, my fiancée is sleeping off a train ride and some fashionable morning cocktails, and I'm getting hungry.

I go to the closet for my fishing rod and reel—vintage Garcia Mitchell—a gift from Amity. She often does that, looks over my shoulder while I'm browsing on eBay, sometimes even snaps a picture, or takes a look at what I've saved for later, and then buys it for me. She knows my passwords for everything (though I don't recall giving them to her). Over the years I've noticed that she likes to go shopping with me in the weeks before my birthday. She's very perceptive, has an excellent memory, and like a good AI program, takes note of whatever I hover over for more than a few seconds in the store. Later she returns to buy it for me. She's very generous in that way—she knows I can't afford much and she likes to be charitable. And so what? I'm selfish. I accept her gifts, but I always feel a little guilty because I can't reciprocate. I'd like to buy her a nice engagement ring, but the cheap ones cost about five grand. So I make a gift of a handwritten score of my original music. She doesn't really know the value of my original scores; how could she? As of today, they have no value. Does that make them invaluable or priceless? I've never understood these negative sounding yet positive words. Anyway, today I take last year's gift of a rod and reel and walk the few blocks to the lake.

The fall wind is picking up and Lake Erie smells like the sea. A couple of ocean freighters that came down the Saint Lawrence Seaway are lollygagging on the horizon. In the thinly wooded area where couples go to make out when the weather is warmer, I turn over a few rocks and find three worms. I remember something about the Shawnee people apologizing to fish they were going to eat, so I talk to the water—the fish in the water—and make a deal: I promise to not catch more than I can eat and promise to not waste any. After four hours, I catch two nice perch and a big bass whose face is sporting a rusty hook that is trailing a few inches of monofilament leader that must have irritated its now-opaque eye for over a year. The hook is thoroughly rusted and easy for a human to remove, so I do, then I free him from my hook and return him to the water. It's his lucky day. Now I'm out of bait, but it doesn't matter—two is about the limit anyway—if you don't want mercury poisoning.

At home, I clean and scale the perch, then fry them in butter with heads-on so I don't waste any with sloppy filleting: I remember and keep my promises. While I am cleaning up, Mrs. Finnegan, much sweeter this time, comes to the door to give me a receipt. It seems that while I was out, "That nice girlfriend of yours stopped by to pay your rent, and then she left." She starts to walk away, then hesitates and looks back. "You're a handsome lad; black Irish are ya?" I shrug my shoulders, she shrugs hers and walks away.

Tomorrow morning Amity will leave for a place she calls "The

Skunkworks," wherever that is. She'll be training or testing or singing karaoke for all I know. She doesn't talk about what she's doing, and it's clear that I'm not supposed to ask. For now, all I know is that she is doing something that involves physics with a group of people, a "cohort of colleagues," one of whom is called ET. We didn't make any plans for the evening, and I have nothing to offer, except maybe a thank-you for the rent relief.

I've cleaned the frying pan and dishes and am about to sit down on the love-seat in the kitchen when there is another knock at the door. It's Amity.

"Hi-ee," she says, handing me a dozen red roses. Then she swings in front of me—like a hypnotist's watch—a car key fob on a ring.

"What's this?" I ask.

"A little present. I got a bonus because the project is ahead of schedule."

"Amity! Why—?"

"Don't you want to see?"

We step out to my parking spot and a shiny new Audi RS 5 Coupe in a metallic cobalt blue—Amity's favorite color. (She says, "Cobalt is disruptive." It's a physics joke of some sort, and I suppose, choosing that shade of blue is her version of a rebellious act.) The sticker price is over ninety grand. At the rate I charge for tutoring piano, when I can get students, it would take me 1,500 hours to earn that much money.

"I just couldn't relax thinking of you driving your old car while I'm away on business, so I traded it in for this. I signed over the old title for you; I hope you don't mind." (I'll bet she got less than a thousand for my 20 year old jalopy on the trade in. I feel humiliated.)

"Amity, I can't accept such a...an expensive gift."

"You haven't even driven it yet. OK. Let's think of it as *our* car, but you drive it and take care of it."

8

Phallacy with Amity

Amity wants to celebrate the arrival of the new car. She's clearly more excited about giving me this extravagant gift than I am about receiving it. Honestly, I've never cared much for cars; I'm not a piston-head, and I also don't care much for driving either unless it's a long road trip or late at night—preferably both. But Amity wants to let me drive her in style. Or maybe she wants to be seen emerging from the tricked-out car that I'm driving. I'll be sure to open the door for her and make a good show of it. She asks me where the "hip and cool" places to go are. I mention that Jimmy Strong is playing at The Phallacy Nightclub and she says, "Take me there."

The car is very powerful and I have trouble getting used to the feel of the pedals and the views in the mirrors. More than once I press the gas pedal a little too fast and lay a patch of rubber on the damp pavement. This time the Lakewood police pull me over. I explain to the officer—very respectfully—that it's a new car and I'm still getting used to it. He looks across at Amity who smiles with all of her allure, and he lets us go. Outside the club I find a well-lit place to park and we walk the rest of the way. Suddenly I'm concerned about the security of the car and the paint-job. I make a mental note of how quickly I become attached to pretty things.

At the door of the Phallacy, the bouncer is a guy who attended high school with us. Back then he was a kind of block-headed bully jock, which made him popular with the popular set. Several times a year, in the heat of his paranoid delusions, he would accuse me of some cardinal offense and challenge me to a fight. I never did, but he could walk away satisfied that he had intimidated me. He didn't, well, not entirely. He mostly just triggered my loathing. Today he recognizes us and acts as if we three were once the best of friends. He wants to exchange numbers so we can stay in touch, maybe hang out and have a few beers sometime. "Sure," I say, "Let's connect on Facebook."

I never look at Facebook.

Inside, the place is dark and dank and smells of spilled beer. Jimmy is on stage singing his hit song, *Cool-Hot*, while lovingly dipping the mic stand like a 1950s crooner. We find a table and order a margarita and a beer just as Jimmy is finishing the song. At the height of the applause, he looks directly at us and says in a deeply menacing, but still musical voice, "Don't think that you can sneak past me." Everybody in the place laughs and believes that he's talking to them, but I *know* he's talking to us. It's time for their break, and while the band is putting guitars into their stands and parking drumsticks, Jimmy works his fans with a technique he calls "touch and go" in which he appears to acknowledge everyone personally but spends less than two seconds on each fan. It's a perfected form of his "sincerity." Ultimately he winds his way to our table.

"You finally bring me the light of my life," he says referring to Amity as he kisses her hand with a gesture so anachronistic and affected that it borders on being campy. Still, she is in a good enough mood to play along. Three musicians from *Shamrock Pluck*, the warm-up band, come over to get some attention from the star, but Jimmy makes wisecracks and then ignores them. The waitress reappears with our drinks and when Jimmy asks her for a kiss, she musses his hair instead. "Five people want to buy you a drink," she says. "Give me a mug of ginger ale and ten bucks," he answers, "You can put the rest in your kitty." She likes that idea and gives him a big, slow, lipsticky kiss on the cheek. "Hey Sunshine," he says to Amity, "Quick! Kiss my other cheek so I don't lose my balance."

"I think you lost that a long time ago," Amity replies.

"Ouch. Are those drinks for you Jack? You got some nerve coming in here for drinks when you know I'm trying to stay sober."

"Well Jimmy, this is a bar after all."

"I'm just kidding. Drink up. And tip too. I gotta stay on good terms with the people here." Then to Amity he says, "Sunshine, do you mind if I borrow your gigolo for a few minutes? I gotta ask him a musical question in private." Amity smiles and shrugs with her palms up as if to say, "Whatever."

We walk over to a dark place near a wall covered with auto-graphed posters going back 40 years or more. Jimmy leans back against that wall and supports his slouch by parking one of his boots on the faces of a 1980s girl band called *Bananarama*.

"Jack, haven't you always felt, deep down inside, that you are just a little bit smarter, a little bit cooler than everybody else?" Waving his hand over the crowd, he looks like Nebuchadnezzar surveying the hanging gardens of Babylon. "Just look at all of these palookas. Every one of them thinks he-she is an artist. But in five years, maybe less, they'll all cave to banausic pressures and give up."

"*What* pressures?"

"Banausic," he laughs. "Look it up. It's a good word—I give you permission to use it." He pauses and looks over at Amity who is engaged in rapid conversation with a small group of grunge musicians. "In fact," he continues, tossing his word salad, "the only one here who's got her shit together is your Baby Einstein over there, and she's got to play Sugar-Mama to your Bohemian groove." I shake my head, "Incomprehensible," I say, but I know exactly what he means. Some drunk patrons spot him and start yelling Jimmy's name. "Let's go into the back room," he says, "It's quieter in there."

Jimmy takes me to the musicians' lounge, but before we can talk about anything, I see, hanging above a nasty old stained couch, on a wall covered with signatures—some famous and some forgotten—the picture of Amity that he stole. The frame has been attached with drywall screws and gobs of hot glue that hang down in suggestive and disgusting drools. Above it someone has written in Sharpie, "Groupie of the Year." Someone else signed on the glass, "I will love you all," and franked it with a big red lipstick kiss. Oh sugar! If Amity sees this, she will be mortified. Jimmy sees me looking in horror and starts talking fast.

"Hey man, I didn't do that. The night I took this picture from your place I came around to see the owner about some money, and I forgot it when I left. One of the sub-geniuses that slithers through here decided to make art out of a found object. I wanted to return it, but man, it's in no condition now. Just look at it."

"Jimmy, you gotta take that down."

"I can't man. You can see for yourself: that thing has been industrially attached."

"Then I'll take it down myself. You can't mock a guy's fiancée like that." I rummage through a roadie's tool box parked next to the door, find a screwdriver and go to work on the frame. Jimmy weakly tries to stop me, but I manage to get under the hot glue and prise the thing off with a lot of damage to the wall.

"Oh shit man! The owner is gonna give me so much grief for this."

"Not half as much grief as I would give you if Amity found out."

"But just look at the wall now," he says.

"Trust, in a slum like this, nobody's going to notice. But if you want to redecorate, you can cover it with a poster of your mother." I pull the picture from the frame, fold it up, and stuff it into my pocket.

"Jack, buddy, don't be pissed at me brother. I swear I didn't do that."

"But you didn't stop it either, did you, buddy? She's going away tomorrow and we came here to have some fun. I gotta go now." I leave the lounge and return to our table where Amity is fending off half a dozen rock 'n' rollers who are pawing her and making lewd suggestions. I steer them away and lead Amity out to the car. She is silently fuming.

"Well, *that* was an experience. I think it's the first time I've ever been surrounded by a real live pack of wolves."

"Sorry Amity. Some of these guys have been out to sea for a very long time."

"What did you tell your friends about me to give them such ideas? And why didn't you do anything to defend my reputation?"

In my pocket I feel the folded picture of Amity and fight the pressing impulse to shred it into little pieces.

9

Nocturne

The short drive back to my apartment is silent. Amity stares diagonally through the passenger window at the closed up storefronts. From my peripheral vision I watch as wedges of light slide across her cheek and over her forehead—a cinematic chiarascuro painted as we glide beneath the streetlamps. I'm sure she doesn't want this—her last night before a business trip—to end so frostily, and neither do I. Any couples' counselor worth his or her salt will tell anyone who wants to listen that the key to a successful marriage is communication. I understand that to mean that I need to ask a well-thought question, and listen attentively to her answer.

Back at my place I decide not to talk about what happened at Phallacy Nightclub, but instead show real interest in what she loves—not me, but her recent obsession: her work.

"Amity, I'm sorry our date didn't work out as planned. Maybe we should have a better plan next time." Amity shrugs and shakes her head as if to dismiss the bad memory. (Funny—and this is the part I really don't understand about her reaction to the lotharios in that club—another woman, a totally different one, might have enjoyed bantering with hipsters like that. But it would be relationship suicide for me to suggest anything of the sort to Amity.) She looks at the wall above the radiator and realizes that something is missing.

"Why did you take down my picture?"

"I didn't."

"Did you invite an orchestra groupie back here and try to hide the fact that you're attached?"

"No, it's nothing like that."

"Then why did you get rid of it? Do I embarrass you?"

"Jimmy stole it."

"Jimmy? Why would he steal it?"

"I don't know. Maybe he's a kleptomaniac."

"Another of his many charming attributes. I like that picture. Where is it now?"

I pull the folded photograph from my jacket pocket and hand it to her.

"He hung it in the musicians lounge at the club. Did a bad job of it too. I had to break the frame to take it down. We almost came to blows over it." A smile begins in Amity's eyes and spreads down to her dimpled cheeks.

"He hung my picture next to a bunch of girly-girl posters?"

"Yeah. Crazy. Right?"

"I don't know. It's kind of fun to think I'm somebody's fantasy."

"I'd much rather have the reality." (Oh that's a good one.) Amity reaches for me and we kiss, but I still have work to do.

"Amity, can I ask you a serious question?" She straightens up and puts on her business face. "What is it about this physics project that fascinates you so much? I haven't seen you this obsessed since grad school when you were writing your dissertation." Amity bites her lip and steeples her fingers looking at the floor like she's praying. Suddenly she lifts her head as if she's just thought of something or just made a decision. The pupils in her eyes have dilated. "Math," she says. "It's the beauty of the math." She gets up from the love seat and goes to the whiteboard on the wall next to my piano. "May I?" she asks.

"Of course." She lifts off a dozen or so Post-it notes I had there and sticks them to the piano. Then, from memory she writes out a small but complicated-looking equation.

"Do you see the beauty in this?" she asks.

"Your penmanship is very neat."

"This is the relativity factor from the Lorentz Transformation. It's a classic bit of physics math."

"What does it represent?"

"Time dilation resulting from acceleration. See, as V, velocity approaches C, the speed of light, time slows down. And it slows in direct relation to the increase in velocity such that when velocity is equal to the speed of light, time stops. So according to the Lorentz transformation, it's conceivable that one single photon is supplying all the light in the universe since, at that speed there *is* no time, ergo that single photon can be everywhere all at once." (I don't know if I'm flummoxed or just flabbergasted.)

''Well, 'Let there be light.' What's that got to do with your project?" I ask. Amity is explaining something scientific to someone outside of her team—probably skating a little too close to sensitive information, and the proximal danger of accidental revelation is getting her excited. Her silk blouse and lacy bra beneath shimmer to her accelerating breath and heartbeat.

"Look," she says, "we always think of velocity in terms of motion between origin and destination, but what if the velocity is obtained through vibration? Maybe forward motion wouldn't be required. Maybe the vibration would be the perturbation that would permit instantaneous travel in space-time."

Amity's professorial display, rich with competence and exuding confidence, is very sexy. She catches me looking at her with a kind of interest inappropriate for the presentation, and halts herself with a jolt and a quick shiver.

"Anyway," she continues, "Music *also* is vibration. Does music have anything this beautiful in its math?" I take the marker and her place at the whiteboard. Then with a paper towel poised above her formula, I seek her permission to erase. She nods. I draw some staff lines across the board and add notation.

"What's that?" she asks.

"An excerpt from the string section of 'Dawn' from *Four Sea Interludes* by Benjamin Britten. Have you ever seen anything like it?"

"Sorry. It means nothing to me."

"Just look at it. The score is as beautiful as the sound it represents, and the sound represents phenomena from human experience that are indescribable in any way other than music." Amity's pupils contract, her shoulders droop, and she exhales with a frown.

"Can you take me home now? I have to leave at six in the morning, and I still have to pack. I'm also kind of hungry—I didn't eat all day; maybe we can get something from the Wendy's drive-through."

It seems like we have been engaged in deep conversation for hours, but when I look at the time, only ten minutes have passed. Tomorrow Amity is leaving for another two weeks. In line at the drive-through, she asks for my phone then installs Signal for secure messaging, and something else to help us communicate when she's traveling. It's a "conduit code" she says—a pipeline to connect us.

We have become two notes, one whole step apart, chiming with unfulfilled expectation. And more and more I realize that where she is going, I can no longer follow.

10

Call of the Wild One

"Jackie boy! It's been almost a week. Are you still mad at me?"

"My loathing for you knows no bounds."

"Great, I love you too man. So get down here right away."

"Where are you Jimmy, central booking?"

"No, you jerk, I'm sober. I'm at the Hungarian place on Detroit Avenue in the eighties. Where else would I be on a Thursday?"

"What's the name of the place?"

"I just told you, The Hungarian. Now get your ass down here on the double!...Sweetheart."

Something's going on for Jimmy to be that serious. It didn't sound as serious as trouble, but it did sound important. I'd better go see. Besides, where else would I be on a Thursday night?

The real name of the place is *Szilvakert*, but very few people know how to pronounce that, so most just call it "The Hungarian." When I arrive, the small place is noisy, hot, and swampy. At one table, old men are drinking Zwack plum schnapps and playing poker for toothpicks. In the middle of the room by the side wall, in a baggy brown suit, sits a burly middle-aged man with wavy hair and a cookie-duster mustache. He is playing

Harry Lime's theme from *The Third Man* on a cimbalom—a kind of zither played with what look like big cotton swabs on the ends of two long wires. An ancient waitress passes in front of me, her arm stacked with plates of goulash, paprikash, and stuffed cabbages. The air is heavy with cigarette smoke even though nobody appears to be smoking. Maybe it's the kitchen crew.

Jimmy flags me to a corner table. Facing him are bare shoulders in black spaghetti straps and long loose coils of shiny black hair. Jimmy, dressed in a vintage zoot suit from a second-hand store, stands to make introductions.

"Julie…"

"Yulia," she corrects, "Yulia Sophia Pasternak."

"Right. Jack, this is Julie. Julie, this is Jack, the composer friend I told you about. He's a wannabe bourgeoisie."

I nod to the side. "Yulia Sophia, *enchanté*. I see you've had the misfortune of meeting my associate, Jimmy the rockabilly. He's a Bolshevik has-been."

"You both are incorrigible," she says.

"Actually Jack *is* a composer, and Julie *is* an opera singer."

"Mezzo-soprano. And I sing more than opera."

"Well now that you've been formally introduced, I'll leave you two alone so you can hook up."

"Sit down chucklehead," I say.

"Seriously, and never take me seriously, I have a rehearsal with the band tonight and she'll be pissed if I'm late."

"She who?"

"Did I say she? I meant the band. My band. Did I tell you Julie that I have a band?"

"Several times."

"Well then why haven't you come to see us perform? Tomor-row, Phallacy, Lakewood, be there." He downs the dregs of a cold espresso, and shivers. "Bah, this sobriety sucks."

"Jimmy," I say, referring to his social alacrity, "I don't know how you do it." He puts his hand on my shoulder and leans in close to my ear.

"Jack, the key to success is sincerity; If you can fake that, you've got it made."

The cimbalom player has moved on to the *Blue Danube Waltz*, and Jimmy weaves his way between the tables to a ¾ beat. When he reaches the aisle where the waitress is delivering a check, he puts his arm around her waist, dances a few turns, then dips her over with a big fat kiss on the lips. When they straighten up, she swats him on the behind with her order pad. Though she feigns anger and insult, her face drops 20 years as she heads back to her corner. Jimmy grabs a shot of schnapps off the gamblers' table, gargles with it, and swallows. The men erupt in cheers and laughter. He's gone—real gone. The waitress smiles and lights up a smoke. Yulia turns her attention to me.

"So is your name really Jack, as in Jack Kennedy?"

"No, actually my name is Jonathan, as in Jonathan Kennedy."

"James is your friend?"

"James? I'll bet no one's called him that since his christening. And friend? I suppose so, but you'll need to define that word before I make a commitment." She raises an eyebrow.

"He seems to think very highly of you. What kind of music do you compose?"

"Orchestral, some chamber, serious stuff."

"Has your work ever been performed?" (I think about my graduate performance.)

"Yes. My *Sinfonietta for Strings* was performed at Severance Hall."

"Oh? I have some interest in that venue. Have you written

anything for voice?"

I think about the assignment Marga gave me recently. I am laying it on thick now, and enjoying the boost it gives my ego. Yulia is smiling with only her eyes while she maintains a lock on my visage.

"As a matter of fact, I'm working on a piece for voice right now, but I doubt it will be performed at Severance."

"Why not? Are you saving yourself for Alice Tully?" What an odd choice of words. I'm not sure if she's speaking English as a second language or if she's making a pass.

"No point in saving myself really; I guess it's just first-come-first-served." (Where did that come from? And did she extract a double *entendre*?) Yulia watches closely and silently for a beat. She's been leaning with her left elbow on the chair back and her hand photogenically touching her chin but not supporting it. She wiggles her long fingers and smiles completely now. I notice, all of a sudden, that she is stunning, with raven black hair and olive colored eyes. She's older than me by a few years, maybe she's hovering around 30, but she has classic beauty and a powerful stage presence that she is now projecting just at me. I feel a little intimidated and think that if she projected fully, I would most likely pass out. She looks down at her phone, then raises just her eyes to meet mine.

"It's getting late. We should go to bed." She pauses, looks. "Will you walk me to the door please? My Uber car has arrived."

I walk her to the car and we say goodbye European style with a kiss on each cheek. And is it my imagination that her kisses feel like she truly means them? When I get home, there are red lip prints on either cheek and my shirt collar smells of lilacs. I feel happy. And guilty.

11

Trolling for Arias

Timo Van der Hout, a guy I met in a music history class and now Special Programs Coordinator for the Cleveland Orchestra, calls me to say that he has an interesting proposal and asks me to lunch. I tell him that I'll go if it includes the lunch. He says, "*I* invited *you*. You be there."

When I arrive, there is no way to miss Timo. He is wearing a white shirt with leopard spots daubed with rainbow colors, and a large opal brooch holding a bolo necktie. His hair is shaved on the sides and piled high on top like curly ramen noodles. He has shaped his eyebrows and powdered his face. I am surprised to see him without eye liner, but this is his professional look.

Over pastrami sandwiches at Irv's Deli, Timo tells me he has a slot to fill in a concert schedule and needs a short piece of new music to cap the program and showcase a singer. He tells me it needs to be somewhere around seven to ten minutes, for orchestra and soprano. Which soprano? He'll tell me later. Something powerful, he says, not light, something real, probably not coloratura—understand: she's a mezzo—so make it serious, not necessarily dark, but definitely serious. The singer has demanded it—wants something new, nothing silly—she's Russian and wants to showcase her art, her soul. It must be as the diva wishes.

"Sounds like she's got some clout," I say.

"More than clout, much more. She comes with an endowment from our newest favorite donor, *and I'm applying for a Koussevitzky grant for you*," he says, that last bit in dramatic stage whisper. "You don't have to thank me—just acknowledge my genius for recognizing genius."

"Who is the donor?" I ask.

"That's top secret, but I can tell you he's got a lot of bread, in fact you could say he's *rolling* in dough. Now, our diva has quite a reputation and is a big draw in Eastern Europe. But that's not the only big thing she has," he says, and holds out his phone with a picture of the soloist—one of those lurid promotional pieces so common these days. (Could this be the same Yulia Sophia Pasternak I met through Jimmy Strong at The Hungarian?)

"I'll do anything to please your sensitive resident diva, Mademoiselle Pasternak. This *is* Yulia Sophia Pasternak," I ask.

"You know her? Has she scorched you too?"

"If she's the same Yulia Sophia I know, then I think we'll get along famously."

"That's wonderful," Timo says flatly. "*Frankly*, she's not my gender."

"She'd be one hell of a soprano if she were."

"Jonathan, what she says is true, you *are* incorrigible."

Frankly, I'm so thrilled to be offered an actual commission to write music (a *paying* gig!) that I'm feeling giddy, like I've just downed a triple espresso. I'm thinking Timo Van der Hout may be the best friend I've ever had, and The Cleveland may just be the greatest orchestra in the world, and I'm feeling like I might be in love with a Russian diva who likes to hang out with an American rockabilly singer. (Whoa, Jonathan, slow down. You're outrunning your headlights.) I take a deep breath and feel the vibe humming through my body. Breathe.

Timo is looking off at a waiter and teasing out his gelled bouffant of caramel-colored noodle curls.

"I'll take the job," I say with as much nonchalance as I can simulate.

"I gave you no option to do otherwise," Timo says. "She insisted on *you*. And the way I sold you to the chairman of the committee for new music, you have no way to back out. *I don't remember what I was drinking that night.* So you have until spring to come up with something brilliant—and nothing that the Merce Cunningham Company would want to dance to, OK?"

"Gotcha."

"Will you have her sing in Russian or French?"

"I'm thinking Latin—Don't want to baby the old horse." Timo shakes his head and smirks.

"Just incorrigible."

As I walk to my car, I'm imagining Yulia Sophia, just a touch *zaftig*, clad in a low-cut black satin gown standing center stage at Severance Hall sucking in all the adulation the audience can give. She's almost my height, and in heels she may be an inch over. Long introductory applause, the conductor (Who? Franz perhaps) raises the baton, gets a nod from the soloist and then the concertmaster (Or is it the other way around?) and then my opening chords, or maybe just a lonely flute, or ghostly high overtones from a double bass—I haven't figured out the music yet.

I get into the car and the autumn afternoon sun has warmed it nicely. In my mind's ear I hear Prima Donna Pasternak opening:

at first slowly, of course, then building to a platform of dramatic emotion, but which emotion? Loss? No, not loss. I want this Russian goddess to feel joy until it oozes from the bows on her patent leather pumps. OK, I'll start with loss, a hint of joy, then more loss, then triumphal joy. I can do all that in about 7 minutes.

But what about the text? I told Timo that it will be in Latin. He's probably already sharing that bit of gossip with his boyfriend, or for all I know he could be on the phone with Yulia Sophia right now, so it has to be Latin. But where will I find a joyful Latin text? Definitely not that stoic Marcus Aurelius. Maybe that little poem by Hadrian, but no, that ends in death and that's way too serious. Hell, the way I feel right now, I could write it myself. I'll write about landing my first commission; it'll be the truth, but the Latin will cloak it in mysticism. I wish I knew a polymath who could do the translation for me—free online services are unreliable, and each gives a different translation of the same sentences. Bertolt Brecht once wrote a play just from lines he picked out of a Berlitz phrasebook. But it's unlikely that there is a phrasebook of Latin for Travelers, and I can't afford to wait; I must start right now—every inch that I move forward, every word and measure that I commit to paper brings me closer to my goal. In a way, we may say, that the ink on the paper is the migration of my work from the realm of ideas into the third dimension. This is what I write into my notebook and translate with the phone:

The heavens are opening for me;
the heavens have opened today.
Sweet little traveling soul,
Come warm yourself in the Light Divine.

Caelos sunt, foramen pro me;
caeli aperuit hodie.
Animula, vagula, blandula
Fove in te spiritus Dei.

Manna from heaven falls on the fields
Collect all His grace in the sun.
Come dwell in the house of the Lord,
Sweet little traveling soul.

Man e caelo cadit in agris
Colligere omnes gratiam Suam in solem.
Venit habitant in domo Domini.
Animula, vagula, blandula.

12

A Little Cocktail Music

This is the social function I have dreaded for months. We are in one of the event rooms of the Ritz-Carlton in downtown Cleveland. It's a beautiful setup with red, white, and pink poinsettias everywhere. The tall French windows are draped with indigo velvet pulled back and tied with gold satin ropes ending in rich knots with braided tassels, and the frosty panes reveal a vision of large fluffy snowflakes swirling in the evening's violet gloam. The entire room is shimmering with hundreds of votive candles in holders of alternating red and green glass—suggesting an authentically secular, Christmas-like holiday. My compliments to the servers and busboys who put it all together with such romantic style. It's comfortable and warm and almost meditative, but relaxing would be a dangerous thing to do. I need to put on a good front to support Amity and to make her look complete and solidly stable.

Amity's coworkers refer to each other as colleagues. Colleagues are coworkers who do not need to punch a time-clock. I'm learning all sorts of things about the business world that I have less than no interest in, such as: most colleagues are either consultants working for exorbitantly high hourly rates (like Amity) or managers, who are classified "exempt salary" which means no matter how many hours they work, they are exempt from overtime pay. Exempt guys get additional perks though like paid vacation time, health insurance, and an employer-matched 401K retirement plan. As a consultant, Amity takes care of all that stuff on her own, which in their view makes her a superhero.

Amity is very popular in this group and they treat her like a celebrity. And I am able to deduce the relative ranks of the individual players here by observing the way that some fawn, and others, like me since my orchestra commission, hum with a serenity born of self-confidence. Amity is energized and more nervous than I've ever seen her, but as far as these kinds of events go, she is giving a stellar performance. There are three solitary people standing against different walls around the room with drink nearby, but never drinking, who look down at their phones if anyone approaches. These I assume are the watchers. Uncle Dan told me that at corporate events like these, someone, probably from human resources or security, is always watching—keeping tabs on who may be management material, and who is a material risk to be managed; who drinks too much, and who refuses a drink; who clings to his spouse's side, and who makes a pass at someone else's spouse. Notes are taken, files are kept, spouses are graded, all in terms of the 3Ms: Marriage, Money, and Morals. Anyone with an obvious, or maybe even not-so-obvious weakness in those areas will be passed over at promotion time, and given unpopular dogs of projects to run in the hopes that he or she will fail and have his or her employment terminated "with cause" so there is no golden parachute to pay out. Amity is doing well, and the more abstract and phony I can play it, the better for her.

Amity introduces me to William and excuses herself to circulate and greet everyone in attendance continental style—cheek-to-cheek with a loose embrace and a kiss to the air next to the ears.

William is an engineer. What kind? Management of wave form turbulence is his specialty. My specialty? Well, in a way, you could say, that I design and manage acoustical wave forms. "Fascinating," he says, "I learn something new about this project every day." (Keep it simple Jonathan: Least said is soonest mended.)

"Quite," I reply.

William is feeling his wine and moves to introduce a singular circulating friend, Delancey, who is carrying a bottle of Heineken with a wet label he has been picking at in a kind of nervous tic.

"Delancey!" William ropes him in to our corral. "This is Jonathan, Amity's Jonathan."

"Delancey," I nod, "Pleasure to meet you."

"Sure you are," Delancey says. "I mean, so am I. To meet you."

I'm starting to feel comfortable in this crowd of neurotics.

"Jonathan is in acoustical wave propagation," William says.

"Close enough. How about you?" I ask.

"Gravitics. I mean anti-gravitics, rather EMF propulsion," Delancey struggles to explain. I'm trying to put all this together, but assume that just like most cocktail party talk, it's mostly bullshit. I cast a brick to see if I can attract some jade.

"Propulsion? Well you're just the guy to make things move." They like this remark. Sip drinks.

Soon, Karl, another wandering colleague, drifts over to see what all the excitement is about. Delancey is picking in earnest at the beer label until he spots Karl.

"Jonathan, this is Karl from avionics," Delancey begins, "Jonathan is in acoustics."

We shake hands. I wish Amity would return so I could hide in her shadow for a while, but I'm enjoying this unintentional deception—which is actually kind of fun. I threw out the thinnest of abstractions, and they are spinning it into the densest of yarns. It's amazing how much we burnish the images of the people we admire.

Karl says to William and Delancey, "I've figured out a work-around for the nav-com issue. We can triangulate off a beacon such as a known cell phone signal without leaving a GPS signature ourselves."

I spot Amity approaching from across the room. There is a tall guy at her right side but a step or two behind. When Amity is walking with a purpose, anyone would have a hard time keeping up. Her companion is spun off by one who is obviously his senior, but half a foot shorter.

"Hi Jonathan," she says and takes my hand; hers is cold and damp. Her radiant smile is frozen. "I see you've made some friends. What were you talking about?"

"Oh just chit-chat. You know, physics sorts of stuff," I say. Amity looks concerned.

"Excuse me gentlemen, may I borrow your friend for a few?" Amity says and leads me away by the arm.

Disarming is what she is. The engineers all smile and are thrilled to have been the target of her pleasant attention even if only for a few seconds. About 30 feet away and outside of earshot, as they say, I can see the guy who was walking behind Amity. He is using his hands to explain something to his boss. He shapes a sphere out of space, lifts it up, then flattens it somewhat to an imaginary pancake shape, makes it wobble a bit, then makes a snapping motion to indicate that it's gone. Maybe they're discussing a magic trick and he's going to put on a show later. Amity grips my arm to draw my attention back to her.

"Jonathan, you must be very careful about what you say."

"Why?"

"I'm an independent contractor and I signed a non-disclosure agreement."

"Well I didn't."

"This is no joke, Jonathan. This is national security."

"Security? What do you know about security?"

"Shh. Let's not discuss that now."

The tall gent with graying temples who just finished miming how he is going to turn a basketball into a Frisbee, has approached. Amity makes his introduction.

"Jonathan this is Edmond Traynor, our project executive. Edmond, this is my fiance, Jonathan Brendel." We shake hands.

The boss character makes a cryptic signal to Amity that he'd like to talk with her. So far the lazy bastard has just stood there in the center of the ballroom all night calling people over to talk to him. In fact, I have noticed that they all watch him peripherally like orchestra musicians watch a conductor, but nobody approaches him *unless* called. Amity excuses herself once again and walks over to the center of the ballroom in a way that is nothing short of seductive. She is wearing a cobalt blue dress of Thai silk with a string of pearls and tastefully muted gold satin heels—an ensemble more fitting to a Hollywood romance picture than an office Christmas party. I watch and am mesmerized by her graceful motion. When I break my trance I see that ET was also watching her every move. He keeps staring for a beat or two just to make it obvious to me. I've already sized up this guy to be a cad, then he speaks.

"So, Jonny, we finally meet."

"I wasn't aware that you were so engrossed in anticipation."

"Surely you were expecting this moment."

"Surely you assume a familiarity that doesn't exist."

"Perhaps. You know, everyone at I.C.I. is enamored of Amity?"

"Is that so."

"Yes. She's brilliant, extremely organized, and destined for greatness. You two have nothing in common, do you?"

"Well, opposites *do* attract. You should remember that from your high school physics. Or did you play hooky that day?"

"I never attended what you call '*high* school.' I had private tutors and went directly to Oxford, then to M.I.T. for my post-graduate work."

"Sounds like you were awfully busy."

"Extremely.

"Pity that."

"Why?"

"You had no time to develop social skills." Amity returns and touches my shoulder.

"Look at you two, sharing such intense dialogue."

"I was just reviewing ET's résumé," I say.

"Oh Edmond, why would *you* need to apply anywhere?"

"All I'm applying is due diligence," he says. "Excuse me." Edmond pivots and walks in the direction of the boss.

"What was that about?" Amity asks.

"Your Oppenheimer was just bloviating about his credentials as an *Übermensch*."

"Jonathan don't you dare sow discord among my colleagues."

"Keep smiling, Amity. I come to your planet in peace, to sow harmony...and occasionally counterpoint."

Our little brouhaha is interrupted by that always annoying sound of someone tapping on, then blowing into an amplified microphone. All attention turns to the front of the room where ET is standing next to the boss whom he announces without introduction as Mr. Baker.

"The director is going to make a speech," Amity says, acknowledging the obvious.

Mr. Baker begins his underwhelming address.

"Thank you all for coming. This is a very special season at the dawn of a very special epoch." (Oh brother.) He continues. "We have here assembled a unique team of specialists to work on a uniquely special project." ('Four score and seven years ago...' The way this guy talks, you'd think he had just invented the iPhone. Oh I'm becoming more cynical each day. Why can't I just smile and let them have their fun, feeling themselves so important?)

"...So stay sharp, stay close, and stay for dessert." Laughter and cheers break out as Baker passes the mic to ET. Well, that's over. Thank heaven for small favors.

"We are very fortunate to have in our presence tonight an entertainer that we might be able to coerce into tickling the ivories for us," ET says, then pointing at me, "This is Amity's boyfriend, Jonny."

"Fiance!"Amity calls out, "And he's a composer...of music."

When the applause dies down, William belts out a belated laugh: "Oh, I get it! 'management of acoustical wave forms!'" Others chuckle.

Amity looks at me and through her forced smile says that now she knows why ET ordered a grand piano delivered to this ballroom. Everyone is watching us as they wait.

"Why is he doing this?" Amity asks.

"You're the psychologist, and you're asking me? What should I do?"

"You have to perform, Jonathan. If not, the loss of face would crush the party."

"So? Crush the party."

Amity looks as though she's ready to cry.

"Do it for me Jonathan, please?"

"For you Amity, only for you."

I despise being asked to perform on a moment's notice at a formal event. The result is similar to what happens when a guy picks up a nice camera at a luncheon to take a few shots of his friends. No matter how important he may be to the organization, once he picks up that camera, in their minds, everyone demotes him to 'just a photographer.' ET plans to demote me to 'entertainer.'

I approach the piano, a Steinway—and from the looks of it, born just a couple years ago in Queens, New York. I sit and adjust the bench, then turn to look at Amity. She uses her fingers to sign that I should smile, then folds her hands prayer-style and mouths, "Please." And I mumble, "Say pretty please, with sugar on top, if you please." William is standing next to her now and from the look on his face you'd think he was at the world series and his team was winning. ET has a waiter bring two votive candles in red glasses to put on the piano's music shelf, which is folded down.

"I thought since we have this piano here..." ET says to the now jolly group. "I've added a couple red lights to improve our maestro's night vision, but don't get any ideas ladies, he's spoken for."

Laughter.

Sometimes MENSA humor is just moronic.

He asks me what I'm going to play, then holds the mic uncomfortably close for my reply. I grab the shaft and push it back a couple inches. (What *am* I going to play?) "The piano," I say to laughter and applause.

I check the A above middle C and it's a little on the bright side of 440, then I run up and down a few arpeggios to warm up while I make sure that it's tuned. I wouldn't be surprised to find that it was sabotaged in that way. ET is standing close with his hand on the lid like he's about to sing a baritone aria, and he comments when I finish my check.

"That's it? You compose scales?" The audience laughs.

"I was just checking to make sure you didn't lose any of your marbles or loose screws in there." Then I motion at him with the back of my hand. "You'd better back up a little there, ET—this could get dangerous." I hear William laughing the loudest.

Now, I am a passable pianist, but for me the instrument is a tool for composing, and I can only dream of having the talent to go on stage. Still, I *have* taken performance classes, and seen enough pros at work that I can act the part for seven minutes. I'm fully confident that this crowd has less talent and knowledge of music than I do. I hold my peace until they are silenced, then I begin with a couple minutes of Debussy's *Clair de Lune* (about as much as I can remember), then I vamp on the theme until I find a way to mix in the best part of Chopin's *Fantasy Impromptu,* and segue into the second movement Allegretto from Beethoven's *Moonlight Sonata* ending in the middle of a phrase on one of the tonic upbeats. I let my hands float up off the keys, then gently place them on my lap and straighten my back while the slightly lubricated crowd of engineers and their polite spouses applaud furiously. I see the pride in Amity's smile and she waves for me to stand and take a bow. Then like clockwork, ET returns with his karaoke microphone to throw some cold water on my moment.

"Not bad." the fool says.

The crowd thinks more may be coming, but I'm shot. ET now acts like he wants to interview me.

"What was that little ditty you played there at the end?" he asks, thrusting the mic in my face. I try to take the mic, but he won't let go. I hold on as if for stability while I feel for the power switch.

"That little *ditty* at the end? Why that was the old Ludwig Van himself."

Then, using a little prank I learned from watching Jimmy Strong deal with a cocky reporter, I switch off the mic as I let it go. As the audience laughs at my Beethoven remark, I return to Amity, and ET stands alone talking into a dead stick.

* * *

Amity squeezes my hand and tells me in a whisper how wonderful I am. I'll accept that. I expect that this event will probably end soon, and I breathe a sigh of relief. Amity's hand goes cold and she releases mine. I look in the direction of her gaze and see Baker walking toward us. She points to herself but Baker smiles and points at me. Amity waves a yoo-hoo to William and Delancey and walks over to their circle.

Baker is a diminutive man with short dark hair, very fit, and very intense, and he walks with a strong and steady gait. I can imagine him in officer's uniform commanding a submarine. He approaches me with a mild smile. His handshake is strong but measured, like what I would expect from an officer or a diplomat.

"Well done," he says.

"Thank you."

"And well done on the music as well. I like how you linked the impressionist back to the classical." I get worried.

"Are you a musician?" I ask. Baker shakes his head.

"Let's say I have a talent for listening. But the key is *understanding* what you hear."

"I once heard a tree fall in the woods," I say. Baker smiles with appreciation.

"Good that you were there; even a falling tree needs an audience." Baker looks in the direction of Amity who is pretending to listen to William while she attempts to eavesdrop on Baker and me. She catches Baker's glance and turns to William with faux interest.

"What has Amity told you about her work, Jonathan?"

"Only that she is training and testing."

"Nothing about the project?"

"She signed a non-disclosure agreement, so I ask nothing and she discloses nothing."

"Aren't you curious?"

"Sure. I'll bite. What are you working on Mr. Baker?"

"Do you know how an internal combustion engine works, Jonathan?"

"Basically."

"If all the plans for internal combustion engines were lost, could you build one from scratch?"

"With the right people and equipment, maybe. Though I have no interest in engineering."

"Well I've brought together the right people to re-create a complex system using only a concept."

"That's definitely abstract enough. I wish you much success."

"Nurture your assets, Jonathan. 'Nothing gold can stay.'"

He shakes my hand firmly, pressing on my knuckle with his small rigid thumb; when he releases, he nods in Amity's direction as if I need encouragement. Amity dismisses William with a touch to his elbow, and William rejoins Delancey. After escaping William's monologue, Amity sidles up to me and asks about my conversation with Baker.

"Nothing important," I say.

"Everything Baker says is important. What did he tell you?"

"He said that ET is an ass-hat."

13

Sector B

Marga's text is very simple:

Free?

Yup

Something 2 show u

K

Broadview & Pearl in 15?

30

c u. BTW wear boots

I am off to another mysterious rendezvous with Marga. (Isn't she much more cryptic than she needs to be?) She doesn't seem to have anything to hide, and doesn't really appear to be paranoiac. So I am beginning to think that she may just be playing. Or is she playing up all the mystery and clandestine behavior as a way to attract attention to her work or to inspire others to create fantasies about who she is—fantasies much greater and far more interesting than the reality of a fine artist surviving on a trust fund left by a wealthy grandmother. But couldn't *that* just be *my* fantasy of who she is?

The truth is, for all the years I've known Marga, I haven't

really known Marga. Still, it's fun to try to figure out what she's all about. Getting to "know" Marga is like doing a scavenger hunt in an amusement park. If you forget the mission, there are still enjoyable things to do. Sure, there are a few things I do know. For instance, I know she has a brain surgeon father who is a pretty interesting and quirky kind of guy, and that they live in a multi-million dollar house, just shy of being a mansion, on the lake in the stratospheric Bratenahl neighborhood. I also know that Marga knows how to put on a formal high tea with fancy bone china, and that they have a nice fireplace, and that it's easy to get snowed in when you're visiting for tea and an arctic storm with lake effect dumps three feet of snow in an hour and you have to sleep in a guest room, covered with full-length mink and curly-wool Persian lamb coats because, for some reason, they have no extra comforters or blankets. (Or did Marga just say that so I could experience the luxury of sleeping under a woman's perfumed furs?) But what I really don't know is what I *don't* know about Marga, and that seems to be just about everything else. Every time we meet, I think that maybe today I will see the real Marga, and every time I am left with more questions than insights.

Anyway, I'm hoping spring will arrive early this year, which reminds me of Vivaldi so I pull up his *Four Seasons* on my phone and play it through the car's audio system. Outside is muddy, and the sun is casting a metallic copper shine on everything. The dirty old snow is finally, almost, melted. I take control of my anticipation by looking forward to a nice cappuccino with Marga in someplace small and warm.

When I reach the intersection where we are to rendezvous, I see Marga posing in front of the Art Deco facade of an old bank building. She's wearing a long, Swedish army overcoat of blue-gray wool and a pair of commando pants and combat boots. She's also got an olive green neck gaiter pulled up as a headband to cover her ears, and her long red pony tail is hanging out the back over her turned-up collar. Today, she definitely looks like an artist. I pull to the curb and she opens the door and heaves a very large and heavy rucksack into the back before she climbs into the passenger seat. Her coat is bulky so she has to wiggle a bit to get comfortable and pull the seat belt across her middle.

"Where to?" I ask.

"Is that the only phone you have with you?"

"Yeah. I only have one."

Marga picks up the phone, unplugs it from the charger, then puts it into a foil envelope and places it back on the console. Vivaldi immediately goes silent.

"I was listening to that," I say.

"If you want orchestra, *Midday Concert* is on WCSB right now."

"You are one inscrutable character".

Marga sits back, looks out the front window and says, "Sector B."

"Come again?"

"You asked, 'Where to.' We're going to Sector B."

"OK, then Sector B it is. But where is Sector B?"

"Kind of in The Flats. Follow the road that runs past the zoo. I'll show you where to turn and where to park and we'll walk the rest of the way from there."

Maybe I was wrong about her being just an artist. She is really unlike any other artist I know. Maybe there is more to Marga than any one person can ever fathom.

She has me turn a few times onto streets I never knew existed. Now I see houses that look like they materialized from Walker Evans photographs of rural America during the Great

Depression—ramshackle places perched on a ridge overlooking the square miles of abandoned steel mills. Places that took sulfur dioxide slaps to the face for a hundred years. All the wood is worn and mean, etched down to the grain from years of acid rain that fell during the Great Pollutions of the 20th century; even the mud is black and gray and toxic.

I park the car, we step over a guard rail, and Marga leads me on a path through a sickly woods to a steep, nearly vertical hill of broken shale. "Follow me," she says. "Do what I do." With every step, the shale slides beneath her feet and she sort of jumps, runs, and turns, shifting zig-zag like a downhill slalom skier on the small crumbly stone avalanches. I follow her down in just about a free-fall. My balance is constantly challenged and I intuitively make attitudinal adjustments several times a second. I am absolutely alive in the moment, and absolutely amazed I am alive the moment we reach the bottom.

"How do we get back up?" I ask.

Marga answers, "We'll take the stairs."

Marga hands me her backpack and signs with hand gestures for me to wait there while she creeps forward to survey the edge of a row of pine trees. She motions me forward and we jump across a little stream in a drainage ditch, climb a small rise, and arrive at the side of an oiled-down dirt road that runs around the perimeter fence of the old Smith and Finnerty Steel Mill. "A couple years ago I was taking pictures around here and some kids on bikes showed me how to get in," Marga says, as she leads me to a place where the chain link fence has been cut. "This hole's been here for years. Mill workers probably used it as a shortcut."

We step through the hole in the fence, and I make a perfunctory effort to close it behind us. The first thing I notice is the rust. Rust is everywhere. There are rusty railroad tracks and rusty rail cars—some derailed. The dirt is hard and matted down and rusty. In the low lying areas there are pools of stagnant rusty rain water and tall plants, some are cattails, others have more fluffy tops; my first thought is papyrus, but I know that doesn't grow this far north, maybe it's what they call pampas grass. All over the railroad track bed are small rusty purple balls called taconite, a kind of iron ore that kids used to pick up from the tracks behind the zoo to use for ammunition in slingshots. There are also chunks of sulfur, some the size of a man's fist, that are bright yellow and provide a striking contrast to the taconite. I wonder how these spilled treasures could still be visible on the surface since the steel mills closed so many years ago. But one look around answers my question: the soil here is so polluted that not much can grow, few plants, no leaves, nothing to cover the ground. It's mostly a brownfield.

From the hole in the fence to the main buildings could be an eighth of a mile, or a half mile—it's hard to judge because the size of the building complex is way beyond human scale. Old smelting and fabrication buildings are enormous, with silos a hundred feet tall, storage tanks the size and shape of sub-marines, a giant sphere with a funnel bottom here, spiral stairs wrap around smokestacks there, and pipes, maybe five feet in diameter, flow from the tops of towers that run horizontally for the entire length of the building. The railroad tracks run directly into the center of the largest one of these structures. And that's where we're heading. I feel like an archaeologist, but then realize that I am just a trespasser.

"Marga, aren't we trespassing?"

"On whose property?"

"The owner of this steel mill."

"Jonathan, the owner of this steel mill left forty years ago, as soon as he opened a replacement factory in Asia."

"Won't the police come?"

"Why should they? They have better things to do with their limited resources."

"Aren't you afraid of running into some bad guys in here?"

"No. That's why I carry this."

She opens her coat and reveals what is probably the prettiest, purplest hand gun I've ever seen.

"Damn! Where did you get that?"

"Birthday present from my ex-boyfriend in California. It's a Kimber *Amethyst* 1911, in 45 caliber. I loaded it with red tracer rounds."

"You know how to use it?" She gives me that look.

"We used to shoot old cars in the junkyard. But I don't have to shoot anybody; just the sight of it will scare off any sane person. Even if I miss, the sound and light is enough to make them pee their pants."

"Marga, you never cease to amaze me." At this she stops in her tracks looking hurt and her bottom lip goes pouty.

"Do you think I'm a bad person?"

"No. Not at all. However, you are unfathomable." She looks relieved.

"Oh, that."

Yes, That. Marga lives in the Mariana Trench of friendship and my sonar doesn't ping that deep.

We move on, following the tracks into the heart of the largest building. There is a smell of rusting iron, of course, but also a strong oily smell, a fishy oil smell. (Did they use whale oil forty years ago?) The roof consists mostly of a heavily reinforced glass skylight that appears to have been retractable once upon a time, probably so they could open it during a pour and let all the sulfurous pollution go straight out into the sky—to be enjoyed by the workers' families at home on the hill. There are catwalks in the sky everywhere in this building. They are next to parallel tracks for a movable gantry that spans the building from side to side and supports an enormous traveling crane that still holds, suspended in mid air, two hooks, each one as big as a Buick. Below the hooks is a crucible, like several other crucibles, that were lined up awaiting their turn at the blast furnace when the last whistle blew and the last shift worker punched out for the last time.

I get a bad vibe in this place; it feels incredibly dangerous on almost every level imaginable. For the most part, silence reigns, punctuated occasionally by the odd sounds of dripping water, and creaks and clanks from metal trusswork expanding or contracting with the heat of the sun. And she wants me to compose bright and happy music for a performance in this place? A requiem or a dirge would be more fitting.

"So, what do you think of Sector B?" Marga asks.

"This is it? You brought me all this way to get depressed over ruins porn?"

"Stop thinking like your mathematician girlfriend. Look at it as a performance space."

"For *whom* will you perform? Ghosts? Pigeons?"

"Do you know we had 25 people in here for a concert last week?"

"You're serious. How did you—" So many questions that they telescope out infinity mirror style.

"You want to know who I meant by 'we,' right?"

"Among a plethora of other things, yes."

Marga reaches out for a two foot long open end wrench hanging on a hemp rope and bangs it on some vertical trusswork:

3 bangs, pause, then 2 more. A window on the side of the crane cockpit slides open and a bearded man calls out in German.

"*Hallo Marga! Wen hast du mitgebracht?*"

"This is my good friend Jonathan. He's American."

"*Hallo* Jonathan! My name is Werner, but you can call me Vernon if that's easier."

"Werner is easy enough," I answer.

"Jonathan is the composer I told you about."

"*Wunderbar!* I was just running sound cable to the mixing board in here. Come up and take a look."

As Marga and I make our way around mysterious pieces of abandoned mechanical miscellany, I tell her that it has always been my dream to work in a steel mill; she doesn't believe me. "Actually, I've always dreamed of composing music for industrial accidents," I say as I kick a chunk of porous rock that looks like pumice, but is probably slag.

"Seriously," she says, "think about the acoustics in here and what might resonate the best. I was concerned that with all this metal around, it might sound too tinny. But the concert last week sounded really good. Werner thinks the rust doesn't echo as much, and might even absorb some of the glassy higher notes."

"Is Werner an acoustical engineer?"

"He's a physicist—electricity is his thing. He was a troubleshooter at CERN for a while and made some money, then he called me and asked if I knew of a squat in America where he could live illegally and do some experimenting. I brought him here."

We start up a spiral steel staircase to the catwalk, and I try not to look at Marga's backside as we climb.

"Why is it called 'Sector B'?"

"We all met in Berlin, in the part that used to be called the 'American Sector.' Since all the guys are from there, we decided to call this place the Berlin Sector, but 'Sector B' is edgier and easier to remember."

"All the guys?"

"There are four others, musicians—rock and electronic mostly, but all artists. Though they don't like to stay here overnight."

"Huh. Little Berlin, right here on the buckle of the rust belt; 'Sector B' sounds made-to-order."

When we reach the top of the stairs, Werner comes out of the crane cab and meets us on the catwalk. Marga makes introductions and walks away to her 'office' to make some coffee.

I'm not crazy about heights, and the builder of the catwalk did not take acrophobics into account when he designed the latticework floor. Werner senses my unease and tells me to focus on the handrails, and not the floor. We enter the crane cab and I'm amazed at how spacious it is; it looks more like the wheelhouse of an ocean freighter.

"Jonathan. Are you really American?"

"American born and raised," I say.

"Americans are direct. I like that—fewer misunderstandings, you know? May I be direct too?"

"Yes, definitely. Please do."

"Are you Marga's boyfriend? I mean do you love her?"

"No. I am not now, nor have I ever been, Marga's boyfriend. I love her like a crazy sister, but I'm not romantically interested if that's what you mean." (What I say is mostly true.)

"Yes, that is what I mean."

"Are you interested in her that way?" I ask.

"Of course! Isn't every man?" Yes. I know what he means. She becomes the target of desire for most men who meet her. It's not her intention, usually, and I'm not sure she understands it either.

"Not every man has your good taste in women, Werner. Just be careful. Marga is like a mustang, you know those beautiful horses that run wild in the American West? They don't fare well in captivity."

"I understand. Thank you my friend." And we shake hands.

Werner shows me the used mixing board he bought from some failed local band, and explains how he has re-purposed many of the cab's switches and levers to handle lighting and effects. (Lighting?) He tells me there are many old generators scattered around, some large enough to power a hospital, and easily brought back to life, but they require too much diesel fuel. It's much easier, he tells me, to tap into the Municipal Power lines—which he has already done. Power lines that, believe it or not, have remained intact, connected to sodium vapor street lamps that splash pools of orange light at random around the factory campus, and stay lit 24/7. Lamps that mostly, even more amazingly, have not burned out after blazing for half a century.

Werner has even cut an access hatch through the wall and into the giant pipes outside where he installed transducers to produce subsonic vibrations with seismic effects. Strange things started to happen. And he was afraid that the tones and harmonics might cause sympathetic vibrations that could cause the steel to flex like elastic. "And it would be an unpleasant concert if the hall collapsed upon us," he says. No kidding.

Also in the cab, Werner has a small keyboard he uses for testing. After apologizing for such low-quality equipment and the fact that the keys are not weighted, he asks me to play something—anything, to hear the hall. The mood of this place is getting to me, that and the fact that the sun is still setting early—soon—affects my choice to play the theme from Howard Hanson's *"Romantic" Symphony Number* 2: sad, challenging, and finally, victorious.The acoustics are what you might expect from Marshall amplifiers in a warehouse, yet there are so many varied angles and surface shapes that the music has no place to directly echo back, so the result is not bad. When I get to the heroic-sounding part, Werner stops me, makes some adjustments to the equipment and asks me to play that note again, just that D flat major chord. When I do there comes forth a solid "whomp" of a sound that I can feel. Werner laughs and tells me to play it again but look out the window of the cab this time. I do, and witness something like a heat wave that ripples through the factory and makes the cattails sway outside.

"Werner, what was *that*?"

"It's something I developed. Holographic sound? 3-D sound? I'm not sure what to call it yet, but it's physical."

"I'll say! How does it work?"

"The note is processed, modulated both in amplitude and frequency."

"AM and FM."

"Yes, but only in the auditory range, not in the radio frequencies. Though I was hoping to drive it up into a plasma."

"Have you played an entire concert through this processor?"

"I have some fears, you know?

"I'll bet you do."

"Don't you think it should be used sparingly, like garlic?"

"Or tympani," I say.

"Yes. Sparingly, like Tympani And Garlic. Maybe I'll call it TAG."

Just about now, Marga appears with an old, sooty-bottomed, Yosemite style percolator full of steaming coffee and three steel camping mugs in chipped gray enamel. With Marga in the middle, the three of us sit and dangle our legs over the side of the transverse catwalk, drink black coffee, and look down the railroad tracks. The setting sun filtered through the cattails casts shadows that look like Slender Man.

"This place must get spooky at night," I offer.

"There have to be ghosts," Marga says. "Too many people died working with fire and steel."

"How many, do you suppose?"

"I have no idea," she says, "but it stands to reason that it was lots of people."

"Do they ever come visit you at night?"

"It's hard to say. But just to be sure, I smudge my office with burning sage."

"There is too much strangeness going on at night," Werner contributes. "Lately I have seen the sharks: black helicopters—very quiet things—hovering around the perimeter."

"That's why we always put our cell phones into foil bags before coming here," Marga says. "The phones ping the cell towers six times per minute, even when they're turned off, and the foil acts as a Faraday cage to stop that." (There's that old boy Faraday again.)

"Why do you want to stop it?" I ask.

"A couple of helicopters with frequency counters could triangulate off of our cell phone signals, identify us, and locate our position," Werner answers. (Where have I heard this theme before?)

I nod as if I understand, though I'm not sure why a group of *avant-garde* musicians and artists would need to hide from black shark helicopters. But then again, I'm not from Berlin.

14

Single Room Occupancy

When the sun sets, Werner puts on a baseball cap with a headlamp that lights up the gantry in front of him. He's decided to go out to a club for some music and beer. Marga and I are welcome to join him; we pass. But we need to head back soon if we want to make it up that crazy hill to my car. Werner's headlamp scans from side to side as it shrinks away along the railroad tracks. Marga lights a kerosene lantern that is hanging on the side of the crane cab. (I note that it makes sense to have things like matches and kerosene and coffee around if you're going to spend any amount of time in an abandoned steel mill.)

She holds the lantern aloft with her left hand and with her right, laces her fingers through mine. She looks like a phantom, or an actress playing a phantom in a really scary film—which just intensifies the anxiety I'm feeling about walking on a corroded metal grid fifty feet in the air. To keep me close, she presses my hand to her hip and we walk together across catwalks, over platforms, and through bulkhead doors. I am practically blind in the darkness, and completely at her mercy. The lantern sways and shadows lurch up the walls, her heavy boots go 'toom', my black slip-on Vans sneakers scuff and I stub my toes on unseen bolts, and something heavy with rope that I suppose is an ancient block and tackle. (I should have worn boots like she told me in her text.) Marga continues to hold my hand against her hip and I can feel her anatomy working as she moves—which reminds me of learning to dance the cha-cha in fourth grade. I am in another world, Marga's world, and it is absolutely surreal.

After climbing a couple short staircases, we arrive at a steel door and have to step up over a ten inch high threshold. Marga communicates the difference in elevations by lifting up my hand and only says, "Be careful." We enter a cocoon of a room with bay windows that face outside on two of the walls and to the left of the door, another window that overlooks the catwalk and the steel-pouring bay. In New York City they would call this an "efficiency apartment" or "SRO—Single Room Occupancy." With a commanding view of most of the premises, this must have been a boss's office. Using a bit of logic, I feel proud to deduce that his title must have been Director of Operations. Marga puts the lantern down on a plank that serves as a desk under the window and asks, "How do you like my office?"

"Cozy."

The first thing I notice is a smell of sage, like somebody is preparing a turkey for the oven, then I smell *burnt* sage which is the anti-ghost remedy Marga picked up on a Native American reservation in Arizona. Next to the lantern is a piece of hundred year-old swag—an ashtray in the shape of a gear sprocket etched with the name of some long-defunct supplier; I can barely make out the words: "Suppliers of Iron and Steel Casings." The stub of sage is bound up with string and resting against one wall of this ash tray, looking like the mummified stogie of some dyspeptic, coarse-talking tank commander from the second world war. The sight and smell of ghost repellent is comforting.

Marga is busy arranging a futon couch so we can sit down. It looks fairly new. (How did she get that up here?) "Use that yardstick to pull the blackout curtains down off that nail and cover the window. And hang this thermal reflective tarp over that, so we can turn up the lights." I do. Marga lights some religious or magic candles she picked up in a bodega. They are tall glass tumblers with things like "Luck," "Health," and "Joy" printed on the sides. Now, the room really *is* cozy. Marga opens her backpack and removes canned food: green beans, chicken soup, corned beef, smoked kippered herring, several kinds of sardines, and even some cans of B&M brown bread with raisins. She hands me a can of the brown bread and directs me to a can opener on a little chest of drawers she uses as a sideboard. From the bottom of the bag she retrieves two glass jars wrapped in paper towels. "I saved these from yesterday's tea: Devonshire cream to go with our raisin bread."

We are picnicking on the banks of the River of No Return.

"When are we heading back," I ask.

"Oh, we can't head back now. Now we have to stay."

15

Midnight on the Perimeter

The brown bread comes out of the can in a solid cylinder that Marga slices into coins about three quarters of an inch thick and lays them, one at a time, on a piece of foil on the lantern's flat top. In a little while, after the raisins are sizzling, Marga turns over the bread. While the second slice is cooking, Marga opens the jar of clotted cream and spreads it thick like butter on the first. She feeds me a bite and waits for my reaction. The bread has a heavy molasses taste that the raisins help to cut, and the buttery cream helps it all go down. I nod till I can swallow. "Not bad, but it can't compare to those little cucumber sandwiches you serve at your tea parties."

"Out here on the perimeter," she says, "sacrifices must be made."

There's not much to clean up, though the can needs to be secured in an old covered fire bucket to discourage any mice. She wants to make more space, so I help to move things around: an olive drab steel chair, a homemade wooden bench, an old steamer trunk full of costumes and wigs. Marga pulls at the bottom of the couch frame and it becomes a full-size futon bed.

"We'll sleep here," she says.

I'm lucky Amity is out of town. I would have no way to explain this so that she could understand. Do I even understand? How long can one play friend to a passionate friend before one crosses one's own Rubicon? Uncle Dan says a relationship is always either moving toward a commitment or toward a breakup. Which way here, which way there? I wonder as I wander.

Marga points out a narrow door to the right of the main door. That's the toilet and sink. She tells me that Werner (she calls him Vernon this time) connected the water pipes to a 55 gallon rain barrel on the roof—so use the water sparingly: "If it's yellow, let it mellow; if it's brown, flush it down. And don't drink the water from the sink because it probably has copper and lead from the old pipes, plus whatever fell into the rain barrel. If you are thirsty, there are a few gallon jugs of drinking water under the table. One other thing," she says, "don't go out without me."

"I wouldn't dream of it."

She steps into the lavatory with a gallon of spring water, and I imagine she is brushing teeth and washing her face—whatever evening ritual wealthy young female artists perform when they are living in a primitive squat. When she emerges, she is carrying all of her commando clothes in a neatly folded stack, and she is now wearing a white flannel nightgown with a sparse pattern of tiny violets and a ruffled hem at the bottom that halfway covers the tops of her untied combat boots. "Your turn," she says. "I left some toothpaste and a new toothbrush for you on the sink."

On a little shelf there is a candle that provides just enough light for me to get toothpaste on the brush and a fair aim at the porcelain throne. Above the sink is a mirror with a beveled edge; the silver backing is so tarnished that I am seeing myself, as they say, in a glass darkly. I meet my eyes in the reflection and wonder what I may be getting myself into, what I am already into. For a fleeting second I consider what I might feel or do if I discovered that Amity had been in a similar situation. There is a flush of anxiety in my face, and my scalp tingles. I shake my head and vocalize a truncated groan to block out the thought. (Reality is, Jonathan, you *are* in this situation.) It's as if I were flying a plane that crashed in a dangerous country and I have to figure out how to stay alive until I can be extracted. Amity would understand that analogy. But I'm *not* a downed pilot and the cavalry is not coming. I rinse my mouth. I have no flannel jammies to change into, and even if I did, I might not, since I feel safer having a layer of denim between Marga and me.

I step out of the toilet and drop my sneakers in front of the main door. The air is redolent of hot wax and kerosene. Marga has blown out the candles and asks me to turn the lantern down to just a glow. In primitive conditions, fire should always be nearby and ready. She is lying, not posing, on the futon. No games, she is ready to sleep. In fact, she looks so calm, that for a while I forget about ghosts and marauders. I put my coat over the back of the office chair and retrieve a small notebook and pencil from the pocket. I should log this strange day. But ach! Less evidence requires fewer explanations. And what would I write anyway? Even the factual sounds fictitious.

I look at Marga. In the lantern glow she looks so soft and warm. (Everyone looks soft and warm by lantern light.) She is asleep. And she is beautiful. (Every woman looks beautiful when she's asleep.) I lie down with my back to her and get as close to the edge of the bed as possible, putting a good six inches between us. I am emotionally exhausted and feel myself dropping off to sleep even here.

And then I smell perfume.

The dream starts out in a field of wild flowers. It is Death Valley in a rare bloom after waiting a century for a freak rainstorm. Yellow flowers as far as the eye can see. The valley floor is a sea of yellow blossoms, the distant hills: yellow and gold. It is a world of gold, and it is warm and fragrant and more real than any flower garden or florist shop I have ever visited. The view has a soul. It is a living experience providing everything one could ever need. But it is morning and the sky is turning red; (Red sky in morning—sailor take warning.) There are red dust clouds rolling in that are beautiful yet strange: terrifying and fascinating at the same time. They are enormous, enormously powerful, and overpowering all the golden blooms. The clouds roll in, seemingly in slow motion, but their power to change the landscape is confirmed by the sight of miles of yellow blossoms getting buried under a beautiful red dust. In the distance there is a flash, a ball of metallic light, then an angry shock wave, and fire in an expanding cloud of thick black smoke that threatens to consume all of the flowers. But instead, the black smoky fires are extinguished by the red clouds—and the red dust covers the sea of yellow flowers and preserves them for the next rain. A shock wave continues to roll through the hills, a thunder rumbles through the valley, and the landscape surrenders to the red dust dream.

When I awake, the office is shaking with a subsonic rumble and pulsating air pressure. I turn to Marga who is barely conscious.

"Marga, wake up! It's an earthquake!" She presses her finger to my lips and shushes me.

"Keep quiet," she whispers. "Sharks. Don't move."

"What are they looking for?"

"Whatever they can find. Don't let it be us."

Yes it's quieter than a regular helicopter, but its rhythm is persistent and cannot be ignored. It's so close. The prop wash undulating the air pressure makes my ears alternately block and open, and even though we're inside, I'm finding it hard to breathe.

It occurs to me that we might die here tonight, and *that* was never in my plans. I am facing the same impossible choice that has challenged humans since our primitive days: fight or flight, and I can do neither, but only remain in place, quiet, breathing as little as possible in the hope that the T-Rex outside will move on to another cave. I feel a sudden panic and an urge to run. Marga senses my crisis and pulls me closer, kisses my forehead, and strokes my hair like Mother calming her child.

The helicopter moves on and away, but my heart is still pounding, shaking my breath, and the adrenaline has turned my fingers and toes an icy cold. I look at Marga and she closes my eyelids with kisses. Now she sings softly to me—children's songs in foreign languages. Several languages, each able to say something with a different shade of meaning. She sings in a whisper so close that her lips occasionally brush against and vellicate my ear while her warm, minty breath on my neck draws goosebumps. I hear some French, some German, some Italian. She seems to have exhausted her repertoire of nursery songs and switches to poetry. Maybe Verlaine. What she is telling me seems complicated and my understanding is limited to the words I know from Verdi operas and Schubert lieder and the common phrases that everybody knows. But Marga is speaking poetry: smooth, liquid, and lovely. I start to drift and dream, then I hear jewels that go straight to my soul: *"Mon amour, mein Schatz, Ti voglio. Ti voglio tanto bene, amore mio."* I don't care if it's poetry or something else; I am alive, we are alive, and Marga is letting me know. Her tears fall on my cheek and she wipes them away with her hair. I lie and float in her embrace till just before dawn when fatigue at last prevails.

16

Breakfast in a Tin

About two hours later I am awakened by sunlight through the open curtains and the sound and smell of coffee perking over an alcohol zen stove. Marga is sketching in her journal, sees me move, and speaks.

"I warmed up the leftover raisin bread and the coffee's almost done."

"How does an adventurer like you suddenly become domesticated?"

"What's domesticated? Everybody needs to eat, and everybody *I* know likes coffee." (So there, Jonathan.)

We share the leftover brown bread and some kippers that we eat straight from the tin using extra chop sticks she saved from last week's takeout. I'm thankful for the salty smoked herring since it cuts through the cloying sweetness of the bread. The black coffee is straight out of a detective *film noir*. Although I am hungry, I'm also careful to be polite and not to eat too quickly or take too much. Marga moves the larger pieces of fish to my side of the tin and gives me the extra share of bread. I'm a little embarrassed about last night, and I avoid looking directly at her.

She on the other hand is sitting very close, looking directly at me and tilting her head to the side to get a better angle toward my eyes. I think she may be playing, so I make direct eye contact. Now that the need to eat has been satisfied, and the desire for morning coffee has been fulfilled,

"How do you feel?" she asks.

"Thick as a brick."

"You look upset."

"You sound like a girlfriend."

Marga wipes her eyes with her fingertips and reorders the few things on the table. Now it is *she* avoiding *my* eyes.

"Marga, there are some things I need to know."

"What specifically?"

"Too many to be specific."

"Pick just one then."

"What happened last night?"

"You had a bad dream, I think."

"Caused by some helicopters, I think."

"Oh, that. Right."

"But I'm not asking about that yet. What happened between us?"

"Nothing happened. You had a nightmare, the helicopters woke you up, and I helped you stay calm."

"Marga, you wore perfume last night." She shrugs. "In a squat in an abandoned factory."

"It's cologne number 4711. I like the way it smells."

"So do I, and that's part of the confusion. And that angelic flannel night dress, was that for me too?"

"Did you like it? Be honest."

"Honestly? Yes."

"Did it make you want me?" (Why should I care about

propriety?)

"I wanted to hold you and kiss you and get as close as I could get."

"Why didn't you?"

"Because that's not who we are. I'm engaged, and you've never really wanted me anyway."

"You're wrong there Jonathan. I've told you so many times that I've always been crazy mad about you."

"But that's just something you say."

"And I don't lie. Not to you."

"So are you trying to steal me away from Amity? It won't work."

"No, I don't want you to leave her. But I need to know that you love me. And you don't have to tell me; I'll know. I need you to always love me. Otherwise I can't create."

"This is messing with my head."

"You are my muse, Jonathan." (How then should I process this?) She continues. "Look, you're safe. Nothing happened last night. OK? Not between us."

"You are so wrong."

Marga puts some wrappers in the fire bucket and covers it. She's nervous. Maybe she's revealed too much. Exposed her soul. She looks directly at me again, runs her fingers through my hair, takes a big sniff of my scalp, then smiles a smile that should be reserved only for lovers.

"I've always been..." she begins, then catching herself, stops abruptly. "Make yourself at home. I'm going down to my studio to paint." She takes her sketchbook and walks through the bulkhead office door. I stand and watch through the reinforced glass as she stretches her arms skyward, prances, then hops and skips like a child, and finally jogs, weightless, down the catwalk toward the back of the factory.

* * *

I brush my teeth and take a huge drink of water, then gather up the few things I had taken from my pockets last night. I look around Marga's office and notice details I hadn't seen before. There are sketches drawn directly onto the wooden table with a Sharpie, measurements for something she was planning to build, but the measurements are not in feet and inches, nor are they metric, but they are plotted out in "hands"—likely influenced by her earlier interest in things equestrian. It's definitely more organic and human scale to use body parts to measure objects. And I'm just a few body parts away from disaster. There are also some lines written on the wall—some lyric or poetry she was working on: "Slip kin sit / Mother chore baby / Chair baby more / Mother milk spill." I haven't a clue what it means, but I know I'm getting a glimpse inside Marga's mind at something she hadn't intended to share.

As I head out to meet the day, there is considerably more light on the catwalk than there was yesterday; it's shining in through the formerly retractable glass skylight. The metal grid walkway is less ominous when lit from above. With a hand on the railing, I focus my gaze forward and occasionally forget that the floor is just expanded metal consisting mostly of empty space. There is some motion in the crane cab, so I decide to visit Werner. He is looking through a tool box full of junk.

"Morning Werner."

"Hallo Jonathan. Do you happen to have any razor blades? I'm thinking of trimming up the beard a little."

"No. Sorry. I wasn't planning to stay last night. By the way, were you here when the black helicopters came snooping around?"

"Ja. I was a little drunk when I came back, and I forgot and took the phone out of the foil pack. Maybe they were sniffing my signal."

"I don't understand. Why are they looking for you?"

"They are looking for this," he says, and pulls from the box a square frame of lavender-tinted transparent acrylic the size of an old DVD case that's holding a clear disk roughly the size of a ginger snap cookie. Enclosed inside the disk and centered in red cross-hairs is a rust-colored pellet the size of a match head; maybe it *is* a piece of rust. Or wood. Or a piece of ancient cloth stained with blood.

"What is it?"

"Some foolish scientists call it 'the relic'; they wanted to use it as a target in the particle accelerator. They believe it will open a hole in space-time and some other dimension. The day they were scheduled to run the accelerator, I lifted their target and took a walk. I guess they figured out that I have it."

"That's some far-out science fiction," I say.

"Maybe. But there is a real possibility that it could cause a localized black hole, and they don't understand the real danger, or they don't care. I thought if I took it, I could remove the risk. But now, the risk is on me."

"So who is in the helicopters?"

"Some sort of paramilitary contractors. They come here and fossick around. Sometimes they land and piss over by the cattails. Once, one of the crew shot a wild dog, and his commanding officer scolded him for making too much noise. 'We're supposed to be invisible, you jackass!' were his exact words."

"You'd better be careful. That thing must be valuable for them to travel so far to find you and get it back."

"It's one of a kind. That's why they call it 'the relic,'" he says. "This is a big facility, so I think it's safe here. Where is Marga?"

"She said she was going to her studio to paint. Where is her studio?"

"Northwest wing, all the way in the back. It has a southern exposure and good light. But Marga doesn't allow any of us to go in there."

"Thanks. I'll remember that. By the way, you might want to find a better hiding place for your relic."

* * *

With the morning sun to my right, I walk north through the main building looking for a room on my left. Water drips down from illogical places, probably leaking in from rooftop puddles of leftover snow melt. I think about how big the snow piles must get up there during the depths of winter when an arctic blizzard with lake effect dumps on the city. To birds it must look like a glacial thaw with plenty of places to splash and drink. There could even be returning Canadian geese up there taking a swim during a rest stop. My daydream evaporates when I reach the end of the building and still haven't found a room with a southern view. I call out for Marga and in a few moments, a wall moves.

But it's not a wall, it's a movable stage set painting of a wall, complete with rusty steam pipes, graffiti, and crumbling brick— all paint, and all *trompe l'oeil*, attached at the top with pulleys that glide along a taught steel cable. Marga is holding three toothbrushes full of paint: one cerulean blue, one pumpkin orange, and another Naples yellow. "What's up with the toothbrushes?" I ask.

"I'm scrubbing the pigment into the primed canvas; it makes the colors glow like a Rothko." I ask if I can see and she tells me not now, not yet. "Someday. One way or another," she says.

17

Revelation in Toronto

Amity is back in town and has the long weekend off, so we take the new car on a little road trip to Toronto—one of my favorite places to go for concerts, museums, theater, and the film festival. Amity likes it for the restaurants, architecture, bilingual culture, and living large at the Royal York Hotel. We leave before dawn and take the long way: to Detroit and over the Ambassador Bridge into Windsor. From there I stay on the less-traveled byways close to the north coast of Lake Erie and soak in the beautiful countryside.

Eventually we turn left onto Route 10, a road that's laser-straight and true, that takes us directly into Chatham where we stop for gas and coffee. Chatham is the town where during the 1850s (according to a plaque on the wall) abolitionist John Brown recruited local men and planned his raid on the Harpers Ferry Arsenal back in the USA. On a bank of the river, we find a bench next to a sugar maple and watch the wind move regiments of little ripples diagonally south across the water's surface in the direction of Virginia.

I've been driving for six hours and I guess I'm getting tired.

Due to the unusually early morning start, my brain chemistry is confused about what phase of the sleep cycle I should be in. I'm experiencing something like jet lag so the world is becoming a little too heavy for me to remain chipper and frisky or to take everything lightly. I was hoping I could get through this trip without going deep, but there are demanding things in the air—a lone robin's melancholy rain song, the smell of wet humus, a restless spirit in a sudden temperature drop— and I start to think about the importance of every seemingly insignificant thing. Amity is doing what she's been doing since we left Cleveland: looking at her phone and answering texts. I catch myself thinking about Marga, and I want to go—now.

We stop at Tim Horton's and get a half-dozen donuts and a couple coffees for the ride. Amity has cut way down on coffee and tea because she says caffeine can create fibroid tumors in women's breasts. Nothing I should worry about, she tells me, fibroids go away when caffeine is removed from the diet, and so she removed it.

For the last hour or so of our trip we cruise in on the 401, the King's Highway that takes us to the Queen Elizabeth Way. As it gets closer to the city, the road widens until just before downtown Toronto where it suddenly opens into eight lanes. The effect this dilation has on me is something resembling a satori. I sigh, feel a wave of peace wash over me, and let the car's GPS guide us straight to Front Street and the parking garage of The Royal York.

At the front desk, I show the reservation on my phone, and Amity pays with her black AmEx card. We stroll around the lobby, down the grand spiral staircase to the underground shopping court, check a few menus, and grab a free magazine about where to go and what to do: Orchestra Toronto is playing Holst's *The*

Planets in a matinee concert at Meridian Arts Centre. We have just enough time to wash up and catch the subway to North York.

It's sunny but not hot. It never seems to get hot in Canada, or maybe I've never been in Canada when it's hot, but every time I've come here with Amity there seems to be a chill in the air or the threat of a chill.

The concert is fine, though I struggle to stay awake, and my stomach grumbles out loud during the quiet moments. I've heard this piece performed many times and by excellent orchestras, so there are no surprises. Still, the performance today is accurate and substantial, though if I were the conductor, I would have beefed it up in the Mars movement—but then again, I'm not Canadian.

When the applause ends, the woman who was seated next to Amity (and who appears to be ecstatic over the music) introduces herself as Chiara. She is tall and stately, with shiny chestnut hair cut in a chin-length retro page-boy style with bangs and sides that curl in toward her face. She could be an extra from a *Great Gatsby* party except that she has a slight accent and uses Italianate gestures when she speaks. Her date is Townsend McGill, a young philosophy professor from University of Toronto. He's about five foot ten, same as Chiara, and he's dressed in blue jeans, a button-down white oxford shirt, and a tan corduroy sport coat.

They are friendly enough and we strike up a conversation. The women take the lead as we all walk toward the subway. Chiara slips her arm through Amity's and chats away as if they were long-lost sisters. Amity appears to enjoy the attention, but from my experience and watching her operate, I know that she is also doing a quick personality study of this unusual subject.

"I'm glad she's found a friend," McGill says to me.

"Glad?"

"She has radical ups and downs, which makes things difficult at times. She's very successful, you know. She's editor of an Italian journal."

"How about you?"

"I teach philosophy at U of T. That's where I did my graduate work on the 'phenomenology of place.' Are you familiar with phenomenology?"

"I only took Intro to Philosophy, so I forget. Is that Heisenberg?"

"You mean Heidegger, but more like Husserl and Merleau-Ponty. It's the study of conscious experience from the first person point of view."

"So it's about living life."

"Pretty much. Except unlike normal people, phenomenologists pay attention."

McGill goes on to give an example to illustrate why this is important. He says one can drive for hours, traveling all day while deep in thought or conversation, or while transported by music, (to this I can relate) but it is rare that a driver is conscious of the act of driving *and* listening *and* thinking—the entire subjective experience all at once. A phenomenologist driver wants to be aware of the totality of the experience of being *inside* an environment (the car) that's traveling *through* an environment (the countryside). I tell him his phenomenology reminds me of Amity's "quantum psychology" and how she observes that most people live in continuous trance states. And me? Writing music focuses me. When I'm composing and in the creative zone, the walls drop away, time refuses to act normal, and either stops or jumps ahead. After an hour of composing, I find that colors are more vivid, sounds more intense, all sensations more focused—in short, when I create, I am more alive. I notice that when McGill is thinking about philosophy, his pupils dilate and his eyes have a far-away look. He asks me nothing about my music.

We walk south on Yonge Street and right past the subway. Amity has asked a few questions, but otherwise shows deference to Chiara and her monologue which resembles an espresso-fueled stream of consciousness. McGill is slower-paced and pensive, but similarly self-absorbed. Chiara—McGill's fiancée, he now tells me—will be going back to Italy for six months to organize a new office for her publishing firm, while he has managed to swing an unpaid sabbatical in order to teach a semester in Jakarta, Indonesia.

"Phenomenologists begin with the principle of *epoché* where we refrain from making judgments," McGill says. (A car runs a red light and narrowly misses him.) "What a jerk!" I say, referring to the driver. McGill, oblivious, continues. "From there, a phenomenologist refrains from judging whether anything exists or can exist."

"What's the purpose of that?"

"It leads directly to a freedom from worry and anxiety thereby inducing a state of *ataraxia*, a kind of mindfulness which allows us to see the world as it really is," he says with that far-away look.

"Sounds like Amity's description of quantum psychology again."

"Or the Buddha's nirvana," McGill says with a wry smile.

"I guess all roads lead to Rome. Have you ever been to Rome? I'll bet they have good pizza."

"No. But after I finish my sabbatical in Jakarta, I'll meet up with Chiara in Venice. Maybe we'll go to Rome after that."

By now I'm absolutely famished, and after a while I stop the group to ask if the couple would like to join Amity and me for dinner. McGill opens his mouth but doesn't speak; instead he looks at Chiara who purses her lips slightly. "I think we have other plans," McGill says, though I think he would really like to have dinner with us.

We continue on in this way for a long while. Chiara has burned off her excess energy and is now speaking quietly and in serious tones. This gives Amity the room she needs for more probing questions. McGill is also speaking, but I miss most of what he says because it's so esoteric, and I am very tired and very hungry. I point out another Tim Horton's donut shop along the way, but nobody gets the hint. "There's a Greek restaurant," I say. "Here's Vietnamese. Tacos. Curry." But nobody's listening to me. In fact, my voice is getting weak and I think I may be talking to myself.

We've been walking almost an hour and I can't really tell you much about the journey except that there are restaurants and gas stations everywhere and we just ran out of sidewalk at the 401 overpass. (Is this still Toronto?) It seems like we're on some kind of endless military hike and may be lost; but no one else is concerned. I can feel that the Chelsea boots I'm wearing have rubbed a couple of big blisters on the backs of my heels. Somewhere near Lawrence station we say goodnight and exchange contact info and promise to stay in touch. I feel slightly elevated by having the professor's embossed business card in my pocket.

The subway is clean, but it has a strong smell of electrical sparks—I'm not really sure what ozone smells like, but it may be that. My eyes are burning and I can't keep my hands off my face; I need them to prop up my head. Amity does not look tired, in fact I can see the wheels are turning in her brain. "You and Chiara seemed to hit it off," I say.

"It's called 'intimacy on encounter.' People often have deeply personal conversations with someone they've just met and whom they are not likely to ever see again. That layer of anonymity affords a feeling of safety and freedom to share their problems."

"She looked OK to me."

"She's beautiful, but dysfunctional."

"Hmm, like piano music by Erik Satie. Is it possible that it might just be a cultural difference?" Amity looks at me like a tenured professor might look at a freshman who's just asked a worn-out question. I change course. "McGill, her fiance, is going to teach for a semester in Jakarta, Indonesia."

"That's about as far away from Chiara as he can travel without leaving the planet."

I'm surprised to hear Amity being so judgmental. The more time I spend with this revised Amity, the less self-confident I feel. She is a new woman, and around her I feel like an immature boy.

I wonder if this is how she behaves with others when I'm not around. I wonder if this is how she behaves when she's with ET. I wonder if I'm holding her back.

18

An Adolescent's Question

In a little while Amity and I are back downtown, and decide to eat at the hotel. I can't remember what I ordered (everything is so expensive in this place) but I chose what I chose because it was the median price. When it arrives, it is shrimp curry with coconut rice and some kind of chutney—Earl Grey or Major Grey, I can't remember what it said on the menu.

"Amity, do you ever wonder about the purpose of all this?"

"I suppose their mission statement expresses a desire to provide the optimum dining experience using the best quality of organically grown ingredients."

"I'm not talking about the restaurant. I'm talking about life."

"Not that again. Don't get philosophical Jonathan, you know it doesn't lead to anything useful."

"Must everything be utilitarian?"

"To prosper in life, one must move toward one's goal, and when it is achieved, set a new goal."

"So you just set and achieve goals until you die? That's the meaning of life?"

"Oh please, Jonathan, don't get morose. I'm talking about

Maslow's *Hierarchy of Needs*. Once the needs are satisfied, one becomes self-actualized."

"So Maslow is a guru preaching 'Get enough stuff, and you'll reach Nirvana?'"

Amity goes silent and parks a stifled frown at the corners of her mouth. I know she thinks that my questioning is just sophistry, but she will clam up rather than risk triggering me into delivering a half-baked lecture on the wisdom of the Sophists. She will remain silent on this and many other topics that she has placed in long-term parking. Soon, she may be permanently mute in my company.

"I've got to figure this out, Amity."

"What is there to figure?"

"Life. Why I write music. Why I want and *need* to create."

"You are twenty-six years old Jonathan. 'Who am I' is an adolescent's question."

"Oh, I see. So you don't know either."

"Are you so unhappy?"

"What makes you say that?"

"Happy people enjoy their lives; unhappy people question the meaning of life. You really have more control over your happiness than you think, Jonathan. You choose to write music, and you choose to live an artist's lifestyle. But somewhere along the path that you've chosen, you bought into the myth that artists must suffer. You don't *need* to be poor. There's no *virtue* in poverty. You can have a *real* career, live in a nice house, and write music in your spare time."

"Right. And I can just as easily become somebody else. Somebody who can provide the suburban bungalow with a little garden, a Volvo SUV, and I can keep the aspidistra flying. Well maybe that's just not me."

I'm not sure what this contretemps is about anymore, nor how it began. I was trying to make a point, but now I feel more confused and misunderstood than ever. Amity's eyes have widened and her face has lost its color. She looks like she's going into shock.

"Who told you that?" she whispers. "William? Karl? My god, did I talk in my sleep?"

"What are you talking about? Told me what?"

"Jonathan, this is not funny. You can throw away your future, but don't destroy mine along with it. It took me months to get my code-word clearance."

"*You* have a code-word clearance?" Amity narrows her eyes. "Bungalow? Your code-word is bungalow?" Amity crosses her arms and stares at the Berber carpet. "Volvo?" Amity covers her face with her hands and considers everything she's worked for, everything she's plotted, planned, and arranged for a decade. "I must have talked in my sleep," she says to herself. "Aspidistra?" I push. "That's it, isn't it?" She reacts, "Who told you that?" I punch the title into the search engine on my phone. "Orwell told me. English Lit, freshman year. Here," I say, "Let DuckDuckGo tell you," and I show her the result: *Keep the Aspidistra Flying* by George Orwell. She seems relieved, then troubled anew. Something important has been breached, but not by a living human. "Don't say that word out loud again," she says. And now she knows that I know, because she's confirmed it.

"ET came up with that code-word, didn't he?" I ask, and get the iron stare. "He's such a putz."

***

Amity walks out of the restaurant without me, and I tell the waiter to give himself a large tip and charge it to our room. On the ride up in the elevator, neither of us says a word. She's slipping away from me. Something is amiss. Amity is clearly having second thoughts about taking me on as a life partner, and it feels like a premarital divorce. I have a strong urge to hash it all out when we get back to the room, but then I remember something Uncle Dan told me: "If it's late at night and it seems important, it's not important." Instead, when we get into our suite, Amity grabs a bathrobe and her make-up kit and heads into the bathroom. I approach the door and am about to knock until I hear her talking. Her phone is on the table near the bed, so she is either talking to herself, praying, or crying. Then she starts the shower and I can't hear anything else.

I lie down on top of the bedspread, fully dressed (sans shoes) and rub together my sore tired feet. When I wake up it is nearly 3 am, and the bedroom smells like a forest. It's the hotel's complimentary shower gel, that piney Canadian brand called *Vitabath*. Amity is asleep. I brush my teeth then sit in the burgundy ostrich-leather club chair and rest my throbbing feet on the matching ottoman while I listen through ear buds to the local classical station on my phone's FM radio. The announcer uses a pretentious faux British accent to name the piece that just ended, then he carelessly lets the accent drop when he reads the news. I turn it off and try to meditate, but I can't focus on "OM" or any other magic word, so I just listen closely to the air conditioner's fan. In a few minutes the sound disappears and I am in the steel mill again and Marga is declaring her love for me while I feign sleep. "You are my muse, Jonathan. *Je t'aime. Ti amo—più di ogni altra cosa al mondo*...more than anything in the world."

About three hours later when I open my eyes, the sun is up. I take a shower to scrub away the residue of the dream Marga. She must have been thinking of me. Anyone who thinks that people can't communicate telepathically or read each other's minds is naive, although usually we ignore the other's mental information as a courtesy and as a way to keep our sanity. As I rinse off the shampoo, Marga's face slides away and Amity's image materializes. When I come out of the bathroom, Amity is sitting at the foot of the bed, fully dressed and scrolling through messages. I ask her if she'd like to go out for breakfast and she tells me she's not up to it, that I should go by myself, and that she can order room service if she gets hungry. Besides, she needs to catch up on some work. I ask if she'd like to head back a day early, and she says, "I think you have a good idea."

Really? Then why don't I feel good about it?

19

Oh the times they are a changin'

Downstairs I wander through the PATH, the underground tunnel system that connects most of the major buildings in downtown Toronto. I've got a dry lump in my throat and a feeling of hunger with no appetite. I'm not sure where to go. I just look in storefront windows as I come to them: cell-phone stores, phone cases, phone accessories, pharmacies, basketball shoes, another Tim Horton's. Then I smell vanilla, and figs, and cherries. It's coming from a tobacconist's shop; must be pipe tobacco. (Who smokes a pipe anymore? How cool would that be?) Prominently displayed in the window is a red box, about as long as, and half as wide as, a shoe-box, emblazoned with a drawing of three clove buds and the word Jakarta. Now that is synchronicity! Just yesterday I was speaking with a philosopher who is going to Jakarta. What does it mean? Who knows? But I'm going to try McGill's *epoché* and drop my judgment for a while to see where it takes me. I enter the store to the jingle of an old-fashioned bell that's attached to the door with a spring.

The walls are glass humidors full of all sizes of cigars wrapped in green, brown, or blackish leaves with visible veining that makes them look alive, like skin. The glass showcase is full of smoking pipes with wooden bowls carved from the burls of briar wood, each one beautifully patterned and unique as only nature can do. The counter-top supports glass jars filled with cut pipe tobacco flavored with all kinds of things, but especially vanilla, rum, cherry, and some mysterious unknown spices. Behind the counter are racks filled with cigarettes. Ancient folk music is playing in the back room; I think it's Bob Dylan: "Oh the times they are a changin."

The clerk comes out wearing a Harris Tweed sport coat that looks like mine except his shows a lot more mileage with a frayed collar and obvious holes in the sleeves from burns or moths—it's hard to say which. His face has a certain tweediness to it as well, having a dry, dusty, leathery look of someone who has absorbed a lot of pipe smoke in his lifetime. I ask him about the red Jakarta box in the window, and he tells me it is only for display, unless I have fifteen-hundred Canadian dollars to spend on it. Why so much? The brand was the most popular *kretek* (hand-rolled clove cigarette) but has been discontinued for some time. This is a full carton of those rare coffin nails. With a hundred twenty cigarettes to a carton, that's more than 12 bucks per smoke. But if I'm interested in Indonesian clove cigarettes, there are other brands that are still being produced. He recommends Djarum.

"What brand do you smoke now?" he asks.

"I haven't had a smoke in ten years," I say, "But I'm thinking of starting again."

"You shouldn't. It's a filthy, awful habit."

"Do the laws here require you to talk customers out of buying your merchandise?" He gets me a pack of Djarum and collects my fifteen dollars.

Back in the PATH outside the store there is no place to smoke a cigarette without offending someone or getting a ticket. So I carefully open the pack—which looks like it has been folded and glued by hand—and smell the spices. I look at the address of the factory: Jakarta, Indonesia, and try to remember what McGill said about the place and what kind of significance there could be to this synchronicity business. I imagine beautiful, lush islands, tropical breezes gently tinkling bamboo chimes, and full percussion orchestras playing exotically-tuned Javanese music late into the night. I put the pack into the outer pocket of my sport coat next to the lapel and just over my heart. Then I ride up an escalator, emerging onto the street and into the sunshine.

As I wander around downtown, I get this strange feeling, actually more like a realization than a sensation, that Amity is no longer my fiancée, and maybe she's not even my girlfriend. Strange to think of her as a girl now. She has become so strong, so confident, and so independent lately that I feel soon she will have no need for me. Need? That's funny. Amity only has goals. She may be ready to graduate from me and move on to someone more equal to her in character and abilities. But what the hell does that mean? Am I not a composer? A creative genius whose abilities cannot be measured on an IQ scale? That's what I tell people anyway. Friends believe me. I'm not sure Amity believes me anymore. Truth is, though we've been growing in different directions for some time now, I can only see *her* growth, but I myself rely on the opinions and feedback of others to gauge my own progress. Fact is, I have my doubts about a lot of things lately, including everything I've just told you.

For a long while now I've been aimlessly meandering through the streets while I mentally trip between fantasies of a brilliant equatorial paradise called Jakarta, and a dark, over-chilled room at the Royal York where my sunny-haired fiancée sits alone, distracting herself from emotional crisis by playing the workaholic scientist. I remember McGill's phenomenology trick, and try to stop judging my own reality.

I pull focus into the present moment and see that I am passing through Chinatown. But soon the buildings lose their Asian reference and take on a hippie vibe with psychedelic graffiti murals. A big Hollywood-type billboard tells me that I have now entered Kensington Market. I sit for a while on a wooden bench as I think about my situation, and I feel overcome with a tight feeling in my stomach. Maybe I need food, but how can I eat when I imagine the whole damn world is falling apart around me?

Before I realize it, I am smoking a kretek that is spitting little sparking embers of clove, and I'm getting smiles from artsy college students who pass by. I start to relax. It's the first time I've had a cigarette since I was 16 when Amity asked me to quit for her sake. She reminded me that, when I was young, cancer had taken my mother and it could be genetic. (What color was my mother's hair? In the only images I can conjure of her, she's bald and wan.) The cloves crackle when I take a drag, and although I know this stuff is deadly, I'm grateful that it momentarily soothes my tight throat, stomach, and nerves. Still, I shouldn't stay here too long or the anti-smoking patrols are duty-bound to show up and harass me.

I crush out the smoke and launch myself into the crowd. There are so many smiling couples and tourists whose cheerful demeanor only shellacs my misery until it is hermetically sealed. But I am determined to shake off the blues. I wander down a pedestrians-only street lined with craftsy vendors of all sorts and buy a pretty pair of handmade dangling silver earrings from a flirty saleswoman, and then immediately realize that they are really Marga's style, not Amity's. I slip them into my pocket and go on a deliberate quest to find a pair for Amity. I look for a long time, but there is nothing on the street that would appeal to her. I literally spend hours searching every table of junk and handling every "artisan-produced" earring that could double as a fishing lure. Eventually I go into a *real* jewelry store and use the remainder of my credit limit to charge a small, simple pair in pure gold. Next, I need to adjust my mood.

A lot of success in life is the result of positive thinking. I've heard that many times. I've never had real success, so maybe that means I've never been positive enough, or positive long enough, for the success to set in. Maybe I should count my blessings: I have a master's degree; that's a certain success. I have a new car, but that's a gift from Amity. I have Amity: voted best looking, best dressed, most likely to succeed. She is a success—always has been. Probably her only downfall is her connection to me. (This positive thinking isn't progressing the way I'd hoped.) But I can start anew with a fresh, positive attitude. I will give Amity the gift and then take her for a romantic dinner. I will ask her about her interests, her work, and then I will just listen. I will not speak unless it is to ask a question. I will be the perfect date and try to win her heart again.

20

The Anesthetic Odor of Clove Buds

I pause in the lobby of the hotel and search up restaurants in the neighborhood. The first result is an Indonesian place called *Warung Nusantara.* Aha! Synchronicity again. What the hell; why not? The write-ups give mostly five stars and everyone mentions something called *rijsttafel* which is a table-full of small dishes, samples of food from many different regions, all eaten with rice—hence the name. This is beginning to intrigue me. Before yesterday I really didn't know anything about Jakarta or even Indonesia except two musical scales called Balinese and Javanese that have an exotic sound but are hard to compose in. That and how a long time ago a huge volcanic eruption there caused a summer snowstorm in London. So it is settled. I will take Amity to *Nusantara* for dinner and romance.

When I enter the hotel room, Amity is sitting at the desk working on her laptop; our bags are packed and standing near the door. "I've found a restaurant we can try for dinner," I say. But Amity says she's already eaten and is not hungry. I tell her I bought her a gift and show her the earrings. She tells me I shouldn't use my credit card because I have no way to pay it back. "I told the front desk we will be leaving early," she says. "We should probably get going."

* * *

I take the short way back to Cleveland, driving at night and passing every car along the way. We roll past Niagara Falls without giving so much as a sideways thought about the falling water. It is not the most enjoyable of return trips I've ever made, in fact I eat my heart out all the way, but it is probably the quickest. Amity pretends to sleep the entire trip, and opens her eyes only when we arrive at her house. I get out of the car to carry her bags, but she stops me and says, "Don't bother. I can take it from here."

All the way home, from the *kreteks* in my pocket, I inhale the anesthetic odor of clove buds.

21

Uncle Dan Interlude

I need to back up for a minute here. I've quoted Uncle Dan several times, and I suppose it's a good time to tell some more about him to show that he is a real man and not just a collection of aphorisms. Uncle Dan is my father's older brother, a veteran of the Vietnam war, who took care of me (rather, he gave me a place to stay) when I was 14 and my father died. How did my father die? How *did* my father die?

We lived on a ranch near Elk Mountain, Wyoming—which is where I grew up. It may sound strange to most people who have real memories of their childhood, or at least some sense of their origin with roots in some location, that I have no fluid memory of growing up. All I have are cognitive snapshots. I do have a sense of being subordinate to everyone who was older—I guess that's childhood—but as to origins, I have always had the impression that I just arrived, fully conscious, in a world of severed connections. I must have spent some time crawling the floors, because I do have clear and detailed images of every inch of baseboard in that old house, baseboard that was covered in dark garnet shellac that allowed the wood grain to show through—if one were to look closely. It could have been a hundred years old, that shellac. As far as I know, nobody uses that stuff anymore. At the end of the short hallway that led to my father's bedroom there was one spot where a carpenter, a painter, or perhaps Pops himself, had touched the wood with a greasy finger so that the shellac did not adhere properly and over time chipped and peeled in a thumb-sized broken bubble that around the edges was sharp to the touch. Odd the things we choose to remember, or the things that choose to impress themselves upon our memory.

I was hardly a toddler when I lost my mother to cancer. Something in her breast metastasized. In the only image I can recall of her, she's bald and her face is an ever-shifting set of features: now ghostly, now pretty. There is a general sense of her fading, not of her being and then being less, mind you, but a weak image that began to fade about the same time that I began to recognize its importance. There was a loss, but I can't say entirely what was lost. Mother. And whether she would have been a good one or bad, we'll never know. In my mind now, she's like a lightning bug: a sudden little flash, a slow fade, and then she's off to somewhere else. I couldn't have saved her, not with love nor wisdom could I have saved her, even if I had thought she was something in need of saving. I know that now. At the time, I didn't even try. I just noticed that something in the house faded, and was gone.

From the time my mother became unable to get out of bed, a group of well-meaning church ladies took care of me, that is, took turns caring for me—taking me out of the house, keeping me away from the sickroom. They taught me how to read and how to sing, but I wasn't a cheery outgoing kid (probably deficient in vitamin D) so I didn't get very close to any of them.

One day when Pops was sure I could walk and talk and didn't need diapers anymore, he stopped letting the aunties take me. But who exactly were they? Their identities are now a mishmash of notable parts: sand-colored peroxide waves dry and stiff as straw, metallic green eye-shadow, corn-row braids, a fortress of padding and lace straining against a tight cotton blouse; each had her own interesting features, but none held my attention as a complete person—none is a complete entity in my recollection.

Only one woman from those years, grandmotherly Sadie Bucknell, holds any solid place in my memory. Auntie Sadie home-schooled me for the two middle school years in every subject but math—the importance of which she thought was exaggerated. She held a mouthful of fluency in several languages and worked those foreign phrases into our conversations. When I told her a story about something I thought was interesting, she would reply with, "*C'est vrais?*" And when she wasn't sure if I understood her lesson, she would ask, "*Verstehen Sie mich?*" She also taught me to play piano and how to tell the difference between Bach and Handel: "Handel-harmony, Bach-counterpoint." When I wanted to skip piano practice she dropped the Latin bomb, "*Ex nihilo, nihil fit.*" One afternoon, she stopped by and delivered scores and books on composition including Rismsky-Korsokov's *Principles of Orchestration* and Tchaikovsky's *Guide to the Practical Study of Harmony*, several vinyl recordings of classical music, a beautiful electric keyboard with weighted keys, and a pair of headphones so that I could listen and practice without disturbing my father. When he asked me where I got all the stuff and I told him Mrs. Bucknell, he said "Oh," and nothing more.

* * *

Pops fed me and taught me how to do chores, but I really don't recall his talking to me very much. He'd sometimes look at me then stare at the wall or the floor. (That's when I learned how to read people's minds, non-verbally, and I can tell you, there's a lot going on inside a man's head when he's picking at the callouses on his hands. And most of it, like music, is impossible to put into words.) I think I reminded him of Mom just by being there, though I don't know if I looked like her. When she died, Pops got rid of every emotionally-charged artifact: clothes, letters, pictures—so there is nothing to go by. He dealt with his grief by riding his horse—a Cleveland bay named Penny—and fixing the fence, while I played the piano and invented musical themes for every object in the house. There was no internet where we were, though we could have had it if Pops had sprung for a satellite dish. So, as weird as it may seem, I didn't play video games, or watch anime or porn like my would-be classmates did. I checked email at the library, but never caught the tech bug.

One day in late winter, after an unseasonably warm spell, we got hit with a sudden temperature drop and a heavy, freezing rain. Pops was out riding Penny, and I was working through chord progressions in a circle of fifths with my headphones on. I didn't hear anything but my music, and was a little surprised when a neighbor in a dripping rain slicker tapped me on the shoulder.

"Where's your old man?"

"Out riding the fence line with Penny," I answered.

"Nah. Penny came over to my place, still wearing a saddle. I just put her in her stall and dried her off. Your Pop wasn't there. If he's not here, I'd better go and look for him." And that was it.

* * *

At the funeral home, I sat in the corner and made myself as invisible as possible. From the conversations overheard, I learned that for some reason Pops had gotten off, or fallen off, Penny and was lying on the ground during that long freezing rain. Penny might have come around to the house, but with my headphones on I probably wouldn't have heard her if she'd come up on the porch and knocked with her front hoof. When they found Pops he was frozen solid as if he'd been coated with glass. They had to chisel at the ground around him to pry him up. There was also a lot of whispering among the women as to who would take care of teenage me, but my Uncle Dan showed up and said that I would live with him in Cleveland. "No, not Texas. Ohio."

Uncle Dan worked out some kind of deal with our neighbor who agreed to watch over everything and take care of the animals until he decided what to do with the place. He told me to take only what I needed, so I loaded some clothes, a sleeping bag, my keyboard, and some music books into the back of his shell-topped pickup truck. Then I went back to the house and under Pop's bed for a small red steel box that originally held road flares, but for all of my life contained some of Pop's treasures, mostly old coins which, because of their circulation wear, held little numismatic value. There were wheat-back pennies and a couple steel pennies from World War II. There was also a stalled railroad pocket watch that was missing the minute hand but which indicated the right hour for two hours each day. But my favorite treasure was a silver dollar from 1910. It was one ounce of pure silver, big and heavy as far as coins go. The only flaw was that somebody, maybe a grandfather I never met, got that coin as a gift and drilled a hole in the top in order to attach it to a string so he could wear it around his neck. Or maybe it was once attached to a key ring. In any event, someone, maybe Pops, decided that the hole was a flaw and filled it with solder. Now it is a silver dollar, slightly less than one ounce, plugged with an ugly gray blob of lead. For whatever reasons, all of these things had value to Pop. I carried the box to Uncle Dan's truck with both hands as if it were as precious as Pop's ashes, and we headed for Ohio.

It was a two or three day trip and we didn't talk much at first. After driving for about six hours Uncle Dan asked me how I was feeling. I shrugged my shoulders. "Yeah, it hurts like hell," he said, "but it don't mean nothin'. Nobody gets outta here alive." Then he signaled for the next exit—Odessa, Nebraska—and reading my mind said, "*I'm* hungry too."

We pulled in to a place with a water tower fixed up to look like a giant coffee pot—the *Sapp Bros* truck stop—for food and fuel. I got one of the "served-all-day combos" called the Trucker's Special that consisted of eggs, sausage, bacon, beans, fried tomatoes, potatoes, pancakes, toast, butter and jelly— everything that a kitchen can serve up for breakfast, all on one plate the size of a truck's hubcap. When I finished, and I did finish—a feat that can be accomplished only by a starving trucker or a teenage boy—Uncle Dan asked if I wanted a bowl of cornflakes. It took a second of shock for me to realize that he was joking, and when I did, I laughed until I cried, and so did he. We both had just experienced the worst of life: I lost my father and anchor, and Dan lost yet another brother. We now shared a bond that Uncle Dan knew from the war—a complex bond that included anger, depression (which Amity says is anger turned inward), and a guilt that conflicted with the relief and joy we felt for having survived. In addition, Uncle Dan had a new source of strength in that he now had me: a wounded buddy to fight for, and if necessary, die for. If I had been old enough, we probably would have gone to a bar and drunk ourselves stupid. On the way out of the truck stop diner, Uncle Dan put his arm around my shoulder like a father would, or should.

* * *

Uncle Dan realized that, at this point in his life, I was about as close to a son as he was going to get, and I sensed that he was stepping up to the responsibility and was going to make the best of it. He began to speak to me in a friendlier tone and shared bits of his history. In 1968 he was about to be drafted into the Army, but joined the Marines instead. Through some turn of events, he wound up going to Guam where he met a fetching Navy cryptologist. After his tour, they married and moved to her hometown where Uncle Dan took a job in a steel mill. "We were both young, and headstrong," he told me, "and I screwed up a lot. She went AWOL and then bugged out completely. A few years later, the steel mills bugged out too—went to China. And I'm still in Ohio. Ain't that a pisser?"

* * *

When we arrived in Cleveland it was dark and cold and the streets were filled with gray slush from a heavy snow and an extra-heavy salting from the city's snow plows. Uncle Dan's little bungalow had a tiny backyard that abutted another backyard behind another bungalow on the next street. I was used to a lot of space and sky in Wyoming, so getting accustomed to this claustrophobic lifestyle would require some mental adjustment.

I guess some people might call it PTSD or shell-shock, but there's no way to accurately describe the emotional wasteland that was my life when I moved in with Uncle Dan. He got me into a small Catholic high school because he had heard that they were really tough and he didn't want me to be coddled. Since I was so quiet, the teachers thought I was a silent genius and were biased in my favor. With no official academic records, aside from Sadie Bucknell's superlative reviews of my homeschool performance, the principal put me into honors classes where I could pull a grade of A or B just by paying attention in class. They also heard my tale of woe from Uncle Dan, and cut me some slack on late homework. I can't really say that they gave me good grades for nothing, but their favor assured that in a tie, I'd win.

It was also in that school that I met Amity. She was president of our chapter of the National Honor Society and was also one of the peer tutors. Although I had trouble with geometry and math in general, I was afraid to ask for help for fear that the teacher might assign me to Amity's tutelage and the secret of my averageness would be revealed. I needed some kind of distinction to bring my status up to par with the honor students, and when I asked Uncle Dan for advice, he told me, "In 'Nam we had an expression: 'Give a man a fish and he'll eat for a day, but give a man a hand grenade and he can catch his own damn fish and eat for a week.'" I pondered that for a while and took it to mean that instead of asking for help, I should ask for something really big. So I arranged a meeting with the principal and explained my reasons why the school should give an award for musical composition and why I was uniquely qualified to get it.

To this day I am the only student ever to win that award.

22

Pre-Concert

It is a beautiful spring day in April—the time when kings are wont to go to war.

I take two comp tickets I got from Timo after the last rehearsal and drive over to Uncle Dan's house. It's been a while since I've visited him, and he is as genuinely happy as he is surprised to see me.

"So, this is the big night," he says. "Sorry I won't be able to make it. But that's not the only reason you came here, is it? You look like you're in a blue funk."

"No. Actually Uncle Dan, I'm scared shitless."

"What are you worried about? Your head has been in longhair music ever since you were a kid. You're smarter than anyone on that stage."

"I'm not so sure about that."

"Listen, this show is guaranteed to be a success."

"I think I'm as afraid of success as I am of failure."

"You could use a tour of duty in Southeast Asia to get some perspective. Look Jonathan, you're in a good place: you're above ground, and you're not cold. What will be, will be: *Che sera,*

sera and all that happy horseshit. Win or lose, you are going to survive this thing. Do you think the orchestra wants bad reviews? Hell no! They won't screw it up. This concert *will* happen and it *will* be good. Right now the gears are in motion. They're going to pull it off and there's nothing you can do to stop it—even if you wanted to. Is your girlfriend coming?"

"No. She's in Texas on business." Uncle Dan nods his head, then shakes it since he's still surprised when life situations turn crappy, and girlfriends go AWOL.

"Well, tomorrow and Saturday you will probably be a wreck. Why don't you come around on Sunday and we'll have more time to talk."

23

World Premier

After three days of rehearsals, the time to debut my first commissioned piece has arrived. It's the last on the program, but it's preceded by some crowd pleasers: Mozart's Overture to *The Magic Flute*, Schumann's *Symphony No. 4* (played without pause), then after the intermission, *La Valse* by Ravel, Fauré's Suite from *Pelléas et Mélisande*, then mine: *In Reverentia Temporis* (*In Reverence of Time*). It's a perfect setup for me to knock it out of the park (Jimmy told me I *must* be good if my opening act is Mozart). My piece is a little longer than I expected, it's just over ten minutes. It also took me longer to write than I had imagined at first, which is good, because if I had been able to turn it out as quickly as I had bragged to myself, then I wouldn't have trusted the result.

My greatest inspiration for this piece was Mahler's work of genius, *Das Lied von der Erde* (*The Song of the Earth*). I've always been awestruck by the sheer beauty of that symphony for two voices and orchestra, and how Mahler built a sonic architecture that suspends the vocals in mid air, and still allows the brilliance of each musician to shine forth. I borrowed that idea and, with the violins and the cellos, built two musical walls to bracket the soloist. I think of it as a giant porch swing to suspend and rock Yulia's voice while she cuts to the soul. (Picturing Yulia in a gingham dress sipping lemonade on a porch swing helps mitigate the intimidating effect of her celebrity.)

I also control the full orchestra by treating it as several chamber orchestras, only deploying the power of the full ensemble for the climactic moments. This arrangement is to honor the talent of the musicians whom I truly love right now. For the dark parts I use pedal point from the double basses and dissonance from the bassoon and French horns. I also keep Mahler's pentatonic scale in order to frame the joyful parts in oriental crystal—hence the celesta. There are even a couple Easter eggs—small musical quotes from Mahler that I incorporate as a tribute; I'll let the listeners figure out where they are. As it is, I am very pleased, and in rehearsals, Yulia Sophia's voice was liquid gold. At one point I offered her a translation of the libretto, and she said to me, "How can an English translation improve the Latin?"

Yulia said she did not want to see me today before the concert since that would spell bad luck for her. She didn't even tell me what she was wearing to the performance. Of course I am in black tie, a gift from Amity which she said I can also wear to dinner when we take a luxury liner to Europe. It's a nice idea, though there is no way I can afford any trip that requires more than two tanks of gas. (I don't know how long it takes to get paid for an orchestra commission, but it's way too long as far as I'm concerned. Still, I didn't want to ask anyone about money for fear of sounding too needy.) I suppose Amity plans to buy the cruise line tickets, or has already bought them to surprise me when she returns from her Texas trip. Anyway, I can wear this tux to any formal occasion including my wedding, if and when that happens. We still haven't set a date. What with Amity traveling so much and my trouble paying the bills, I can't even think about planning a wedding—at least not the kind that Amity expects.

God, I'm a nervous wreck.

I walk around backstage where the musicians are changing their clothes behind their big old wardrobe trunks; most congratulate me though some make jokes intended to calm my nerves—fat chance of that. "I didn't see the diva," a violinist says, "maybe she got cold feet and went back to Moscow." "What if she doesn't show, Jonathan?" asks another, "Think you can sing her part?" "Not unless you've got some hormone injections in that trunk," I reply. Everyone laughs. While she straightens my bow tie, the young violist Mary Ballard tells me how honored she feels to perform in the "world premier" of my new opus. My scalp tingles and my face blushes. Speechless, I simply smile and place my hands over my heart. I have finally made the team. They are genuinely happy for me. "There's no need to be nervous now, Jonathan," Mary continues. "Your work is done and your piece *will* be performed tonight. At this point it's like a snowball rolling downhill, and there's nothing you can do to stop it. But— just make sure that you smile when you come out for the curtain call because I heard the music critic from New York Times is in town. He's a big fan of Yulia." She points toward the audience: "Fourth row, right of center, next to some donors."

I peek out from the wings near the harp where I think no one can see me. Although there are some familiar faces I can't place, there is no one who looks to me like a critic for the Times; I imagine he'd be in jeans and a black t-shirt under a black sport coat. Nobody big or scary anyway, the crowd looks nice. I see two of my former professors. They have come to be supportive,

I'm sure, but it's got to be tough for them to see me—so green from their point-of-view—being showcased at Severance Hall in such a big way with the hottest new talent from the Russian opera circuit.

I scan for other recognizable faces, but see mostly couples in business attire coming from early dinner and wine. Throughout college I spent many a Thursday night at Severance Hall in a great seat I bought at student discount rate because there was always one single chair, stranded between couples, that the box office couldn't sell. And always, I could smell the wine and garlic on the breath of those around me. I never drink before a concert. I think it is sacrilegious.

When Mozart, Hayden, Beethoven, or even Shostakovich put a pen to paper they were connecting to something much greater than themselves. From this higher power they were able to commune with the spheres. It's something sacred; it's even holy. When you, the composer, connect with the music, when the music enters your soul, or comes from your soul, when, for a time outside of time, you forget all the rules you learned in class—yet they still find their way in somehow—it becomes Art with a capital A. And I believe that the audience has a responsibility to approach Art with a sober head so that the message from beyond—that music of the spheres—can make its way in and hopefully enlighten the listener's soul.

I remember a lecture I once heard on "The Spirituality of Listening." The speaker is director of an organization dedicated to enlightenment through listening, and she believes that all listening is a spiritual experience. I agree, but only with a couple conditions. First, there is a difference between listening and hearing. The hearing part requires a certain amount of under-standing and feeling. Without a modicum of understanding and feeling, the listener might just as well be hearing static. Secondly, in order for the hearing to be transcendent, what is being listened to must be in some way sublime. In every score that I write, I aim for the sublime, and if Providence chooses to add something divine, all the better. Ergo, critics will call it sublime, but only if they are hearing and not simply listening.

Someone waves to me from the audience. It's Dr. Lance. He's talking to an old woman with purplish-tinged silver hair who may be his lady friend from Boston. There is an open seat next to him that must be for Marga. She's probably in the ladies' room, or running late and will meet him here. Amity said she would try to make it, but I told her not to bother. Irving, Texas is a long way from Cleveland, Ohio and with the taxis and the after-concert celebration, there is no guarantee that she could make it back to Irving in time for her morning presentation. Some things aren't meant to be; *es lo que es*—that's just the way it is.

* * *

The orchestra files onstage and begins tuning. After the house-lights are flashed a couple of times and the audience is seated and settling down, a local classical radio celebrity comes on stage to share historical tidbits about the pieces to be performed. There is a lot of activity backstage and I'm having some difficulty hearing him. At the end of his lesson he briefly describes "Brendel's newest, an aria from an oratorio," (I guess he called it that because of the Latin) "which, after his *Sinfonietta for Strings,* is the second Brendel composition to be premiered at Severance Hall." After some polite applause, he continues and describes the soloist as, "A continually rising superstar, a fellow-in-residence, and a Russian temptress *extraordinaire*, Yulia Sophia."

At this the audience bursts into laughter and applause since the description fits the social media persona that her publicists and paparazzi have ginned up to promote her career.

As he exits stage right, the radio host winks at me then shares nods with the conductor who straightens his back, smooths out his tuxedo jacket, and makes his entrance to a polite serving of applause. The orchestra begins, and I feel my heart pounding against my shirt; I take deep breaths in an attempt to control it. Except for the stage hands who are playing poker for stacks of dollar bills, I am now alone backstage. I'm feeling dizzy from hyperventilating when Timo shows up carrying a glass tumbler covered with a linen napkin. "I've brought you some refreshment," he says. "An extra extra dry Rob Roy with a twist. Basically it's half a pint of Dewar's with a little lemon peel for vitamin C." I thank him for being the life-saver he is. "I got you into this," he says, "now I've got to get you through it." I take a sip and decide that the bartender must have just touched the vermouth bottle for good luck, because this drink is pure Scotch whisky. I set it down on the road case for the unused tympani.

Intermission comes quickly and the musicians make the best of their short time by drinking bottled water and answering texts. Yulia Sophia is nowhere to be found. I interrupt Timo, who is flirting with a bassoon player, and ask if he has seen her. "Oh, don't worry, you'll be seeing plenty of her when the time comes," he says, and they both laugh at some inside joke.

The intermission is now ending and the stagehands are flashing the houselights again. My perception of time is heavily distorted and it seems to me that people are moving very quickly and I'm processing activity and people in little snapshots that rotate like bits of colored glass in a kaleidoscope. Panic is setting in. I'm not exactly sure what I'm afraid of; it may be failure and the embarrassment of being exposed as a fraud. Amity has told me about a psychological insecurity known as the "impostor syndrome" that attacks otherwise capable CEOs and Hollywood stars between pictures. Or it may be a fear of success and all that comes along with that: a new class of friends, travels far and wide, television interviews and guest lectures, money, boredom, and a lack of inspiration—success could ruin me as surely as failure. This makes no sense, I've just got butterflies, like every aspiring actor or actress called in for a second audition. I find the glass of Scotch and swallow a big mouthful.

Pizzicato bass notes float in from the stage and I realize that *La Valse* has begun. A flash of insecurity peeks through again followed by the thought, almost audible, that *even* Ravel was once a goofy kid. (The whisky is doing it's job.) Not much of a waltz, I say to myself. In parts of it I hear, and find impossible to clear out of my head, the song "Pure Imagination" from the movie *Willy Wonka & the Chocolate Factory*.

More polite applause separates Ravel's impertinent exercise from the glorious harmonies of Fauré. I really can't tell if being last in this arrangement tonight is an incredible blessing or a horrendous set up. As a tonic I try to envision myself in the pantheon of great composers with these others who were nothing if not human like me. If the encyclopedia of great composers is in alphabetical order, I will stand after Bach, no wait a minute, after Beethoven, and before Chopin. No, wait a minute, Anton Bruckner should appear before Chopin; but I want to be next to Chopin—maybe they'll leave out that choirboy, Anton. One of the stage hands offers me a chair while the others look on. I politely refuse, and half of them chuckle while the other half pays out. It's probably the whisky, but I laugh along with them. These guys will gamble on anything.

As *Pelléas et Mélisande* rounds the bend to the final chords, three of the stage hands stand, button their jackets and straighten their ties, then head over to the soloist's dressing room. They knock, get a response, then enter and close the door behind. What in the world is going on here? Why are these guys going into Yulia's dressing room, and why isn't she out here? My piece is next, and she has to make it fly or we'll both have egg on our faces.

The applause is rushing in as Yulia's door opens and a stage-hand backs out carrying a scepter and a golden *globus cruciger*. Yulia appears next in a purple satin gown—really just a long, unlined silk slip, cut low in the front and high on the leg—mostly covered by a spotted faux-ermine robe she must have rented from a theatrical costume shop. Behind her the long ermine train is carried by two very serious-looking stagehands. When she reaches the stage door and sees me standing there, she squints me an evil eye and says, "*Ire ad infernum cum latinis,*" telling me to take my Latin and go to hell. She must have been practicing.

When the stage door is opened and the conductor glances our way, the first stagehand gives Yulia the scepter and the orb, and she makes her entrance, literally like a queen, with the other two stagehands carrying the train of her robe. I have no idea what this selection of costumery has to do with my music, but the audience loves it and they applaud furiously and even whistle before she has so much as exhaled. She has become someone else altogether, a character of her own devise providing backstory to my music (a backstory I didn't write). And she has so entirely entered into, or been taken over by this character that she is controlling the audience with her intense presence. Some in the audience, I suspect, think that she is an actual queen and would bow and scrape or curtsy if the space between seats permitted. I look at the audience through the stagehands' speakeasy peephole to see if Marga is catching all this, but see that her usual seat next to Lance has been taken by the silver-haired woman.

Yulia approaches her mark beside a stage prop—a standing four-foot section of a broken marble column (actually plaster painted to look like marble) covertly placed by the stagehands during a brief curtain drop after the Fauré suite. She must have requested that for her royal antiquity theme, something to touch and maybe lean on for effect. She is deeply in character in a world of her own making, and acknowledges neither the conductor nor the audience. She has made her entrance not as a soloist at a concert about to begin, but as an actress into a play that is already in progress. She remains frozen, expressionless, and silent. The statuesque tableau she creates with the column drives the audience wild and they applaud with a fervor rarely witnessed *before* a symphonic concert. Her stillness soon inspires an attentive hush followed by anechoic quiet. I am extremely concerned about what might happen next.

The conductor decides not to wait, and instead uses Yulia's silence to form unwritten beats (rests) which he counts with his raised baton before launching into the work. (This is not what we rehearsed.) I see his left hand cue the French horn and am startled when I hear that eerie opening note, even though I wrote it, already coloring the air. While enjoying the pureness and truth in that singular timbre, I hear it thicken as Yulia's voice folds in with an otherworldly crystalline jewel. What a surprise! When I wrote the score, this is how I imagined the opening, but after all the restrained rehearsals, I'm ashamed to say, I didn't think Yulia would deliver the goods. She must have been protecting her voice for tonight. The audience is transfixed; there is not a cough nor a throat clearing in the house.

Yulia is singing, adding color to the instruments, which—as far as I'm concerned—she, as the diva, is within her rights to do. After all, not wanting to insult her intelligence or art, I left so much of the interpretation to her. Maybe it's because I got in over my head with this assignment, or that I just got lazy or scared as I ripped through the daily calendar sheets leading up to the first rehearsal, but I made generous use of *tempo rubato*, allowing her to steal time and adjust her delivery speed to make the Latin phraseology fit. She slowly lifts her head and makes a graceful sweeping motion over the audience with the scepter. Then as a continuation of that sweep, she holds forth the golden orb and considers it like poor Yorick's skull. The ermine cape slips off her shoulder and folds deliciously onto the floor. At this moment, in this house, she is queen of the world. And then her opening lines:

"*Quid quid latet apparabit*" [Whatever is hidden will appear]

"*Nil inultum remanebit*" [Nothing will remain unpunished]

Those who have read the lyrics and translation in the playbill gasp at the feeling Yulia is able to impart.

I think of Auntie Sadie and how she used a little book of foreign phrases to teach me a smattering of Latin, and I feel her presence and her love. The orchestra is filling the hall with sounds so vibrant that they trigger a synaesthesia in me, and, for a while, I see vividly colorful geometric shapes filling the air like an animation of a painting by Kandinsky. For a moment I feel I have left my body and am watching the scene from the air near the proscenium arch. The musical shapes, my shapes, pour through me and echo with their original archetypes in my soul. Yulia slides into the next phrases with clarity and fluidity as if possessed by Caesar's ghost—and he can sing.

Aprilis, tempore quo reges bellant [it was April, the time when kings go to war]

Profectus cum militibus [he marched with soldiers]

Tutor et ultor [defender and avenger]

Et fortissimus erat [and he was most courageous]

Spes sibi quisque [each man is hope to himself]

I look at the audience and see eyes wide open and jaws slackened. Nobody (including me) is blinking, and my face is wet with tears.

Relicto corde suo [he left his heart]

Et ferri eius ferro. [and carried his steel]

Posui ferro in risus [I put steel into my smile]

Flores levaverunt sua petala [flowers waved their petals]

Ubi bene, ibi patria [where it is well with me, there is my country]

The tempo changes and the melodic theme returns. The orchestra swells and crescendos, the opposing chamber-like sections answer each other's calls—the sonic walls build and suspend Yulia's incredible voice.

Omne corpus mutabile est ["Every object is subject to change"—Cicero]

Tempora mutantur, et nos mutamur in illis [now times are changed and we are changed in them]

At this point Yulia changes to a timbre that I can only describe as pastel and powdery.

Dixerunt quod futurum esse, futurum esse sed non erat [they said whatever would be would be, but it wasn't]

Venenum in auro bibitur [poison is drunk from a golden cup]

The darker bass lines form a foundation calling forth images of oak, then leather, then stone. Yulia now turns on the afterburners of her directed, projected presence.

Veritatis simplex oratio est ["The language of truth is simple"—Seneca]

Vive ut vivas [live that you may live]

Vive memor leti [live mindful of death]

Et si diis placet [and if it pleases the gods]

Vade in pace [go in peace]

Valete ac plaudite [farewell, and give applause].

Yulia added that last line. It wasn't printed in the lyrics on the program and I wonder who, if anyone, caught it. As the orchestra goes silent and Yulia holds holds forth her last note, she glides back into her opening tableau pose and freezes. When the sonic dust has settled into the upholstery, the conductor drops his head which the audience takes as a signal that this unfamiliar piece has ended. After what seems like an eternity to me, the hall explodes with applause and cheers of every kind including whistles and shouts and the stamping of feet. The din is so raucous that it takes a few seconds for me to register that it is positive—a sign of approval. The conductor, beaming a colossal smile, turns and holds out both hands in Yulia's direction. By now the standing ovation is thunderous, and I have trouble connecting this praise to my work. Yulia takes a deep bow, and while folded over she turns her head to look at me standing in the wings and reaches out her hand beckoning me to join her. I'm really not sure what's going on until I feel the stagehands pushing on my back and telling me to get out there. "This moment won't last forever," one yells into my ear.

Yulia is blowing two-handed kisses to the crowd until someone hands her a big bouquet of roses. Single flowers are flying up on the stage from all directions. After my first stumble, I become giddy, begin laughing, and jog out to center stage and

Yulia. She takes the bouquet in her right hand and throws her arms around my neck lifting most of her bare left leg behind her for balance (and to provide a cheesecake moment for the paparazzi). By now I am completely surfing on the adoration filling the house and put my arm around the small of Yulia's back and dip her deeply for a theatrical kiss. The audience loves it. Even the orchestra is standing and applauding and smiling with joy.

Yulia turns to her faux column and retrieves the scepter and globus cruciger which she presents to me—one for each hand—and then steps backward to leave me front and center for the applause. As I face the hall, I notice that the critic from the Times is on his way out with a donor. Oh well, screw them if they can't take a joke.

The audience doesn't want to leave, and the conductor tells us we should get off the stage while they're still energized. We take a few more bows, then Yulia takes my hand and we exit stage right to further applause and congratulations from the musicians. She will not let go of my hand and stands so close that I can feel her warm skin through my tuxedo. She's acting like a teenager in love. "Let's go to the green room and get a drink," she says into my ear. She leads and I follow.

Champagne toasts are made with everyone in the green room. Yulia swallows a full glass each time, and I follow her lead. There are so many people in the room, it seems everyone involved with the orchestra has come. I recognize even the young guy who drives the instrument truck on tours. It's a party that nobody wants to end. There are selfies and hand shakes, slap-on-the-back congratulations, and unfunny jokes that I laugh at nonetheless. And when my energy starts to wane, Yulia tickles my ribs and laughs deeply and seductively as she nibbles on my earlobe.

She pulls me by the hand leading me through the dark hall to an even darker limousine, and we're off.

24

Aftermath

Today I feel pretty awful. I've come to expect an emotional letdown after a concert of my music, but after all the preparation, writing, revisions, and rehearsals, then the tension of waiting, and the concert itself, followed by the congratulations, compliments, and minor criticisms (couched as tedious, manly-type sarcasm and passive-aggressive jokes) my psyche is pretty well scoured. Then, following a late night of endless champagne-fueled idiocy carried out in a fugue state, what I've got today is a spotty memory and a disgusting *Katzenjammer* of a hangover. I remember a few embarrassing moments with Yulia—toasting each other's success, success with the next, each other's health, the orchestra's health, meaningless things said in thinly veiled seductive tones, and double entendre inserted where none logically fits. Then I remember trying to bribe the conductor's chauffeur into giving us a ride to a bar somewhere where we toast some more. At some point we get really stupid and fill fluted champagne glasses with vodka to toast Mother Russia and God Bless America.

Shortly after that, (and here's where it gets blurry) Yulia

becomes very friendly (nude and all under that silk satin dress), and I get morose and tearful (enough booze can do that) and she begins to mother me, and rock me in her arms in that dingy booth in a campy nightclub. Then I wake up in my own bed, fully dressed (sans bow tie) with shirt undone and no memory of how I got home. The headache and nausea are to be expected, but the intense shame and guilt are enough to make me a teetotaler. After a few trips to the bathroom, I kick off my shoes, put a pillow over my head, and swear I will never speak with Diva Pasternak again.

I lay there all day, and only get out of bed at 4 AM because my kidneys are swimming and I am absolutely famished. After brushing teeth and showering, I finally feel human again, so I go to the Greek diner and order an Irish breakfast: three eggs, three bacon strips, two sausages, back and white pudding, home-fried potatoes, fried tomatoes, beans, toast, black coffee and a tumbler of OJ. It may only be relative to the suffering I endured yesterday, but as I eat and drink, I feel elated. Through the Cleveland Orchestra, I just successfully delivered the World Premiere of my second, brilliant orchestral work (my first vocal work!) and judging by the duration of the applause, the concert was a hit. But I make a conscious decision to avoid all news today—why open myself to the slings and arrows of jealous critics (if there are any) only hours before my next concert?

25

Performance Day

For most of the rest of the day, I listen to the recording I made for Marga's performance. It's pretty good for a fake. What I mean by "fake" is that I cobbled it together from small parts performed by groups of student musicians. A friend who teaches violin in Cleveland State's music department asked for volunteers to, "Play a new work by Jonathan Brendel—the composer who was commissioned by The Cleveland Orchestra to write for that Russian singer who is so hot on the social media." So the professor put together a small string section and we recorded in a studio at WCSB—the university's radio station. The general manager there, a young classical music enthusiast, helped me to overdub on multiple tracks until we had what sounded like a full string orchestra performing a reasonable interpretation of my score. Young musicians almost never get paid, but in exchange for producing a canned version of my follow-up opus, they were given complimentary tickets to my World Premiere. They all declined my invitation to Sector B.

By about two in the afternoon I start to second guess my tempo choices but decide to leave well-enough alone. Tonight, everyone at Sector B will likely be an artist who will use Marga's performance as inspiration for their next painting, drawing, video. I might as well wear black—it's always in fashion with the art crowd. So I put on a black dress shirt, my black Wrangler cowboy jeans and a black jean jacket. And just to connect with my Wyoming roots, I wear my Justin Roper boots. Amity would say that I look like a Wild West mortician. Marga will love it.

26

Setting the Stage

When I arrive at the Soldiers and Sailors' Monument, our rendezvous point downtown, Marga is in disguise so that I hardly recognize her. She is dressed in a hotel housekeeper's uniform with sagging, flesh-colored, knee-high nylon stockings that hang at mid-calf above worn-out, dirty-white sneakers. To accurately describe her look is to use up my normal allotment of hyphens. Marga is holding a folding hand-truck against her knees, and my brain—always looking for patterns (as brains are wont to do)—sees it as an old person's walker. Her hair is covered in a washed-out blue terrycloth turban and she's dusted her face and eyebrows with oatmeal-colored talc that visually flattens her features and renders her essentially unremarkable to any passersby. I would have driven around the block several times looking for my friend had I not recognized the old wardrobe trunk she is sitting on. It has several worn decals from the glory days of ocean liner travel: the Cunard and United States Lines, Hotel Monopol-Leipzig, the Excelsior Palace in Venezia, and one, a new one—the kicker—a bright red and yellow wiener in a bun from the Currywurst Museum in

Berlin.

Once I realize that Marga is going incognito, I pull up to the curb, beep the horn, and pop the boot, but make no effort to help—which might draw attention. I treat her like the character she is playing. Anyone viewing the scene would get the impression that I am the trust fund progeny of Pepper Pike royalty come to collect the latest live-in charwoman who is about to be subjected to multiple rashers of abuse—dished out with gusto.

As Marga pretends to struggle with the mostly empty steamer trunk, I get out and stomp around to the back of the car making a big show of impatience while warning her that any damage to the Audi will be deducted from her pay. Two grandmas at the bus stop shake their heads with disgust directed at me. The trunk doesn't fit, and eventually, with grunts and cussing, I work it into the back seat. The more contempt I show for Marga, the more realistic her disguise becomes. She couldn't ask for a better supporting actor.

As soon as she's in the car, I quickly drive away with as much attitude as I imagine my character should have. Marga says I did a good job, and that I'm finally beginning to understand her. At first I head east, in the direction of Pepper Pike, to keep up appearances, then circle around and head for the industrial valley and Sector B. Marga leads me to a different route that takes us to the steel mill's old truck entrance; this is the way tonight's crowd will come in.

As we approach the factory campus, Marga tells me to proceed with caution. The car's low profile and thin "performance" tires are built for a racetrack—the Autobahn—not the deep ruts and buckled asphalt of this old service road. Marga says, "You should have asked for a Jeep." I ignore her impertinent remark and drive slow and easy, sometimes riding the berm to avoid bottoming-out and losing the muffler or goring the oil-pan on a chunk of concrete. Under Marga's direction all the way, I maneuver the Audi to the side of the mill closest to her studio. She has me wait with the car while she runs inside, returning with a long roll of the Belgian flax linen she uses for her paintings. I can tell the cloth is expensive; it is a tight weave that is soft to the touch and has more shine to its surface than a typical cotton canvas. After we remove her wardrobe trunk, we cover the car with the linen—the gray and earth tones of the fabric transform the car's shape into just another anonymous piece of post-bankruptcy factory detritus. Marga opens her folding hand truck and we wheel the wobbling trunk along a gangway toward the stage area.

The mill is alive with activity—it's like watching roadies and roustabouts setting up a carny. There are structural things being assembled—a sound system and some kind of practical theater rigging to make someone, I assume Marga, fly. Steel beams ring with hammers and men shout to one another in exaggerated tones—a soundtrack reminiscent of Harry Partch. Everyone seems to know exactly what to do, but I'm sure it might seem different to me if my German were better and I understood what they were saying. Marga jogs up the spiral staircase and a Berliner friend uses a block and tackle to hoist her trunk up to the office level. Outside, four men in dirty sweatshirts use iron bars as levers to tip a battered, small-gauge gondola off the tracks. It falls on its side with a deep boom sending a cloud of orange rust and black coke dust wafting into the cattails. (Time for a high-five.) Now the audience will have a clear view of the performance from the railroad tracks.

An eight foot tall crucible with an opening seven or eight feet in diameter, probably weighing ten tons, has been dragged on skids to just outside the furnace building. A small stage built from planks has been placed on top of the crucible's opening. Werner is in his gantry testing red and yellow lights wired inside the crucible. These will shine like molten steel up through spaces between the planks to light Marga from below. By now she has pulled the wardrobe trunk over the railing near her office and calls for me to come up.

Running up the spiral stairs, I catch myself laughing. It's hard to describe the feeling, but I'm ticklish inside, and antsy—I *need* to run. Before my World Premiere with the Cleveland Orchestra, I was petrified, but today, anticipating tonight's performance in partnership with Marga, I'm nearly ecstatic. *In Reverence of Time* was a success, and the audience loved it even if the Prima Donna turned out to be a virago. Maybe if I were to spend a few years working with her, we too would become friends. But in the circles Ms Pasternak travels, the air is rare. She can have it. Today I know I am rolling with an inertia that can't be stopped. There is an unusual high-voltage running through my system— everything is positive and amped-up. Even the funk in this old steel mill—a stench of iron and sulfur and whale oil—is glorious, equal in its transcendental power to the Niagara Centennial Lilac Gardens in May. I feel emotionally effervescent and I'm afraid I may not be able to handle much more.

Might this be joy?

At the top of the spiral staircase I turn and see Marga sitting on her trunk on the catwalk outside her office. She's holding her left hand with her right, trying to stop the dripping blood. "I need your help," she says calmly. "When I swung the trunk over the railing I sort of smashed my hand on some rusty steel, or old paint—something sharp."

"Wow! That looks really bad."

"That's just blood. I haven't seen the cut yet."

"I'll take you to the hospital."

"No. Under the desk there's a 50 caliber ammo can. It's full of first aid stuff. Can you get it? Please?" I run to get the can and return just as fast. "Inside is some Bactine disinfectant with lidocaine. Rinse the cut with it."

"Marga, this is going to take more than some sunburn medicine."

"Just squirt it all over my hand so we can see what's going on." She's amazingly calm. I follow her instructions and she sucks in a deep breath through flared nostrils. When the blood is rinsed off I see there is a diagonal, jagged cut about three inches long. "Good," she says, "It's just a laceration. Missed the veins."

"Marga, you definitely need stitches, and a tetanus shot."

"I just got a tetanus shot last week after I stepped on a nail. Use some of the smaller band-aids to pull the wound together temporarily. You'll need to make some butterflies from the cloth tape; I'll talk you through it." I make the butterflies without her help, and do my best to pull the skin together—roughly where it belongs.

"This is just a temporary fix, Marga. If you don't get it done right, it could leave a big scar." She shrugs. "You really should be more careful."

"It doesn't matter. Nostradamus predicted that California is going to fall into the Pacific Ocean and a tidal wave will go around the world and pretty much destroy all civilization."

"Really? But you can't count on that Marga. If it doesn't happen you'll wish you had taken better care of yourself." Another shrug.

"Now, put a non-stick pad over it and wrap it with that gauze.

Not too thick, I need to put a glove over it."

"Are you still going through with the performance?"

"Wouldn't you?" We lock eyes in silence, Marga deadly certain of her commitment, and me, fairly certain of my doubt.

I unwind the roll of gauze gently and slowly around her hand, and she watches me with the eyes of a little girl in love with her savior—her surgeon father, Lance.

"I'll need your help to get into costume," Marga says, "but first you need to help me get out of this one." I jokingly ask her if she hurt herself on purpose. "Ask Freud," she tells me. "You're the only one, Jonathan...who can help me." She lets silence fall for a beat, then, "Please open my trunk and get my bathrobe."

Marga's old housekeeping uniform is held together with real mother-of-pearl buttons up the front. She makes no effort to help me. I try to focus on the mechanics of unbuttoning rather than on what is being revealed—though it is no surprise when I discover that Marga has gone all-the-way with the costume and is wearing an ugly old cotton bra and bloomers, possibly something from her grandmother's cedar chest or an Amish Victoria's Secret. She slips her right arm out of the sleeve, but I have to rip the left sleeve to get it over her lacerated hand without exacerbating the injury. When I go behind her to help with the robe, I notice wide scars across her lower back—not narrow like a whip, but about the width of a leather belt.

"Marga, what happened to your back?"

"Be grateful, Jonathan. Sometimes a living mother is worse than a dead one."

Marga takes three wigs out of the trunk and puts them on Styrofoam mannequin heads on her makeshift table. One is a platinum blonde shoulder length flip with bangs, another is a purplish-tinged silver old lady curl, and the third is an anime style, cartoon-blue with long bouncy curls, a side part, and a swoop over the left eye. "I'll go with the blue," she says.

"Who's your character tonight?"

"The Chinese goddess, Kwan Yin. She comes down from heaven to pour out a blessing."

"Aren't you afraid people will accuse you of cultural appropriation?"

"Never fear your audience, Jonathan. Once the show starts they have a steep learning curve to contend with. If they don't understand what you're doing, it's not their fault—they're probably victims of fashions and trends, or maybe they're just slow. And don't ever give credence to any critic; every one of them is impotent and unimaginative." (How has she garnered such a mature philosophy in the few short years she's been performing?) "Can you take out the powder blue gown and lay it over the chair, please?" The gown is alternating layers of fine translucent blue and transparent white fabric. She reaches into a little drawer in the trunk, takes out lacy red silk wedding lingerie with garters and silk stockings and lays them on the table. "I can take it from here," she says, "I need to get into character."

Stooping to walk through the doorway, I think of the scars on her back—and maybe others that can't be seen, and I feel that I've just met Marga for the first time.

27

Visitation

On the catwalk outside the office, I lean against the iron handrail and watch the activity all around. Smith and Finnerty Steel has not been this busy since 1985. Attached to the transverse bridge next to Werner's control room there are two seriously thick braided cables that run the length to the cauldron stage outside. At the top of these cables there is a circular wooden platform made to look like a giant lotus flower wrapped in clouds or emerging from clouds. There are small grooved wheels hidden on the bottom so that it can ride on the cables. Across the back of the platform there is a T-shaped bar to give the passenger something to lean against or hold on to for the ride down. A pulley attached to the bridge connects this rolling sled platform to several sandbags and counterweights that can be adjusted for Marga's exact weight. One of the boys from Berlin is testing the platform and rides to the cauldron a little faster than he expected. He tells his helper to add a couple more kilos of iron to the counterweight and it should be just right.

I hear a familiar laugh and voice asking for "Red." It's Jimmy Strong looking like he just returned from a gig in a Las Vegas casino. He's dressed in a pale tan check sport coat over a black shirt with a long, pointy collar that sticks out over the lapels. The top three shirt buttons are open, revealing a surfer necklace of turquoise and white pukka shells. His hair is brushed straight back in a high pompadour. He is standing next to the cloud-rider who points up toward the office. Jimmy looks up and sees me. "Jackie baby!" he yells.

"Stay there," I say, "I'm coming down." When I get downstairs, he embraces me like a long lost brother. "Where the hell have you been?"

"Off the grid. I lost my phone and couldn't get a new one."

"How did you do that?"

"I think somebody stole it when I was in rehab."

"So you got the cure?"

"Ninety days clean and sober, Guvnor."

"Congratulations. What brings you here?"

"Shit man, I came to see you. Just kidding—I wouldn't steal a motorcycle just for that. Actually, it's my brother's bike. He won't miss it. How did you guys ever find this place? Isn't this where the mafia dumps bodies?"

"I had nothing to do with finding this—that was Marga and her German friends. But now that I've been here a few times I kinda like it."

"It must grow on ya like a crotch-rot fungus."

"So seriously Jimmy, what brings you here?"

"I'm your opening act. Didn't Red tell you?"

"No. But I'm honored man. Truly. Where's the band?"

"They wouldn't come here—no sense of adventure. The scientist, Vern, he's pretty good with a keyboard, and there's another guy who plays guitar. Maybe you can accompany us and bang on some anvils and such."

"Whatever it takes. You know I'm here for you baby."

"Ha. ha. ha. You remember that."

I show him around the exterior of the building, the parts that I know, and explain where the audience will sit and how Marga will make her entrance down from the sky. Jimmy shakes his head slowly with a look of amazement. "To think," he says, "while I was out there making money and pissing it away on booze and junk, you guys were doing stuff like this. Tonight will be my first truly clean and sober gig. It's a new start for me Jonathan." (Yes, he called me by my real name.) "I gotta get out of the clubs. There's just too much temptation to backslide. I've been lucky, real lucky, but I don't know how long it can last. Sooner or later luck runs out."

Jimmy tells me that he will perform some new songs he wrote while he was in rehab. Marga came to visit him there. How did she know where he was? He doesn't know. Why did she come to visit him? Again, no idea. But on one of her visits, she asked him if he could write some new music, "something deep" she said, and sing at her performance. That assignment kept him alive, and focused. And now, here he is with nine new songs, and ninety days clean and sober.

"What if the crowd doesn't like deep stuff?" I ask.

"Jackie, no matter what you do in life, some people are gonna love you for it and others are gonna hate you for it. So you gotta stick with the winners."

"That's why I'm sticking with you, Mr. Strong."

"That means a lot," he says and puts his arm around my shoulder.

I take him on the grand tour, show him the cattails, and point out the slag pits. I explain how the city never turned off the power, and how the squatters make it all work.

"This place is amazing—it's like a whole unknown world down here."

"Play your cards right Jimmy, and someday all this could be yours."

"You're too good for the orchestra scene, Jack. You should learn a trade—become a plumber, or better yet, a honey dipper." For all of his sobriety, the man has not lost one bit of his inebriate charm.

* * *

Werner pages me through the sound system, and soon I'm in the control room. He's opened my audio file and is playing it through the control room monitor. He tells me it's brilliant. He got it this morning, and he's listened to it all day. He likes the complex layering and "tonal echoes" as he calls them. How were the overtones achieved? I can show him the score— sometimes the written notation is nearly as beautiful as the sound. He asks if he can supplement with his keyboard. Sure, I say, as long as the improvisation is consistent with the mood that Marga requested—bright and optimistic. He may use his holographic sound conditioner to drive home the crescendo. Fine, but remember—sparingly, like tympani and garlic. Our brief *tête-à-tête* ends when Jimmy and one of the Germans—a musician—enter to force an impromptu rehearsal with Werner. Jimmy is more nervous than I've ever seen him. He has nine new songs, filled with truth, to debut for Marga and me, and he wants them to be knock-outs. "Hey Vern," he calls. "I brought some charts for my songs. You can read charts, right?" Werner is excited to see real handwritten songs scored jazz style with chords spelled out with letters instead of notation—and by an

American rock-n-roller. He beams, and treats the papers as holy scriptures.

Out on the lot, I forget about Faraday and the foil envelope signal blocker, and place a call to Amity. It goes directly to voicemail. "Just calling to say hello and I miss you. I'm going to watch an art performance tonight at a theater space called 'Sector B'. They're playing a new composition of mine. It's bright and optimistic—you'd be extra proud of me."

About two minutes later I get a text: "That's nice."

And that is all.

28

Overthrown by Art

The show is scheduled to begin at 8 pm, but as these things often go, it doesn't. Marga's announcements on social media told people to assemble near a corner bar at the foot of Valley Road. She also made a deal with a gypsy bus company to drive them to the venue. This way, none of the audience knows the actual location of Sector B until they arrive. The bus driver takes the outer roadway that circles around the mill so he won't have to back up when it's time to leave, and he stops near the truck gate to unload about 50 passengers. One of the German artists unlocks the gate and leads the audience to their seats on stacked railroad ties and old oil cans. Anything like real chairs, even beach chairs, would be insulting to these cultural dissidents and iconoclasts.

Once they are seated, some reach into their backpacks and pull out things to drink and smoke. Werner and the guitarist are doing a soundcheck and accidentally pump out a sixty Hertz tone at about 120 decibels, courtesy of the Municipal Light and Power company. When that's corrected, the guitarist plays a few bars of one of Jimmy's songs, which get warped by the TAG sound conditioner. The cattails rattle and the crowd yells, "Yeah!" They will be lucky if they have any eardrums left to listen to my composition. Jimmy climbs to the stage from a ladder beside the cauldron. Three clip-on aluminum dish work lights loaded with 150 watt bulbs illuminate the master.

Jimmy is standing in place, yet moving slowly. His shoulders dip and rotate in extreme slow-motion. It's as if he is taking an inventory of each muscle—like a pilot flexing the rudder and flaps during a pre-flight check. The music, slow and haunting, provides the rails upon which his grooved soul will run. He extracts a wireless mic that was wedged in his belt like a ceremonial dagger and starts to hum in harmony with the lead note. Werner accompanies on keyboard while the guitarist plays just the bottom note of the chords on the wound strings. When experienced *in situ*, the effect is like watching an illegal production of contraband music on the Public Broadcasting channel—some rogue government is about to be overthrown by Art.

Jimmy's song is unlike anything he's ever done before. It is minimalist—extremely slow and hypnotically repetitive, as haunting as if it had been written by Arvo Pärt while pining for the Highlands. Werner and the guitarist are getting their money's worth from the echo effect and take a full eight or ten minutes to develop variations on the basic theme. Jimmy has been breathing deeply and completely so that when his time arrives, and he grabs an F and slides up to A#, he uses an entire lungful of air. I was definitely not prepared for this beginning. When his words reach the part of my brain that translates sounds into meaning, I break out in goosebumps—his text is uncanny and bewildering and Jimmy takes more than a half minute to articulate:

"If you

by desire

could stay warm."

His breathing and singing are synchronized with the music and his tone is so pure and in such perfect pitch that it is impossible to tell when his voice begins and the keyboard or guitar ends. At times he makes ever so slight adjustments to his vocalization so that the voice and instrument go into phase and send an acoustical surf washing over the audience. I see motion in the control room and realize that Werner is going for the sound conditioner. He dials it up slowly as Jimmy navigates the vibrato and when he catches the phase, Werner amps it up just enough that the audience gasps. A few begin to cry. The song contains every broken heart and every *Sunday Morning Coming Down* that Jimmy has ever lived.

It is a beautiful idea, well-executed, and energized by the Almighty. But Jimmy doesn't seem to have an exit plan. For about an hour he has been experimenting and improvising on the fly, and his years of experience on stage are informing every alteration and every gesture. The audience is fused with the performance, and pouring its magnetic energy back into Jimmy's feed loop. Time has stopped, and we are experiencing a kind of group enlightenment or at least revelation. I break free from the trance and think of Marga and wonder how in the world she is going to top this. Then I see her in the shadows next to the control room stepping over the railing and onto the cloud elevator.

29

Marga's Huzzah

I remove my phone from the foil again and begin recording as Marga, *dea ex machina*, slowly descending, breaks the air. Werner fades in my music. The string section in my recording is playing *lento*, with no expressed beat, so the sound hangs like a watercolor wash providing a temporal space for Marga to arrive and for the audience to focus on her ethereal presence. I've also combined the violin section playing the major key with the bass playing in a darker minor. By alternately shifting from the latter to the former, I build the conversion from doleful to optimistic— a sonic metaphor for Marga's journey. Jimmy senses the change and disappears while all eyes are on the alighting goddess.

When she steps onto the cauldron stage, Marga moves on ballet slippers with a slow, fluid gait that is hidden by her floating, diaphanous gown. I look for her wounded hand, but she is wearing white cotton gloves that extend past her elbows. In her left hand she holds the hollow gourd which I assume contains the blessing she will pour out, and in her right, she carries three incense sticks that lay thin trails of smoke as she walks. From where I'm standing, next to the overturned rail car, the effect is chilling: she really appears to be a disembodied spirit—gorgeous but ghostly. The incense smoke and gauze of her dress float like a disintegrating fetch in the still night air. Marga has gone fully *outré.*

A single violin rises above the rest playing the song of a thrush. On another track, a recording of an American robin's morning song provides counterpoint—soon the strings' dawn chorus will begin, and the shift is having its intended effect: the audience is sliding uphill into ecstasy. The transition from Jimmy's long song into mine, and Marga's entrance from upstage, seem to have been carefully calculated and rehearsed—neither of which is true; it is just the result of five people pouring their talents and their souls into the work.

Out of the blue there is a powerful smell of electrical sparks in the air—maybe from Werner's jury-rigged sound system, or the lights—but it seems to be coming from all around. It's that odor of ozone that I remember smelling in the Toronto subway. It fully overpowers the old factory smells that are usually very strong. Then I feel it. All the hairs on my body are standing up. Is my music that powerful? Has Werner engaged his TAG, 3-D sound multiplier? No, the static is from above us. Marga stops her hypnotic dance routine and is staring at the sky behind the audience's heads. Sector B turns a rich deep purple color. Marga's gown and hair glow like she's just descended from heaven, which is her character's story line after all. The crowd takes notice of the strange ultraviolet luminescence when it reveals all the stains on their clothes.

I don't know how they managed to pull this off. The entire place is glowing. Marga throws her props to the ground and uses her good hand to pull her dress up to her hip holding it there with the wrist of her injured hand. The audience goes wild when they see her lingerie. But she is not playing the seductress—she is reaching for her pistol. The audience loves that too. My prerecorded music is building to a crescendo of optimism as she aims at the sky above our heads. I look up and see a dull white sphere hovering just behind us. It looks to be about 20 feet wide and just about that far away. About one-third of the way down from the top there is a darker line, maybe two feet high, that runs laterally around the orb and, for some reason, reminds me of the tinted side windows of a stretch limousine.

The bright violet glow that lit us a few seconds ago is coming from an aureole or corona that surrounds the object. This radiance is mesmerizing; it's not like light from a bulb, but more like bio-luminescence. The orb is bathed in a billowing plasma and it's shedding a luminous gas or vapor that slides around the sphere and hangs briefly in the air like a dry ice fog before it dissipates. It's hard to get a clear look at the thing because these vapor clouds that surround it make the shape appear to rapidly modulate...visually *warble* is the best way I can think of to describe it. At first I think this is some surprise invention of the B-sector boys: a weather balloon and a dry ice mist lit with black-light. But I feel the static lifting up my hair, the smell of sparks getting stronger—and it's coming from the ball.

I hear an ambient crackling sound, but otherwise the thing itself is silent. My music is still building, but the audience is mute. Then, with her blue hair rising upright from static, Marga, angry and out of character, fires.

30

No Greater Gift

Marga is a good shot, and the first red tracer round is placed for a bull's eye, but it curves to the left of the sphere. Some in the crowd, who are familiar with guns and ricochets, immediately run for the exit gate. The rest of us can't stop looking at this thing. My music has moved on to the pizzicato movement and Werner has pumped up the TAG effect so it can be felt inside the skull—as if the violinists were plucking on our brains. Someone, probably high on hallucinogens, lets out a panicked scream: "It's a demon!" Marga fires again, and this time, at the orb's perimeter, the bullet curves straight up. I watch it climb for a few seconds until the phosphorus burns out. Where it lands, nobody knows, and that's not good. By now it's clear to all present that this aerial phenomenon was not part of Marga's show—it is now—but she did not design it nor invite it. I like to be in control of my work, that's why I score everything; however, Marga always leaves a little bit to chance, so that when the unexpected occurs it becomes a part of the act. But that's the problem with incorporating aleatory elements into your score: a soloist may do a bit of grandstanding and take the piece in a direction that totally overpowers your theme. Tonight this hot-dogging blue ball is hijacking Marga's artistic *tour de force.*

Before Marga has a chance to aim and fire again, the orb turns a deep red—like steel that is red-hot, not molten, but redder—more like a waning ember, and then it flies straight up. In less than a second, the object is so high that it looks like it's going to be just another of the distant stars. The only difference is that Marga's star is a warped Red Hots cinnamon candy heart.

For a few seconds, I watch the thing and wish it would return so that I could get a second look. No sooner have I made that wish than the ball drops back to where it was before. When I say "drops," that's not entirely accurate since this sphere of light moves too fast for its motion to be seen. It's more like it disappears from there and, with a streak of color, instantly manifests here. But now, here it is again, maybe 20 feet away at the altitude of a housetop. And it is unsteady—it's moving jerkily, haltingly, up and down from housetop high to three feet above the ground, as if it's being driven by a manual elevator operator who's had too much to drink.

It finally comes to a rest on the ground or just above. For some reason, I'm not afraid. There is something familiar about it, like I know it, or I should know it. The purple aura is gone and there is no wind. It's just sitting there like a big dimming nightlight. The red glow deepens to a burgundy and begins to emanate heat until it turns invisible. But it hasn't. It has become a lens— a solid transparent circle that inverts the view of everything behind it. It is perfectly clear, like somebody cut a hole in our picture of the fence and the pine trees behind and flipped that picture upside down. Although there at the top, one third down from where the top was, the band of dark limousine windows is reflecting the stage lights.

There is motion in that window—behind that window—there are figures lit in pale green glow, like that seen through night vision goggles, or lit from the panel lights of a car's dashboard. They are dressed in silver jumpsuits and wearing what look like silver baseball caps. They are very busy, but one looks in my direction and our eyes meet. He turns to another and gestures with a silver glove. The other locks eyes with me and then quickly turns away, her blonde ponytail swinging from the back of her cap.

In my mind's eye I see a man picking at the label of a beer bottle, and a woman in a cobalt blue dress.

I have forgotten about Marga and her performance, upstaged as she was by this interloper, until she takes another jealous shot, this time low, which ricochets off the orb's personal gravity field and buries itself—still burning—in the slag and gravel beside my feet. You don't need to be Sun Tsu to understand that this is now a war zone. Even the most intoxicated of the audience members are looking for the way out. Jimmy has climbed back onto the stage to disarm Marga, but I can't hear what he's saying over the triumphal sound of my musical climax. Marga lowers her arm, but does not surrender the weapon. I crouch down next to the steel gondola for cover. I look back and see the ball is shifting back through the color spectrum and when it becomes a gold color—like 24 karat gold—it flattens to a cigar shape, or maybe a pancake, about one-fourth of its previous height from my side view of it, and slowly rises about a hundred feet in the air. It then slides north toward Lake Erie at the speed of a slow bicycle, trailing a smudge of luminescent gold in the sky behind.

I look back at the stage where Jimmy is pleading with Marga. She looks away from him and back to where the orb had been, raises her pistol again and fires. I feel the thumping pressure waves before I see the two black helicopters—that sound resets the pulse of my heart to an uncontrollable tympanic polyrhythm and I feel panic like the audience must have felt at the premiere of Stravinsky's *Rite of Spring.* Four men in black commando clothes step partly out onto the helicopters' running boards and shoulder their rifles. Marga's tracer rounds pass between the choppers and Werner pumps up the TAG power which causes the sharks to wobble and the commandos to miss with the first of their return fire. When the helicopters get close to the spot where the orb had been, the mercenaries jump to the ground and take aim. Jimmy grabs Marga in a bear hug and swings her away from the shots. He is hit in the back and—locked in an embrace—the two fall off the rear of the stage.

Inside the rail car I can't stop shivering. I feel a mentholated chill in my veins and a kind of paralysis that began the moment the shooting started and I dove inside this filthy steel box. I can't seem to do anything, but I still try: try not to move, try not to breathe, try to see what is happening in the mill by squinting through perforations where the ancient rust has given way. I can hear talk, but not words—just voices, coarse, with military-like bearing. Werner yells something in German that sounds like he is surrendering. Boots give a dull ring on every tread as the men run up the steel staircase then down again dragging Werner and his belongings. They are now standing so close that I'm afraid they might hear my heart beating.

"Gag the kraut professor, and give him a shot of Seconal. They can wake him up for rendition."

"What should I do with all his boxes and crap?" one asks.

"Bring it all. You can dump it into the body bags—I brought extra. Where's Annie Oakley's ghost?"

"She's hit, won't get far. What about Elvis here?"

"Zip him up and load him in. We'll drop him near the projects and then run disinfo that he was killed in a drug deal." (Jimmy—he was clean and sober.) "And don't get any blood on my fine Corinthian leather interior."

"Captain, you are one sick bastard—Sir."

"That I am."

My cell phone is laying face-down in the cattails right where I must have dropped it when I dove into this gondola. Someone is calling—light shines from under it and the phone begins to vibrate. One of the contract soldiers shoots a bullet right through its back. (I can now confirm that silencers don't make a rifle silent.) The captain barks at his subordinate.

"What the hell are you shooting at?"

"A rat."

"What'd you do that for? That rat never hurt you. Leave 'em alone."

The mercenaries laugh as they load the helicopters.

"We'd better hurry it up. That UAP probably drew some attention."

"Who's orb is it? One of ours?"

"Who knows? Could be from the universe next door. I've never seen one like that. But they're always coming up with some new gimmick."

"Strap in the nutty professor—he's our meal-ticket.

In a minute or less, they are aloft and heading east by north-east.

* * *

I stay inside the coal car rocking to the pounding of my heart, listening to my breath and the ringing in my ears, waiting for some sign, some special kind of silence or sound—the voice of a friendly—that will signal an all-clear. I don't know what it will or will not sound like. With all the unreality of this day, I wonder how I can be so focused and hyper-aware.

Above all else, I just want to live, and for that, I feel guilty.

31

Remote Humanity

There is only so long a human being can remain motionless in a fetal position inside a cold steel box. After what seems like hours, I lightly run my finger tips over the scaly blistered rust of the gondola like I'm reading an incomprehensible Braille, and stretch my leg which has fallen asleep. I inventory my circumstances: Truth and reality have gone to hell in a rusty crucible. My perceptions, like my memories, are sun-bleached in the middle, singed and deckled along the edges: the original hues tinged by the caustic dyes of time—those revisions of the past necessary for the preservation of ego. I flashback to a time in fourth grade when I played hide-and-seek with a group of classmates who weren't really friends. I hid so well that they couldn't find me, then they forgot about me and went out for ice cream. The next day one of the kids asked me why I didn't go to Dairy Queen with them. I lied and told him that my mother had called me. My late mother—she will always be late—like my late friends of late.

Random sounds come from inside the steel mill. I hope it's just the cooling and contracting of the structure. I wait some more, the muscles around my ears flex to tune in every anomalous drip, click, and ping. Peacocks at the zoo—they must be a mile away—call out with mournful wails like the screams of some tormented woman. Somewhere above and beyond me, a pack of motorcycles races across the Dennison Avenue bridge, their motors whining through the gears for minutes at a stretch. A car horn. A dog bark. Elsewhere, a siren. All are distant—nothing near. For all of the night's terrors, the normal sounds of remote humanity are barely comforting. And then a small, single-engine propeller plane flies in low from the south, and I freeze again. It doesn't stop, it doesn't circle, it just flies straight on over toward Burke Lakefront Airport. When I'm sure it has passed, I roll out of the rail car and find my phone. As I look back to where the orb and the helicopters had been, it's as if I'm observing everything through the wrong end of a telescope, then I sprint for the hole in the fence in the dream-like slow motion of hyperperception.

When I reach the fence, I can't find the hole. I thought it was directly in line with the opening to the furnace building, but it's not there. I run to the west, pulling on the chain links to find the loose ones, but no joy. I run back toward the east, half-pulling myself along with fingers through the links. Frustrated, I stop to look around, scaring myself with the loudness of my breathing, and jerk my head like a nervous squirrel as I survey the fence-line. There is no cover here; the fence is topped with barbed wire and too high to climb over, and it is too risky to run back to the gondola. Then I see it—something odd on the wire thirty feet away. I run and find that someone has used a length of bent and dented copper pipe to weave the sides of the fence together like a suture. It must be to keep out the wild dogs. I slide it up and out, and the fence wound gapes open. Freedom and safety are just across the road.

I rush to get through the hole and catch the shoulder seam of my denim jacket on a jagged piece of fence wire. I pull and cuss with equal ferocity until the seam gives way. Across the road I forget about the little drainage ditch, and fall right into it—stagnant water comes over the tops of my boots and my hands land on pine needles, then I crawl on my hands and knees until I am hidden under the low wide branches of a tall evergreen. I feel safe until I remember that the black shark helicopters probably have heat vision that can see right through the pine canopy.

For a second, the wild thought comes to me that I can go back to Marga's office and retrieve her thermal blanket, but then I am struck—like a plank to the side of the head—by the reality of what an open run to the furnace building would entail (and what I might find there), and my shivering starts anew. It's too dangerous to go anywhere tonight. I'll curl up under this tree and make myself as small as possible so that maybe—to the thermal vision helicopters or drones or satellites—I might just look like a sleeping deer. I should wait in *here* until dawn, then get my car and get out of *here*. My mind races with seemingly random and unconnected thoughts. Occasionally they revert back to Jimmy and Marga, and I shake uncontrollably until my teeth clatter.

I force my thoughts back to music. Pachelbel's *Canon in D* comes first, but brings with it scenes from a foreign film about upper-class sophisticates at a flowerful wedding in a sunny Italian garden. I think of Amity and what we once wanted, the illusion that I—we dreamed about creating, then, like a wrecking ball, a flying saucer enters the frame and the film is taken over by Federico Fellini.

I wait for dawn, and I shiver.

32

Night of the Shooting Stars

Under the skirts of this fragrant pine there are some small gaps between the low branches, and from my vantage point, if I crane my neck and move my eyes close to the opening, I can see a fairly large piece of sky and a small part of the factory. The stage lights, still shining, are now pointed in odd directions, and one dish is bent, folded like a big aluminum taco shell beaming a line of light onto the ground. There is a faint hiss of static from Werner's sound system. As my eyes focus in, I begin to make sense of what I'm seeing: a piece of linen blocking the view of some junk behind the cauldron stage, backpacks and trash dropped by the fleeing neo-hippies, something that looks like a kid-sized red canvas tennis shoe. Then, with a clunk, the power to the entire place shuts off and everything goes black and silent.

Was it at just this moment that the power company discovered that the steel mill is forty years delinquent on its electric bill? Could it be that the mercenaries still have boots on the ground? I refocus my hearing toward the darkness, but there is nothing. I listen closely for boots. Boots. I remove my Justin Ropers and dump out the slimy water, wring out my socks and hang them on a nearby branch, then put the boots back on just in case I need to attempt a futile run up the hill.

A slight rattling of steel fence against steel pipe seizes my attention. I'm beginning to see again now that my eyes have adjusted to the partial moon and starlight, but the pine branches block my view of the fence where the hole is. Closer, there is a little splash of water in the ditch. I struggle to focus, and see a figure crawling through the dead weeds. Whoever it is must be as full of adrenaline as I am because I can hear the breathing in snorts. The thought of fighting, rather losing, hand-to-hand combat with a seasoned war veteran-cum-mercenary instantly overclocks my heart rate, makes my wide eyes water, and gives me cotton-mouth. If fear really has a smell, then I reek of it.

The sound is getting closer and closer, so I brace my back against the pine, reach up and grab two branches, and prepare to kick like a mule. As the intruder crawls under the branches, I make out that it is the ugliest cur I have ever seen—a mauger and mangy dingo with scabby bald spots that pattern its rotten fur with smutty polka dots. A battle with a rabid dog could be as fatal as a bullet. So I raise up and kick it with both boots which knocks it with a yelp out of my timber tepee. But this son of a pup is either hungry or crazy—it won't go away. So I channel all my fear into blasting the deepest, loudest sound I have ever produced from my lungs, while shaking the branches as if Bigfoot himself were about to bring down the whole forest. The dog lopes away sideways like a coyote, looking back in three-quarter profile, the scant hairs on its spine bristling.

* * *

After the distant and lonely howl of a freight train, there is no more sound. The city has quieted down. I haven't heard a jet plane fly over or take off for about an hour—which means it is after midnight when the last flight departs from Hopkins International. I feel a cool breeze on my right arm and realize that my shirt got ripped along with the jacket and there's a nasty scrape on my shoulder. Once I see it in the moonlight, I feel the sting for the first time. I start to feel the cold again so I button the jacket and turn up the collar.

Jimmy's song begins to play in my head: "If you / by desire / could stay warm."

I try to think of all the things I've ever desired: a piano, a wind-up wooden metronome, cowboy boots, a master's degree in music composition, a beautiful girlfriend, a peaceful home with love and affection, good friends, Marga. I choke on the last two and switch back to the present moment as a distraction. And warmth I think, yes, I now desire warmth. I think about the full length fur coats in Marga's guest room, try to remember that warmth, and then I feel it—a wave of warmth—whether it's the power of desire or of suggestion, I feel it.

But I'm not out of the woods yet, and this gig is not over, though I feel relatively safe now, here under this mother-of-all-conifers. The ground beneath me is padded to about a foot thick with layers of fallen pine needles accumulated over the years. The air is still and quiet and smells like Christmas. I wonder if Marga ever camped out beneath this tree. I sit with my eyes closed and try to catch the saturated color images that flash through my mind from left to right. One of them slows down long enough for me to observe it—my childhood tutor, old Sadie Bucknell. I realize now, at this moment, that she really loved me, no matter how many times I screwed up or tried to cheat on my piano lessons, she loved me. I can hear her voice encouraging me to compose music, all the time compose. Why? "Because *ars longa vita brevis*, your art will outlive you, so seize the day—*carpe diem*." And the oddest thing is that for the first time that I can remember, there is no music playing in my head. Not mine, nor Mozart's, not anyone's. There is only peace, or maybe exhaustion.

I lean forward and peek out at the sky. I look for one of the dippers, and think I've found it, when this needle of light streaks by so quickly that I question whether I really saw it. I see another, and a few seconds later, another. It is late April in the northern hemisphere. I can't remember much from the astronomy course that I took to fulfill a science requirement. Is this the time of year for a meteor shower? What am I seeing? Is this the Perseids? No. The Lyrids? Amity?

Where is Amity?

I curl up on the pine cushion with an eye to the sky.

I will never look at stars the same way again.

33

Red Morning

Just before dawn, a barking squirrel crashes my drowse. I retrieve my slightly damp socks and pluck out the pine needles before returning socks and boots to feet. A robin is the first to sing—a melodic, joyful, and questioning song. Then a thrush spools out curlicues from its tubular flutes. A cardinal trills sharply into audible primary colors, and nature clocks in for work. It's still dark. I peer out through the branches—there is a thick fog loitering in this low industrial valley, and every struggling weed is glistening with dew. I listen for any unusual sounds, but the birds are making too much noise. I thank the tree, (she and I have been through so much together), and push out through the branches into the misty morning air. I clomp stiffly down the slight hill and make sure to stop before hopping over the ditch water and climbing up to the damp but still hard road, and back through the fence.

Someone is watching. I can feel the eyes on my back. I do an about-face and look toward the hole in the fence, the fence line. Nothing. I look up, the moon has set, but through the fog I can make out the diffused deep red luminescence of nautical twilight and sunglow soon to emerge at the horizon. Nothing is moving. Still there is someone or something watching. It may be that mongrel dingo or that barking squirrel, a person or a drone, but... I turn back toward the furnace building and the crucible stage. It seems to be a mile away and barely visible in the fog. My leg muscles, cold and heavy and stiff, won't move. This is where artists and musicians come to die: This is the valley of the shadow of death, and I have to walk through it to get to my car.

It is here that I realize the inadequacy of words. How can I convey what I am experiencing right now? If I should describe patchwork emotions, raw grief, continual pain that forms a new baseline for normal, cold that numbs and stiffens muscles, the fluid experience of timelessness, and fear—a grue that drives to distraction and apathy—with only a thin, sharp sliver of a will to live, wouldn't I be telling, and not showing? In a body not entirely my own, isn't a mindful awareness simply dissociation? Take the walk, then *you* judge.

You are walking next to the railroad tracks, toward the furnace building, and away from the fence line. Your toe kicks something small and it rings metallic—the brass hull of a rifle round. You stop to pick it up and find another as well. At the cauldron stage you find more—these are shorter, must be Marga's. You pick them up too. One has fallen into a puddle of blood the shape of Ohio. You hold the brass and try to register the life in the coagulating red, but it is meaningless. It gets on your fingers and you wipe them on a shred of linen torn from the backdrop, convenient, as it is, right there behind the stage. You put the brass hulls into the cloth and fold it into your pocket. You no longer know why you do anything. There is no reason. You say the only prayer you know: "God help me." You wander around in circles, and now you are back at the spot where the orb first appeared.

As I step from one railroad tie to the next, I gradually come to accept that I am no longer a trespasser: I belong here. If some bored mercenary wants to shoot me in the back, well, so be it— all of my friends are gone. And if a rotten rabid cur wants to attack me, well, he'll get the worst of it, because I'm in no mood for invasive species in my sector.

Before I realize it, I'm back at the tipped gondola and the patch of cattails. A curved triangle of glass from my fragged cellphone reflects the reddening edge of approaching daybreak. I halt abruptly when I see the inexplicable little red canvas tennis shoe. There were no kids here last night. I take a closer look and see that the rubber toe is all chewed up—the dingo must have stolen it from someone's backyard and dropped it here when he came looking for me. I cross behind the stage and see a large stain, darker than the rusty earth around it. I feel dizzy, like I'm about to swoon, and walk behind the linen curtain. I stabilize myself by grabbing the long wrench that's hanging from the rope. Then comes an inspiration: What was the code? Three bangs on the vertical trusswork, pause, then two more. Silence. There is nothing. It's over.

Evidence of former occupation is clear: the wrench for one thing, and the hole that Werner cut through the wall as an access hatch into the giant pipes outside, and empty beer bottles neatly lined up on an I-beam—"dead soldiers" I think that's called. I'm still dizzy. Thirsty. It just now dawns on me that I haven't had anything to drink since yesterday afternoon. My lips are cracked and my tongue is swollen. Nothing can dehydrate a body like a night of terror. Marga keeps, kept water in her office. I climb the spiral staircase and try to ignore the evidence of her hand injury from yesterday. Sitting atop a paint can on the catwalk is a box of matches and the old yellow Dietz kerosene lantern. I light it to keep from stumbling in the dark—there is nobody left in this place to help me if I get hurt.

I step through the bulkhead door and unhook the curtains to let in a slightly brighter gray.

The bay windows facing out over most of the mill's campus allow me to scan for the last time this demesne of long art and short life. The early fog is slowly thinning and the dew evaporating. As the horizon gradually gains color, I have a more complete view of this vast curtilage of toxic tundra—oiled earth burnished to a dull shine in some places, dust devil twirled piles of granular rust in others. Soon, the city will be awake and it will no longer be safe in here.

How's that? Safe? When was *this* place ever safe?

Marga's office is a mess. I brush aside her blue wig and pull out a plastic gallon jug of water from under the table. It's unopened and clean and I drink about half before pausing to catch my breath. Three Styrofoam heads—two bald, and one with a blonde flip hairdo—watch me as I fall to my seat on Marga's futon couch. I think of Amity; she may be my last remaining...(I almost said "friend"). But she, assuming she's alive, has a lot of explaining to do if she wants to get back to normal.

Normal.

Huh.

What an absurd concept.

Sensation is returning to my hands as they warm up, and I notice the delicate softness of Marga's silk chiffon dress lying next to me on the futon. I stroke it and roll the expensive fabric between my thumb and forefinger, then I cover my chapped hands with it. My back is warming from the futon and I feel exhaustion settling in. I'm very comfortable and feel myself nodding off, until I get a psychic slap and bolt upright with an electric shiver: *I've got to get out of here!*

Get a grip. Think this through. Take the lantern. Duck through the squat bulkhead door. Which way is the car? Just keep going. On my left: Werner's crane room—keyboard, guitar, and TAG— all smashed to bits. Uncle Dan's voice yells inside my head: *"It don't mean nothin, Drive on!"* Where is the car? Right!—Outside Marga's studio. Where is Marga's studio? Panic. Don't panic. Nothing looks familiar. Stay calm. Stop. Breathe. Marga's studio has...southern exposure! Walk to the north side of the building. Put the sunglow at my back. Turn left through the fake wall. I'm in.

There is a hiss of silence.

34

A Flicker of Red

Marga's studio is right out of Cleveland's Grand Era of Industrial Pollution. It's about twenty feet wide by thirty feet long, with a twenty foot high ceiling. Most of the southern wall is windows—large reinforced glass set in groups of six: three over three, which swing out for air circulation. (This room must have cost a fortune to heat when the furnaces were down.) The other walls are cinder-block painted battleship gray. The floor is crumbling concrete and rusty dirt. The whole place smells of machine oil, mildew, and sour rust.

Just through the door there is a steel workbench about ten feet long and four feet deep, tall enough for a regular sized man to work comfortably while standing. The table's legs still retain part of their swirly metallic blue, factory paint job—the rest is covered in surface rust. Underneath, connected to the legs, is a steel storage shelf that holds wrenches, hammers, wood-handled screwdrivers (mostly bent), and boxes of Marga's painting supplies. Mounted on the right side of the workbench is a large vise that's shaped like a small anvil. In front is a five foot tall platform step ladder that Marga has clearly been using as a chair when working at the table—a zippered gray hoodie bearing a few strands of red hair is draped over this ladder. On top of the workbench are coffee cans half-filled with turpentine, and about a dozen pie tins holding diluted oil paints and worn-down toothbrushes. There is also a box containing a gross of personalized (but misspelled) "Dr. Toothi" dentist giveaway brushes that Marga must have bought at a closeout store.

I've sort of forgotten why I'm in here when I look to the right and see, leaning against the wall, twenty, maybe thirty large paintings partially covered with a splattered plastic drop-cloth. They are mostly the same size: roughly five feet square, stretched and stapled on wood frames. Didn't Marga say that someday, somehow, I would see her paintings? Well, isn't this someday? When I pull off the cover, I'm stunned to see a portrait of me in a suit I've never worn, sitting at a grand piano, pen in hand, making revisions to a score. The next is a painting of me asleep on her futon. I can almost hear her voice whispering in my ear that night, "*Je t'aime. Te voglio.* Always been..."

There is also a dark painting: two black helicopters descending into a mess of purple and blue swirls, the canvas edged in long green pine needles (she *did* stay under that tree). Here I am pictured again, asleep on my bed as viewed over the rim of a Wedgwood cup half-filled with chamomile tea. (The woman must have had a photographic memory.) Still others: a portrait of Lance in a lab coat, Marga and I at one of her tea parties, me wearing a tuxedo next to a woman in a wedding dress clutching a bouquet of flowers— the bride's face obscured by a potted palm. There is one more, maybe a work in progress. I recognize it right away—it is Severance Hall from the perspective of Lance's seats: walls of Naples yellow and chairs of crimson velvet radiate from the paint-scrubbed canvas. And there, center stage in front of the full orchestra with the conductor and Yulia Sophia smiling on, stand I, holding the props: the golden scepter and orb. (The diva, slightly behind and to the left of me, has been rendered more corpulent and blurry than I remember her.) Above us on an ornate proscenium arch that exists only in Marga's mind, in Romanesque lettering is the abbreviation A_B_C_M_A_Y:

Always Been Crazy Mad About You.

A truck horn in the distance snaps me back to my primary mission which is to get the hell out of here. And as soon as possible. But I can't abandon these paintings to rot, and they are way too big for my car. I could pull out the staples, but there are hundreds on each painting. I know! I can cut the canvas where it meets the staples. Maybe I can use a shard of glass from a broken window. No, the stuff is reinforced with chicken wire—I'd slice up my hand trying to get a piece. Marga must have a knife here somewhere. Rifling through her boxes, I feel like a burglar. Tubes of oil paint, brushes, charcoal sticks, Conté crayons, glue—nothing sharp. (Jonathan think! How did she cut canvas?) There, on the table, a partial roll of her expensive Belgian linen, and next to it: Eureka! A box-cutter.

Over at the stack of paintings, I realize that to cut off a couple dozen canvases, roll them up and stuff them into the Audi— if they even fit—would take all morning, and I don't have all morning. I decide to take only the paintings that could somehow incriminate me. I begin with one I actually want to keep— the picture of me standing for applause at my world premiere. Slicing with the box cutter, I find that gessoed linen is harder to cut than I had anticipated. About halfway across the top, the blade hits something hard under the canvas. I tip the frame forward for a better look and see the lavender acrylic of Werner's relic jammed between the canvas and the wooden stretcher. The mercenaries didn't get it—not yet anyway. The poor guy was willing to be tortured, maybe killed, rather than give it up. Or maybe he is about to give it up. Or maybe he *has* told them where to find it and they're on their way back to get it now. Thank God for the thick fog. They can't fly a helicopter in the fog.

But they can still drive.

I wiggle the plastic square out of its hiding place and take it to Marga's workbench. Maybe I can smash it to bits on the anvil or crush it in the vise. No, they will just scoop up the pieces and make a new one. I look along the edge of the relic's case and see that it is two pieces snapped together with the targeted relic sandwiched between them like an ugly coquina. Using the razor from the box cutter, I spread the two halves and get to the object within. Up close, it really looks like an old piece of crumbling cloth, woven fibers of cotton or flax, I suppose. And it is the color of dried blood—or rust! I lift the relic out from its little center bubble, and carefully carry it on the razor's edge out of Marga's studio to an area of the steel mill where the floor is the rustiest and muddiest. Then, with a gesture pious and respectful, I place the crumbling relic onto the muddy rust, and grind it into obscurity with the heel of my boot. Then I do a little cha-cha over the area until even I can't tell that anything was ever there.

Back in Marga's studio, I take the blood-stained linen rag out of my pocket and rub it on every rusty thing I can find. When the color approximates that of the relic, I slice out a smidgen of the right size and shape, then plug this doppelganger into the target and gently squeeze the acrylic frame back together—making sure to not leave any fingerprints. After I liberate the rest of my painting from the stretcher, I wedge the relic back to where it was between the wood and the remaining scraps of canvas, and lean the entire thing against the left wall—far away from the other paintings—where the mercenaries will be sure to find it.

While slicing off the portrait of Lance, I begin to panic. My ESP tells me that my time is up, I've got to go—now. I put Lance's empty stretcher frame with the other paintings, roll up my two canvases, and set them by the door. Then I douse the lantern, open its fuel cap and pour the half-cup of kerosene over the remaining paintings. From Marga's supplies I get a liter can of turpentine and another of mineral spirits and add them to the artistic kindling leaning against the right side cinder-block wall. Once the paintings are gone, there will be nothing flammable left except for the empty stretcher frame I moved to safety at the left wall. From my jacket pocket I retrieve a book of matches marked *Tobacco Toronto*. I light the mess and wait a little while until the bonfire is a roaring blaze. The canvases burn reddest, soaked as they are with scrubbed-in oil paint. I think of all the hours of work and talent that Marga put into the creation of these. At this point, to the law, I'm probably just an arsonist—but in the world of conceptual art, there hasn't been creative destruction on this emotional level since Bob Rauschenberg erased that drawing by de Kooning. I grab my paintings and go.

Outside the building, I pull the linen cover off my car, wrap the paintings in it, and stuff the whole bundle onto the floor and the back seat. Smoke is beginning to pour out of the building as I start the Audi. (I should have considered that it might not.) It starts. By now, the paintings must all be consumed, and the wooden frames burning well on their own. A quote from Gustav Mahler comes to mind: "Tradition is not the worship of ashes, but the preservation of fire." Through the mirror as I slowly drive away, I see the smoke blending in with the fog, and from the studio windows, a flicker of red that fades the farther I go.

Once I exit the mill property and turn onto Jennings Road, I feel a sense of freedom that seems too good to be true. At a red light, I pull up behind a BMW and feel an ancient pang of envy; I wonder how a normal person without a wealthy girlfriend can afford such luxuries. An unmarked police car with flashing lights pulls up and blocks the intersection ahead. My heart is pounding, but nobody exits the police car. Instead, he blocks traffic for a line of six blacked-out suburban SUVs with smoke-tinted head and tail lights roaring down Valley Road. I watch them in my rear-view mirror as they turn onto the Smith and Finnerty Steel Mill's property. The police car follows them. I turn up Valley Road and into the neighborhood of Old Brooklyn. I'm having an out-of-body experience again (or still) and driving on auto-pilot. I stop the car in front of Amity's house where men are unloading furniture from a moving van. I ask the neighbor where the Halifaxes have gone. Moved, she says, two weeks ago. To Connecticut, she says, and that's all she knows. Such useless information. I am undone.

35

The Long Way Home

The car drives—somehow I am participating. On the Shoreway, I turn on the radio for something to anchor me in the moment. It's Sunday morning. The classical station has two holy men slurping a thin broth of theology in the practiced cadence and hypnotic tones of a National Public Radio propagandist. There should be a warning about listening to this kind of pablum while you're driving or operating heavy machinery. I switch to AM radio and get a cranked-up duo that sound like they're auditioning for a job as the weekday morning drive team.

"Well, Preston, did you hear the one about the UFO?"

"No Jules, what's the punchline?"

"No punchline, it's true! Several people on the west side reported seeing a UFO last night."

"Why do the really strange things always happen on the west side?"

"One person said it looked like a red beach ball, another guy said it was a golden banana."

"I think they must be smoking bananas on the west side."

"Seriously Preston. You gotta let go of your regional bias.

Here's another one: a man who was fishing off the rocks downtown last night said this ball of light floated overhead and made everything glow purple, then it dropped into the lake and popped up about a mile farther out."

"Whack a Mole!"

"Yeah, then it shot off to the west."

"There we go again, 'off to the west.'"

"Wasn't there a meteor shower last night?"

"I think so, but it's pretty hard to confuse a glowing Whack a Mole with a falling star."

"Not if you live on the west side."

"Oooh! Now who is the biased one Jules? Huh? Huh?"

"Well, on a sadder note, Cleveland lost one of *its* stars last night. Jimmy Strong was killed in a drug deal gone bad."

"On which side of town was that?"

I yell at the radio, "Are you serious?" and the voice of an electronic wench answers from an invisible speaker overhead, "This is Siri. How may I help you?"

I tell her to go to hell, and she obediently goes. The radio jocks return.

"You know all of his music was about drugs." (Liar!)

"Or sex. Maybe now that he's gone, you can get a date."

"Oooh! That's just wrong!" (And very rehearsed)

"On a lighter note, today the city begins demolition of the old Smith and Finnerty Steel Mill."

"No kidding? Does that mean the steel mills are not coming back?"

"You got it Sherlock. Apparently a Neo-Nazi biker gang was using the place to manufacture meth. One of their stills blew up this morning."

"Do they make meth in a still?"

"Don't ask me, I'm not a Neo-Nazi."

Who writes this stuff? I switch off the radio and open the windows. It is much too chilly to drive *al fresco*, but the scent of Lake Erie is washing the fog out of my mazard.

I exit the Shoreway onto Clifton Boulevard and get a fleeting image of Napoleon's ghost riding Marengo's ghost down the Champs-Élysées. I feel as if there are steel bands strapped tightly around my skull. I am exhausted and my brain is hissing with white noise. The car is weaving a bit within the lane so I lean forward to stay focused and not fall asleep in the comfortable heated seat.

When I arrive at my apartment building and pull into my parking spot, two men dressed in black suits and wearing sunglasses approach the car. I stand next to the driver's door, turn to face them, and activate the lock and alarm. The car chirps.

"Are you Mr. Brendel? Mr. Jonathan Brendel?"

"Yep. And this is my car, and this is my parking spot. Is there a problem?"

"We'd like to ask you a few questions."

"Are you cops?"

"Not exactly."

"Then what are you, exactly, besides manly men in badly-fitting suits?"

"We're with the Special Response Team."

Mrs. Finnegan is peeking out through the curtains. I press the key fob in my pocket to chirp a few more times as I look at her. She quickly moves away and returns with her cell phone to record the activity—as I knew she would. A couple more curtains move and one reveals just a hand holding a phone. Thank God for all these computer nomad neighbors of mine hoping to make some cash on a viral video.

"Excuse me," I say. "I need to get something from the trunk." I walk toward the men forcing them to step to the side. "On second thought, I don't need it," I say and castle to change positions. I've just upstaged them so that they are now facing the windows. "You said you have a question. Well, ask it. I'm tired and need to get some sleep."

"Where were you last night Mr. Brendel?"

"That's my business." The other man in black must be a rookie. He gets testy and threatens to haul me in. "Where to?" I ask. "You're not police."

"Don't make this difficult, Mr. Brendel."

"I'm not making anything. But a lot of my loving neighbors are making videos of you, so you'd better keep it boring or your cover will be blown on YouTube."

"No trouble Mr. Brendel. We just need to know where you were last night."

"Camping."

"Where?"

"Under a pine tree under the stars." The rookie agent looks at the roll of linen stuffed behind the front seat and says, "Tent."

"What did you see?"

"Stars. Shootings. Shooting stars."

"What else did you see?"

"A dingo. A rooty dingo. I almost got killed by a rooty dingo. I had to fight it off. It had rabies." The rookie agent looks at my scratched arm and takes a step back. The first continues his interrogation.

"Did you see anything else? Anything unusual in the sky?"

"Shit."

"What's that?"

"I didn't see shit. There isn't shit up there."

"Good. Thank you Mr. Brendel. Sorry for the trouble." And they start to walk away.

"Officer," I call, "When you see her…"

"See who, Mr. Brendel?"

"When you see her, tell her *that* was a shitty thing to do. And tell her I'm sorry. Just tell her that."

He nods his head and walks away.

* * *

When I walk through the door into the laundry room, Mrs. Finnegan startles me almost to a heart attack. She's standing off to the side wearing a floral patterned cotton dress and a long, stretched-out, Kelly-green cardigan with sagging pockets; under her arm she holds a large manila envelope. Dryers hum and thump with the dulled taps of damp towels and socks; the air is thick and smells of tropical fruity fabric softener. For the first time since I've known her, Mrs. Finnegan calls me by my first name.

"You don't look well, Jonny. Are you in some kind of trouble?" (I lean against the laundry folding table for support.) "Is it because of that Russian tart? I saw your pictures in the paper. They didn't say much about the concert, just said that you must be the playgirl's new boy-toy. I didn't believe it." (I feel an out-of-body experience coming on, like I'm watching myself in a droll community theater stage play.) "Jonny, you've had an accident! Your arm is bleeding."

"No I'm OK—it's just a flesh wound."

"Come up to my apartment, I can put a bandage on it, fix you a cup a tea."

"No, no thank you Mrs. Finnegan."

"Call me Colleen. I have some good Jameson whiskey—that should fix you up."

"I'd better not."

"How about a bottle of Guinness? It's good for what ails you."

"Mrs. Finnegan, Colleen, you're the best, really. But I'm fine. I just need some rest."

"You need a friend Jonny."

"That too, Colleen, that too."

"It's Sunday, are you going to church?"

"Wait, it's Sunday? Uncle Dan is expecting me today!" For some reason this triggers Mrs. Finnegan's spleen.

"Well then, you wouldn't want to keep your Uncle Danny waiting. Oh, and by the by, a messenger delivered this envelope for you this morning, but you should wait until you meet your uncle to look at it. I know it's illegal to open other people's mail, but this came by courier service, and it seemed important, then I resealed it."

36

Uncle Dan's Sunday Morning Service

Back in the car, with the manila envelope as passenger, I head to Uncle Dan's bungalow in the Ohio City neighborhood. He's not home, and I can't call him because my phone has an exit wound the size of my thumb. I park in front of his house, close my eyes, and cover my face with my hands. Instantly a parade of sordid images passes in front of my mind's eye: grisly wounds, a decaying zombie dog, ghosts of men in silver asbestos suits pulling long steel rakes to scrape slag from a glowing cauldron of molten iron, Amity and ET with lurid, ribald smiles toasting with champagne to the successful maiden voyage of the Aspidistra.

I am definitely unmoored, adrift and rudderless, bobbing in the doldrums at neap tide where sight of the coastline has been lost. I jolt awake with the sensation that the car is floating away. It's not. I just can't trust anything anymore. Where is Uncle Dan? My hands are shaking, I feel light-headed, cold and sweaty, and have a craving for something sweet: candy, a donut. I'm starving. I drive over to Brewnuts and see Uncle Dan's truck. I forgot, and now remember, that Dan Brendel's Sunday morning service is meeting with other Vietnam vets and shooting the breeze over coffee and donuts. I park askew and enter.

Four guys are sitting at a table; the one in a plaid shirt with his back to me is Uncle Dan. I must be a real irritation to sore eyes, because when one of the men looks at me, he raises an eyebrow, another gives me the once-over. Uncle Dan notices the direction of their attention, and turns around to find me standing ten feet away. "Jon, my boy, what's happened to you? You look like you've been though purgatory." Two of the men make their salutations and decamp until next week, the third says that I look like I could use a donut and a drink and asks do I want coffee or beer. Uncle Dan says to get a large coffee with cream and a maple donut. I don't know if his selection is a result of his clairvoyance or if he's driving my appetite with neuro linguistic programming. The bands around my skull get tighter.

"Sit down, Jon," says Uncle Dan stroking the back of my head with his big hand. "This isn't a bender, is it?" he asks. I shake my head. The other vet returns with my breakfast. "What is it then?"

"National security," I say, because that's the first thing that comes to mind. The vet and Uncle Dan share a look. I eat half the donut in one bite.

"Come on Jon. You can talk freely—Richie here spent two years with me in the jungle." I pull the rifle cartridges from my pocket and put them on the table. Uncle Dan picks them up and smells one, hands the other to Richie who looks at the bottom and says, "NATO, five five six. Definitely not a standard gang-banger." After a short deliberate pause, he adds, "Well Dan, it's a nice day. I want to get down to the lake and do some fishing. Call me later if you get a chance." Dan nods and Richie exits. Uncle Dan leans in and looks me closely in the eyes, reading everything. "Don't say a thing. We'll talk in the truck."

I follow Uncle Dan to his house and park my car in his garage as he tells me to, then I get the envelope and join him in the pickup truck. He looks at the nasty scrape on my arm—no mollycoddling from Uncle Dan—he says it looks fine, no infection, he's seen much worse.

"Now, you want to tell me what this is all about?" I tell him I don't know where to begin. "I saw you on Thursday before your concert," he says, "you were fine then. Why don't you pick it up from there."

I tell him the whole story: Severance Hall, the concert, the partying, the hangover, Sector B, Jimmy, Marga, my music, the Germans, the relic, the flying saucer, the sharks, the shooting, the pine tree, the dingo, the shooting stars, the fog, the paintings, the fire, the SUVs, Amity's exodus, the men in black, Mrs. Finnegan and the manila envelope, Brewnuts, and now.

"Damn! You've been through more in one weekend than most guys experience in a lifetime. Paintings still in your car? Show me." I retrieve the paintings and unroll them in the back of the pickup. In the late morning sun they radiate a rich spectrum of colors as if lit from within.

"Who's the brain surgeon?"

"Her father. How'd you know he's a brain surgeon?"

"Because he looks like one." Uncle Dan unrolls the other painting of me at Severance Hall. "This was Thursday night?" I nod. "You look a lot better in the picture than you do right now. What does this A.B.C.M.A.Y. mean on the arch above you?" I explain. "She didn't need to spell it out for me to see—this girl loved you. Some of this paint is still wet." I feel myself getting weepy.

"I'm sorry Uncle Dan. I wish I were more like you. I should be made of sterner stuff."

"Don't apologize Jon. I'm no stronger than you, just more calloused."

"I feel like I may be losing my mind."

"Don't surrender your sanity just yet. You've presented a pretty factual case so far. Let's see what's in the envelope."

Inside the envelope is a manila folder with photographs printed on eight by ten inch glossy paper: professional color shots, likely taken with a telephoto lens from the back of the auditorium at Severance Hall. The crazy part is that there are only a few, and they were taken right after the concert when Yulia and I were clowning around for the audience. In one she has her arms around my neck and is staring at me, in the next, she kisses me, and in the third I've dipped her over for what looks like a passionate kiss (which I can testify—was all theater). These are probably not the best shots for documentation of a successful world premiere. In fact, the actual point is kind of lost on me until I open a smaller envelope in the folder and find five by seven inch glossies in grainy black and white. These were taken in the bar and are far more incriminating—a photo montage of the memories I lost in my besotted fugue state. They look like Cold War era spy photos: vulgar, louche, and compromising, intended for blackmail. There's one of Yulia tipping up a vodka bottle to my mouth, one of us in a passionate kiss (not theater), Yulia with hands inside my shirt, both with hands all over each other, me with glossed eyes and a cigarette dangling from my lip, and the *coup de grâce*—Yulia with one breast exposed holding me across her lap like a blasphemous redux of the *Pieta*. I feel a rush of blood to my face and scalp. After last night, I didn't think I would ever again be capable of feeling horror. I was wrong.

"This looks like a classic, old-fashioned blackmail package," Uncle Dan says. "The kind that threatens to break up a marriage. But you're not married, so are they asking for money? We gotta figure out who's the enemy." There is a printed letter, short but devastating, and signed by Amity. She thinks in the light of recent events, it's better that we go our separate ways. She feels sorry for me because I don't want to grow up, but she cannot continue to play mother to me. I should consider all the things she's given me to be gifts, including the car—which has a twenty-five thousand dollar balance due on the loan note signed in my name. She will return the score I gave her as a birthday present, since it may have some value to me. Uncle Dan says, "What's with the passive aggressive litany of injustices? A simple, 'Dear Jon, Piss off!' would have sufficed."

The letter is dated Friday, the day before her aerial visitation to Sector B.

I guess she didn't have any other cell phone beacon to use for triangulation. Well, I hope she made it home after the mercenaries snuffed my Samsung. (That thing was only four years old.)

There's one more item in the folder from hell: a wedding announcement page from the newspaper *GreenwichTime* of Connecticut that reads, "Amity Halifax, PhD of New Haven to Wed Edmund Traynor, PhD of Waterbury Next Month."

"Huh," says Uncle Dan, "Unless this girl is also a time traveler—which wouldn't surprise me at all—I'd say she's been planning this for some time. How are you feeling?"

"I feel like my entire life is one big wound that's being debrided."

"Well, un-brided anyway."

"Do you think this whole situation happened because I was

unfaithful?"

"Maybe I'm just becoming a fatalist in my old age Jon, but I think everything happens for a reason."

"There's no deep reason, Uncle Dan. I just got drunk and cheated on my fiancée."

"That you did, but if your fiancée had been there to see your world premiere, you wouldn't have been boozing it up with that Viking broad."

"She's Russian," I say, struggling to keep a straight face.

"What, you think the Russians didn't have Vikings?" I laugh for the first time in a long time.

"Listen Jon, sex is almost never about sex."

"What does *that* mean?"

"Just what I said—sex is not what most simple-minded humans think it is. Sometimes it's about companionship, or fighting loneliness. Sometimes it's about control, or power. And, believe it or not, for some people it's still about reproduction. In the worst of cases it's two people trying to fill a God-sized hole in their souls—and that's just impossible. But in the best of all cases it's about a love that just defies understanding, when you want to get so close to your wife that there just can't be any empty space—and that's the only time it's really worthwhile. The rest of the time it's just mistakes, or worse. Sure, at the moment it seems like it has value, but once you get some time and perspective on it, you realize that your life would have been much simpler if you had just gone straight home after work." He looks back into his history and says to himself, "Maybe she wouldn't have bugged out." He pauses for a moment then shakes out the thought. "You were pretty drunk that night, weren't you?"

"Yeah, but that's no excuse."

"How much do you remember?"

"Not much."

"So how do you know you were unfaithful?"

"Look at that picture, Uncle Dan."

"I did. And what I see is a stoned opera singer wanting to breast feed a grown man who is three sheets to the wind. I doubt that either one of you were in any condition to rumba"

"You have a way with words."

"What I really see is a woman who desperately wants to be a mom, and a boy who never had one."

37

Sack Cloth and Ashes

Mercifully, there is no additional insult in that dossier of indignities. Uncle Dan tells me that I must be the most interesting person he knows, and that as long as we are on a roll, we should confront all the demons because that is exactly what they would not expect us to do. He tells me to lose the torn jacket and shirt, then hands me a red plaid flannel lumberjack shirt from a bag of dirty laundry in the the pickup truck. I change right there in the street in front of his house. He also gives me his olive green M65 Army field jacket and a trucker's hat with the Freightliner logo. I don the duds and look like a different person—one who smells like Uncle Dan. I feel safe, and confident, like I could go into battle—with or without fear. He starts the truck and asks where Emily lives. *Who?* Your ex. *Amity.* Whatever.

I get the feeling that in spite of the evidence that I've presented thus far, Uncle Dan is still incredulous regarding my story, but he is having so much fun investigating, that he is intent on retracing the entirety of my journey over the last 24 hours. He insists that as long as we are going to Old Brooklyn, we should stop at Jack Frost and get a dozen donuts. The cashier gives us a baker's dozen, and when we get to the truck, Uncle Dan puts a big fat jelly donut under the front tire, drives over it, and then snaps a picture of the tread marks. When he gets back into the truck, I stare at him with raised eyebrows, seeking an explanation.

"Tradition," he says. "One day back in '68 after a night patrol, we came back to the base and it was raining like the hammers of hell. Somebody had some donuts flown in from the Red Cross. Don't know how they did it, they didn't taste frozen, and pretty fresh too. Anyway, there was just enough left for us— one each. We were running through the muddy camp back to the barracks when Richie slipped and dropped his donut in the road. It probably would have been OK because it was wrapped in wax-paper, but this wacky sky-pilot, a chaplain named Jeddy, was hauling ass in his jeep, driving like it was a Bugatti, and ran right over Richie's donut without even slowing down. When Richie picked it up it was loaded with mud and pressed with tire tracks." I stare at Uncle Dan trying to find the connection. "Well, inside we were laughing hysterically, but nobody ever said anything to Richie, because back in those days he had a really bad temper. He was also superstitious about religion and was too afraid of cursing his soul by belting a man of the cloth. When the chaplain learned what he had done, he was horrified, but pretended like nothing happened when he was around Richie—I mean, it *was* an accident, and he wouldn't have known if we hadn't told him. Besides, he didn't know if we were telling the truth or setting him up for a hazing. The guys used to do stuff like that. After the war, that chaplain moved out to Hollywood to become a pastor-actor. And ever since then, about once a month I send him a picture of a flattened donut." (I'm still staring.) "Besides, thirteen is an unlucky number, and I hate jelly donuts."

"That's conceptual art," I tell him.

"Is it really? Then call me Picasso," he says, and we drive on.

* * *

In a few minutes we arrive at Amity's former house. There are two Asian children playing in the front yard.

"Is Amity Chinese?"

"No. English."

"Then those are probably not her kids." A man comes out of the house carrying a bundle of flattened moving boxes. Uncle Dan waves to him and the man comes over to the truck. "Welcome to the neighborhood," Uncle Dan says.

"Thank you. Do you live on this street?"

"Close enough. We're from the local paranormal society. we're looking for the Halifax family who used to live here."

"They moved out a few weeks ago. We were lucky, they had to move in a hurry so we got a good deal and moving right in."

"That's swell. Congratulations. Do you know where the Halifaxes moved to?"

"Somewhere in Connecticut. I don't have the address, only the phone number. She wants me to call if any important mail comes for her or if there's an emergency. Is this an emergency?"

"No. We're just conducting an investigation into a UFO sighting and thought the Halifax daughter might be able to help us."

"I see. How very peculiar."

"If you speak with her, and you will, tell her that Dan Churchill from the paranormal network stopped by."

"Churchill?"

"Yeah. Churchill, like in Winston."

"OK Mr. Winston, I will tell her." The man goes to play with his kids while Uncle Dan and I drive away.

"What do you think he's going to tell Amity?" I ask.

"Nothing. He's not going to tell her anything."

* * *

As we near the mill road, Uncle Dan pulls the truck into the parking lot of a small abandoned factory. He takes a screwdriver from the glove compartment, goes behind the truck, removes the license plate, and throws it onto the back floor. "I got to get that thing fixed as soon as we get home," he says. I ask about the front plate and he says, "Gotta fix that one too," and we drive on toward Smith and Finnerty Steel. My fingers and toes turn icy and a shiver begins that I can't control. "Uncle Dan, do we really need to do this? I don't know if I can."

"Do you trust me, Jon?"

"Sure I trust you."

"Then trust me." He turns onto the entrance road.

About halfway down the road is the police car I saw earlier this morning. As we approach it, an officer, one of Cleveland's finest in a glorious uniform, steps into the road and orders us to stop. By now, my shivering has turned into clanking. Uncle Dan whispers to me to play it cool. I fold my arms. The officer is tall, with gray and white hair visible from the sides of his cap. He is clearly inches away from an overdue retirement, and working an extra job right now. He approaches our vehicle slowly with his hand resting on the butt of his pistol. There is an occasional hack of white noise from the squelched radio on his other hip. Uncle Dan speaks first and friendly.

"Good morning, Captain."

"Let me see some ID." The policeman stares at me while Uncle

Dan presents his drivers license and military ID. "Brendel, huh? You served in Afghanistan?"

"No sir. Marine Corps, Vietnam, 1968. One war was enough for me."

"You working here today?"

"No sir. This steel mill laid me off decades ago." (I'm now rubbing my face with my hands to control my shakes.)

"What's wrong with him?"

"Poor kid has PTSD. Now he's gone and lost his dog. He's coming apart at the seams."

"Let me see your ID too, son." I proffer my driver's license. "Another Brendel. So you got the whole family out for a Sunday drive?"

"Pretty much it, Captain. Just me and the boy—now that the dog's run off."

"Well, you can't go in here. There's an investigation going on. Something to do with Neo-Nazis."

"Damn! Didn't we put those guys out of commission back in the 1940s?"

"That's what we were told, anyway. But you guys are going to have to turn around. This area is off limits." Uncle Dan salutes and the police captain returns our IDs and steps aside so we can do a u-turn. "Say, in case I see him, what does this dog look like?"

"He's a medium-sized mutt, mostly bald with patches of nasty fur and scabs, and he's got a scruffy strip of hair along his spine that stands straight up like a Mohawk—kinda looks like a hyena with his tongue hanging out to the side, and he's got a bad temper to match." This information jams the captain's cognitive gears and he swings his eyes toward the woods. Uncle Dan leans way out the window as if to prevent me from hearing.

"Oh, and Captain, do me a favor—If you see that ugly cuss, shoot him. I think he's got rabies."

The captain's radio squawks and a voice says, "Found what we were looking for, Tom. Let's wrap this up and go home." As Uncle Dan pulls away, the captain saunters over to his cruiser with a backwards glance at the woods.

"So I guess they found the relic, huh?" Uncle Dan says.

"*My* relic."

"Took 'em long enough. Not very bright—must be FBI. How about we go visit the brain surgeon next? You said you were friendly with him. He might be needing a friendly right about now. We can deliver the painting."

* * *

As Uncle Dan pulls out of the steel mill's driveway, the late-morning sun in the now clear sky hits me square in the face. I squint, pull down the brim of the trucker hat, and close my eyes. Immediately I'm dreaming that I'm at party in New York City. It is a crowded old apartment filled with local composers and performance artists, but there's only one whom I recognize from his videos: Laurence Gilderman. He talks like a jazz musician and he's arguing with the building superintendent about the sounds coming from the radiator: "Man, it's just got way too much percussion!"

The ceilings are pressed tin tiles with a complex, repeating geometry of acorns and live oak leaf clusters. Ornate woodwork decorates all the walls—chair rails, picture moldings, and crown moldings—but their original form is obscured by countless layers of lead paint applied over more than a century. At the doorway to the kitchen I see a spot where a triangle of paint was chipped off down to the wood by appliance movers. (Don't ask me how I know that they did it, I just know). As I look closely at the damage and the dozens of different colored layers exposed, I am looking back through time, and I am mesmerized. While picking at it to expose more colors, I hear Marga's voice behind me say, "If it's so beautiful, why do you want to change it?" When I turn, I see her hooded figure—Little Red Riding Hood—leaving the kitchen. I follow her down the corridor until she turns and vanishes into a sitting room. In that room are Mozart, Mahler, Tchaikovsky, and a few others whose names I immediately forget. (I'm not sure what Charles Ives is doing in there). They are passionately discussing and debating their ideas about harmony when old Pyotr Ilyich straightens up and says, "Monsieur Brendel! You've finally made it!" I tell him that I'm looking for a friend. Mahler says, "Aren't we all?" And the composers crack up laughing. Uncle Dan leans into the room and asks, "Jon, where to next?" I open my eyes and I'm back in the truck. "Rise and shine. We're in Bratenahl. Where to next?"

I guide him through the residential streets until the homes grow larger and farther apart. At Dr. Lance's manse we pull into the semi-circular driveway and I carry the rolled up portrait to the side entrance and ring the bell. The door is answered by a cleaning woman who is obviously the character Marga studied for her maid disguise. She talks to me through the locked door. I tell her that I am a friend of Doctor Lance's daughter, but she shows no reaction of any kind. I'd like to see Dr. Lance. But he's not in. When will he return? She doesn't know—he rushed off to Paris on a private jet to do some emergency surgery, maybe send him a text. This is his daughter's painting—I'd like to leave it for the doctor. "Lean it against the wall," she says, "I'll get it after you leave."

Back in the car, Uncle Dan says, "I never knew the life of a composer was so deranged."

"Neither did I."

"How much do they pay you for a concert?"

"I don't know. I didn't ask."

"You mean you didn't get paid yet? Why not?"

"My friend is in charge of that. Said he would call me when he had the money. That was three months ago."

"You did your part, now he has to do his—it's a contract. Where is this friend now?

"It's Sunday, he's probably working the matinee." Uncle Dan drives.

At Severance Hall, the rolling door to the loading dock is open, and five stagehands smoking cigarettes loiter just inside. (I wish I could avoid them and call Timo directly, but my phone is defunct.) I approach the stagehands and once they notice me they make obscene gestures and one simulates pole dancing at the side of the gate. They're having a good time at my expense, but then slap me on the back and congratulate me, all talking at once so that I can only catch a few words of their jocular stew. "Get any pastrami with your Russian dressing?" "Does Yulia know the words or is she a hummer?" "Want a cup of coffee, or a White Russian?" "Careful with that cigarette Bobby, this guy's loaded with vodka, he might burst into flame." (Ha. Ha. Ha. So. Very. Funny.) I smile to acknowledge that I was a jerk the other night, and ask them to call Timo down here for me.

The stagehands toss their cigarettes and go back to work. When Timo arrives, he is clearly uncomfortable and guides me to a spot next to a Dumpster full of trash where I will be less noticeable.

"Jonathan, what are you doing here?"

"I've come to see my good friend Timo about a matter of great import."

"Well, you should have called. Don't you know how radioactive you are right now?"

"Why should this day be any different?"

"Didn't you read the review by that critic from the Times?" I shake my head. "He praised the orchestra, gushed over Yulia, and trashed you mercilessly."

"Can't be as bad as all that."

"Oh it's plenty bad alright."

"It's pretty common knowledge that the critic has a crush on Yulia. He's probably just jealous."

"Well, what do you expect? After the way you debauched the poor girl."

"Timo, please don't chastise me with morality, you—of all people. If I were to follow your example we would spend eternity shoveling hot brimstone."

"Of course it's not *me* who's offended. But we lost a good sponsor because of your antics. He pledged a lot of money for Yulia's and your concert, but after Thursday night, he cut us off."

"I'm sorry Timo. I had no idea. We were just having fun."

"Yeah, well, I told you Yulia is poison ivy. But that's probably the last we'll see of Baker."

"Wait a minute. Who is Baker?"

"Well *hello*, Jonathan! Baker?—the new donor? I told you he had a lot of 'bread,' 'rolling in dough,' is what I said. How unsubtle do I need to be with you?"

"Short-ish guy, about fifty, black hair, looks like a soldier?" Timo rolls his eyes. "Was he sitting next to the critic at the concert?" Timo nods. "Damn!" A convoy of flashbacks rolls through my consciousness. "Can you send him a message from me?"

"Look Jonathan, I don't know your relationship with this guy, but I'm not going to triangulate between you two."

"Just send him one message—from me—tell him I'm, *Brendel* is, 'no longer interested in engines or the engineers who fly them.' Just that one line. It'll placate him." He writes it down.

"OK, one email only—and I'm putting it in quotes. And I'm giving you notice Jonathan, if this backfires on me, I swear, friend or no, I will blackball you to every orchestra in this hemisphere."

"What are friends for?" Timo gives me an icy stare in profile, then walks back into the concert hall.

When I return to the truck, Uncle Dan asks rhetorically, "No joy?"

"No. No joy."

"What did he say?"

"Amity's boss was the Viking's sponsor."

"The submariner?"

"Yeah. And he torpedoed my funding."

* * *

Uncle Dan insists that I visit Jimmy's family—not for me, but for the family—because that's just what comrades do. Mrs. Strong meets me at the front door but does not invite me in. When I tell her how sorry I am, she tells me that I am the only friend Jimmy had who always brought him home in better condition than when he left. (Not this time.) "I think," she says, "that you may be the only real friend he ever had."

I remember how I introduced him to Marga and how infatuated he was with her, how she helped him stay clean and sober in the rehab, and how he wanted to impress her. Then the first time he performed clean and sober, it was at an abandoned steel mill, and he got killed. My legs go weak all of a sudden, so I sit down on the Strongs' front porch steps and close my eyes to the physical sensation of rotating in wide, fast loops—like riding the Scrambler at Cedar Point Amusement Park. There is a hissing sound of ocean waves crashing in rapid pulses on sloppy sand, and when I open my eyes, the world looks distant and foggy. The vision triggers a full-on *déjà vu* and a flashback that transports me to the misty dawn in the woods behind Smith and Finnerty steel mill. I jerk back into the moment with a feeling of uncertainty—a distrust of time and my fixity in the now. Uncle Dan helps me back to the truck. He asks me if there is anything else I need to do today.

"I just want to go home, Uncle Dad. Please take me home." I hear my Freudian slip, and leave it there, deep and true.

"Sure, Son. Let's go home."

38

Sanctuary

At the bungalow, Uncle Dan tells me to "crash" in his room, and gives me some of his clothes from the days when he was about my size. They are so old that they are back in fashion. "One more thing, Jon," he says, "there are no atheists in foxholes." And then he goes out.

Sitting on the bed's edge, I look at my hands—scratched and chapped with broken nails—and I wonder how they got to be so stained with grease and filth, and whose the dried blood may be. When I rub my hands together and palm my eyes, abstract shapes slip through my mind like scenes viewed through the window of a train barrelling through Ohio farmland at reaping time—scenes that follow so quickly that no specific vision can be maintained long enough to identify, but only serve to produce a lateral disequilibrium and nausea.

Now I don't care who you are, or how strong you are—or how strong you think you are—there will come a time in your life when you will meet your limitation, even the inadequacy of your human abilities, and realize that you are not in control of everything, but in fact, you are powerless over most every thing, and you will pray for help. And if you were obdurate enough to have gone on long enough, you may beg to understand and simply pray, "Why?" And if your loss is severe and deep and primal, your prayer will be a profound and unintelligible groan that arises from the very atoms of your corporeality.

And so, with the uncontrollable monomania of one facing judgment, I groan myself to sleep.

* * *

After repetitive dreams of eating gravel and glass, I wake up parched and drink handfuls of water from the bathroom tap. The city water drawn from Lake Erie's five-mile crib is heavily chlorinated and off-gasses in my face making my eyes water. I go back to bed feverish and exhausted. My dreams are wild and vivid and violent. I continue on this way for what seems like days—I can't be sure how long. I strive to be honest, but my perception seems to be as irrational and implausible as my memory.

When I finally get out of bed, it is because my back hurts and my stomach is audibly growling. Uncle Dan asks if I am hungry. "Starving." He says I should take it easy at first, and drops a hard beef bullion cube into an empty mug with a loud clink, and adds some hot water, forming the saltiest, most delicious soup I have ever tasted. While I sip it and enjoy the smell, Uncle Dan soft scrambles a half dozen eggs which he serves in a bowl with crushed soda crackers and Sriracha on top.

"Vietnamese hot sauce. Tasty stuff. Eat that and you should be good-to-go. I cleaned out your apartment and set up your old room here. No sense in going back to heartbreak hotel. I saw the Finnegan lady and told her that if she had any complaints, she should tell them to the Army because the Marines are just too damn busy. She's probably still chewing on that one."

"Thanks Uncle Dan."

"I also picked up an unlocked phone. Your sim card is still intact, so you get to keep your old number. I told the guy to set up that Signal app for you, so you might be able to retrieve some of your old messages."

When the phone powers-up, a voice mail is waiting—not from Amity or Marga, but from Yulia.

"Hello Jonathan. This is Yulia. It's Saturday night and I am at the airport. Um. What can I say? I'm so sorry for what happened yesterday. I didn't mean to embarrass you or bring shame to us. My benefactor told me it would be good publicity to create a scandal with you. But Baker is a liar. I don't want to play the "bad girl" anymore. I wish I could be more respectable, like you. The critic is a liar too. Your piece is beautiful. I have been moved by music before—many times—but yours brought me to a kind of...heaven and led me to find eternal things inside of myself. But I have fallen, and right now I want to go home to Moscow for a while to heal my soul. I hope that you are not mad at me. Maybe someday we can work together again. I think—artistically—we are good for each other. You are a wonderful composer Jonathan, and even better person. I will not say goodbye, but *Da skorava*—see you soon—and I hope that is true. *Da skorava.*"

39

10 Degrees, 9 Kreteks, and 4 Topics

The spring days pass quickly—as they always do in Cleveland. I've stayed inside and mostly off-the-grid, re-reading the books on composition that Auntie Sadie gave me and, in my mind, repeatedly playing Satie's *Gymnopédie No. 1* in a *grave* tempo. It's getting warmer now, and I've got to do something before I wear out my welcome with Uncle.

In my room, I dump out the large, black trash bags that Uncle Dan filled with clothes from my old apartment. I have never really thought much about clothes—my clothes—but seeing them all spread out on the bed now, I realize that my style was really whatever pleased Amity. In fact, she bought most of my wardrobe. I'm not sure how I will appear to others without her— what will be the outward appearance that people will use to judge me.

Looking now at this frippery, I can assume that everyone thought I was well-to-do. There's the Brooks Brothers suit that I wore once to a pointless job interview for a sales position (I just couldn't wind myself up tightly enough to work with those sporty jokers). And the "casual" 200 dollar khaki pants, 100 dollar polo shirt, and shiny Bass *Weejuns* penny loafers to wear (without socks) to someone's birthday party at the yacht club—a half-thousand of Amity's dollars worth of clothes purchased just to make a favorable impression on one of her friends whose name I forget. Seeing these clothes makes me sad, not so much for losing Amity, but to think of how much she invested into making me into someone else. (From somewhere subconscious comes the memory that the German word for poison is *Gift*.) I guess now I can be whoever *I* want to be, whoever that is.

I stuff all of the regalia back into the trash bags to be deposited in the Goodwill used clothing donations box. Wearing Uncle Dan's outfits feels more natural anyway. The only one piece I save is the Harris Tweed jacket. Though Amity paid for it, I chose it. It's perfect for Cleveland's frosty fall weather leading up to Thanksgiving. It doesn't make me look wealthy, but it does accent my intellectual side. I can wear it with anything—even jeans, a tee shirt, and cowboy boots—and still look like a composer. In every way, it still fits.

Uncle Dan stops by my room and notices the herringbone tweed jacket I'm wearing. He says that I look like a young Jordan Peterson, which makes me think of another professor from Toronto. I reach into the jacket pocket and come up with the business card for Townsend McGill. Huh. Synchronicity again. Uncle Dan asks me to come outside and help him with something.

Out front, Uncle Dan is leaning over the fender of his truck with his head under the hood. He has one hand on a bundle of wires and the other on a futuristic-looking chromium gun flashing a strobe light. "Point this at the harmonic balancer," he says handing me the strobe, "that disk just behind the fan. See the mark on top, that's top dead center. When the timing light flashes you'll see a number that lines up with it. What's that number?" "Six." "I've got to get it to ten degrees below top dead center, so I'm going to turn this distributor and tell me when the number gets to ten." I do, and he tightens the screw. "Sounds much better. See Jonathan, just like everything else in life, it's all about timing." He unclips the timing light's wires, then wipes his hands on a red grease rag; I get a flashback to the steel mill. "So what are your plans?" I shrug. He closes the hood and shuts off the engine. He's nodding his head and biting his chapped lower lip. I can see the wheels turning in his brain. "Let's go inside and put on a pot of coffee."

* * *

Uncle Dan uses an electric percolator from the 1970s, its chrome finish still shiny. Although its profile is somewhat squat, its roundness allows it to hold a lot more coffee than one would guess—8 (short) cups to be exact.

"Your grandfather used to say that to make a good cup of coffee, you should never wash the pot, but instead let the patina of oils build up inside. With all good respect for my Pops, that's bullshit. I clean this thing everyday, and my brew tastes better than his ever did." He shovels the ground coffee from a bright red Hills Bros can into the percolator basket, snaps on the domed top with its little glass bubble, and plugs it in. Instantly it emits an electric growl.

Uncle Dan asks about the skinny pack of cigarettes sticking out next to my lapel where a pocket square should be. I explain that I secretly started smoking at 14 after Pops died, and cigarettes helped me to think through difficult problems. Uncle Dan, also an ex-smoker, must agree to that one benefit of the habit. I tell him how I gave it up at 16 for Amity's sake, then picked it up again briefly in Toronto when I was working through my conundrum regarding Amity. Uncle Dan says cigarettes are a slow suicide that hopefully gives you enough time to change your mind. "You should put them down before they put you down. What brand are they?"

"Djarum. They're Indonesian, with cloves and spices." I hand him the pack and he smells it.

"Festive—smells like Aunt Betty's mincemeat pie. Or maybe an Easter ham. It's a small pack."

"Yeah. There are only ten to a pack, and I smoked one in Toronto."

"So, four for you and four for me and one for emergency."

"How's that?"

"You said they help you think through difficult problems. Let's take your four biggest and talk them through in a tobacco trance."

* * *

We sit at the kitchen table, an oval job from the 1960s in swirly pearly gray Formica with a center section that can be removed to make it smaller and round. It's edged with a shiny, grooved aluminum band with random scratches and dings, and the four legs are chrome plated steel with some surface rust.

Rust.

I smell the perked coffee and have another flashback to my first night in the steel mill, and I'm finding it hard to escape. Uncle Dan fills two blue and white tin enamelware camping mugs emblazoned with a stylized red rope lasso font that spells out the word "Wyoming." The name of that state trips me back another 12 years. Uncle Dan looks at my eyes, and although he doesn't know the specifics of my thoughts, he recognizes the feelings.

"These things are hard to shake, Jon, but you've got to try. Otherwise you could wind up spending the rest of your life on a psychiatrist's couch taking their voodoo mind-control drugs."

"How do I break free, Uncle Dan?" I take up the cup and smell the coffee. It triggers another sense memory of sitting on the catwalk with Marga and Werner.

"Well first, realize that even though your head may be in the past, your *real* head, the three dimensional one, is always in the present. Memories are like ghosts, they can haunt us and even spook us. These kind, the war kind, are the worst. They're like *magnetic* ghosts—it feels like they have real power over us Jon, and they're always yanking on our chains, trying to pull us back there, back to the images and the guilt. But in the end, they are only a vapor, just smoke." He hands me a clove cigarette and takes one for himself.

"But how do you keep them from coming back," I ask.

"Yeah, that's the bitch of it—you *can't* stop them from coming back. But you also can't let yourself dwell on them."

"Easier said than done."

"Look Jon," he strikes a blue-tip match off the rust on the table leg and lights my cigarette, "you can't stop a bird from crapping on your head, but you can stop it from building a nest in your hair." He takes a drag of the cigarette—a clove bud crackles and spits out a spark. "Lively little devils, aren't they? Tasty too. Pretty good though, sweet."

We sit in silence. In my head I'm watching reruns of the black helicopters on their angle of attack with smiling men firing red tracer rounds. I feel like I know those men personally, and I do, because they now live in my head. Without trying, I rewind the flashback to the orb and zoom in through the limousine windows to Amity's eyes—deep with fear, and sadness, and love remembered, and dreams forfeited for a better plan and a new roll of the dice.

Uncle Dan jerks me back with a very immediate and present question. His voice is serene and clear, with a rich, hypnotic tone.

"You hear that, Jon?"

"Hear what?"

"Listen. What do you hear?" He angles his head in different directions; I search for the sound.

"Some kids playing. A motorcycle."

"Closer, what do you hear?"

"The percolator is still grumbling."

"What do you smell?"

"Smoke. Cloves. Coffee. An overripe brown banana on the counter."

"Taste?"

"Black coffee, cigarette, something metallic—must be the tap water."

"Touch? Feel?"

"The table top feels cool, the plastic chair seat hot and sweaty."

"What do you hear now?"

"The fridge motor and the coffee pot."

"Welcome to the present, Jon. Fighter pilots call it 'situational awareness'—my cardiologist calls it 'mindfulness.' Put it all together as best as you can, and look straight at it. When you feel yourself slipping out of time, check your senses in the now." He snuffs his cigarette on the saucer we're using as an ashtray, and walks out of the kitchen.

I look around the room, at the old Kenmore refrigerator plastered with magnets advertising a locksmith, a Social Security benefits hotline, slip-and-fall lawyers, and souvenir magnets from Pelee Island and the Rock & Roll Hall of Fame. It's like I'm seeing this room for the first time. My eyes are wide open and I shift focus to the worn asbestos floor tile in a black and white checkerboard pattern. The stub of the kretek begins to burn my fingers—the pain is a reminder that I am alive. I quickly crush it. Uncle Dan is in the bathroom and I hear the flush, and then water in the sink. The stench of cold ashes—devoid of soul and languishing in a saucer—differs from the organic aroma of burning tobacco, and cold coffee is an aberration unlike the fresh brewed stuff. The closer I look, listen, and feel, the more I notice how much variation there is within this experience—and there seems to be no limit to the sensual subtleties. With this focus I have effectively shut off the internal monologue that has been pulling me back.

But something is arising from inside. It is a visceral sensation that wells up into my mind's ear, it is the most beautiful chord of indescribable timbre, having a color that fluoresces in my mind's eye as a triad blend of crystal emerald, aquamarine, and citrine with an overtone the color of amethyst. How can I speak of a sound (an internal sound at that) in terms of illuminated gemstones? Don't people talk about undertones of chocolate, flowers, and even cedar wood in the taste of their coffee? Why not? It's *their* coffee. And *my sound* is crystalline. It is an extraordinary, inimitable blending of timbres and frequencies that I seriously doubt I could ever reproduce. It is also the first time in a long while that I have thought about music. And the vibration of that chord triggers memories of timeless things I can't recall ever having experienced, but I feel and recognize them as familiar—archetypes, I suppose. The brilliance of this elemental radiance effectively pulls me out of my mindfulness and back into my imagination and Amity's eyes, Jimmy's smile, Marga's whispers, and I'm gone. I try to re-focus on the chord, but it tumbles and disintegrates and flees from me like the fading call of a red-wing blackbird through the window of a speeding car. Uncle Dan breaks my spell.

"Jon, the past is history, the future's a mystery, today is a gift—that's why we call it the present."

"That sounds like a cliché, Uncle Dan. Did you invent it?"

"Nah. I heard it from a guy named 'Left-nut Louie'. He had some good ideas, but he wasn't all there."

"I can tell that from his name."

We light our next kreteks. Uncle Dan does most of the talking on the subject of "earning a living" and "real" work. He's 74 years old and still drives a truck delivering zinc-plated machine parts to the few factories remaining in Cleveland. I mostly smoke and struggle to relate what he's saying to my own situation. I tell him that I've never had a *real* job—any kind of exhausting work that would make me sweat. Who would hire a guy like me to do physical labor? One look at my CV and they would make me out to be a dilettante, and they wouldn't be far from the truth. My best course of action would be to lie on the application to downplay my education, try to make grammatical mistakes, and use slang during the interview.

I announce to Uncle Dan that I will take a job as a stock boy at the 24 hour hardware superstore. Of course, after that declaration I lapse into my now familiar trance, into reveries some good and some terrifying, and resurface only—with much effort of will—to focus on his words. It's significantly, though not entirely, unpleasant to tour the contents of my soul, and Uncle Dan is a proficient medicine man who deftly balances life lessons—happy and sad—with affirmations of health and self-worth delivered in his signature style:

"Are you out of your fricken mind?" He calls me to attention. "Jonathan, look here, a guy can't abandon his dream of becoming a marathon runner just because he lost his foot to gangrene or whatever. At some point he has to stop blaming himself for stepping on that punji stick, and get on with his life like Burroughs did."

"Burroughs?"

"William S. Burroughs, that beatnik writer who got drunk one night and tried to shoot a whiskey bottle off his wife's head. He was high, but his aim was low."

"Did he change his name to William S. Tell," I ask. Uncle Dan takes a drag from the cigarette and rolls it in his fingers while looking at the crackling ember. He shakes his head with a grin of appreciation, and continues.

"Anyway, after Burroughs got that straightened out with the law, he should have given up the booze, but more importantly, he *didn't* give up writing. And neither should you give up composing. Your music has been performed by the greatest orchestra in the world and the greatest opera singer of this century."

"The century is still young."

"And so are you." That statement hangs in the air and slowly twists like a wisp of ectoplasm. Lately I've felt like an old man dying of a spiritual consumption, and it's hard to return to my former age. Uncle Dan continues. "So you had a bad rap. You lost a few friends. Would you believe me if I told you you'll get more friends? That you still have friends? That I'm your friend?

Listen Jon, everybody has somebody they call a friend, but how many *real* friends does a person have in his life? I mean a friend who, if you called and asked him to meet you tomorrow morning in Seattle—no questions asked—would do whatever it takes to be on that plane tonight?"

"Jimmy might have. Amity would—if her schedule permitted. Marga. Yeah, Marga would have."

"And so would I. Be grateful. You've had two real friends. Some people live their whole life and never find one friend of that kind."

Uncle Dan asks me something about my social life, and lights our two kreteks off a single match. For a fleeting moment I get a sense memory of sitting in muddy, camouflaged, combat uniform, smoking cigarettes with a buddy while waiting for a helicopter dust-off—I take the memory to be radio frequency interference bleeding in from Uncle Dan's psyche, and I let it pass through.

I mention that Amity and I have, *had* been an item for ten years. "Ten years? Shoo! That's a long time," says Uncle Dan. "That's longer than a lot of marriages last. That's longer than my marriage lasted."

"Without her, I'm not sure *what* kind of social life I can have. I'm not even sure that I could carry on a coherent conversation with a woman right now."

"Why would you want to? You haven't been single since you were sixteen. Give yourself a break. At least hold off until the dust settles."

"How long is that?"

"How can I calculate the expiration date for a dust storm? I just know that the bigger the explosion, the longer it takes for the dirt to settle. I would think, with what you've been through, you've got to give it at least a year."

***

I'm suddenly craving fresh air and step out onto the back porch—really just a landing made of rotting old wood at the top of five wide wooden stairs, also made of rotting old wood with a flaking, battleship gray paint job. It's late spring. A wiry and unkempt lilac bush—planted too close to the house by Uncle Dan's ex—holds out the blossoms of a few late bloomers that were shocked shy by a vindictive Cleveland cold snap. Their perfume sparks the beginning of a memory of Yulia that I forcefully veto with an act of will, creating space for a deeper souvenir to surface.

It's fifteen years back, and Auntie Sadie is performing Chopin at a The Gryphon Theatre in Laramie, Wyoming. She's wearing, a long black skirt, shiny black pumps called 'character shoes,' and a white silk blouse with a big collar that's ruffled high around the back of her neck and makes her look like Mary, Queen of Scots. Her bun of silver hair looks powdered. It's my first time hearing her perform outside of class, and I fully expect her to be wonderful. I'm her 'date', eleven years old and standing stage-left in the wings where she can keep an eye on me. When she recovers from an emotional crescendo and floats back to a softer melody, she catches my eye from across the stage, smiles, and winks. After the concert, a local reporter searching for an angle to his story, asks her if I am her son or grandson. Sadie Bucknell, still glowing euphoric from the performance, says, "He's a prodigy, my protégé, and my muse."

There is a long wheeze as the rusty door spring stretches, and a jarring report when the old wooden screen door slams against its frame. The spongy planks of the porch sag a little as Uncle Dan steps out and hands me my Wyoming tin cup filled with coffee. He sees me staring at the lilac bush.

"I'm surprised that crotchety old thing is still alive, let alone growing flowers. Neighbor said I should rip it out and start afresh. I don't know...If a thing wants to live, who am I to kill it?"

"Uncle Dan, did you know my mother?" My question snaps him back into the moment.

"A little. I first met her at your Pop's wedding in Rawlins. Couldn't stay though cause I had to get back to work at that damned steel mill." He sets down his cup on the two-by-six plank capping the stair rail, and starts picking at the calluses on his hand.

"What was she like?"

"I didn't know her too well. Rawlins is about fourteen hundred miles from Cleveland—though it seems farther when you have to drive it. So mostly I came to visit on the Fourth of July when your Pops and I would do some fishing and shooting near Elk Mountain. Anyway, I didn't spend much time around her." Uncle Dan looks up to the left, and straight through the sky. "What little I remember about her is that she was a strong, Wyoming kind of girl. Irish stock, I think, but sort of homey—you know, not the flashy movie star type." He looks left toward the lilac bush, but not at it. "She was quiet, didn't talk much. She liked to sing though, had a very clear voice—I don't think that she ever smoked or screamed, nothing that would damage that voice. Your Pops was a quiet man too, though he was deep, I mean he thought about deep stuff, like something had a grip on his guts. And *he* had never even been in the war."

"Yeah. He was like that." I take a sip of the coffee which tastes tarry from being continuously reboiled. "Do you remember how my mother looked?"

"Like I said, she was a Wyoming girl. You know, the kind that might have won a 4H ribbon at the county fair for 'Best job of caring for a red heifer', but wouldn't consider running in a Miss Wyoming beauty contest. I'm not saying she wasn't pretty, she was, but in that natural way—never wore makeup except for some lip-balm on her wedding day."

"What color was her hair?"

"Funny you should ask that. I really don't know. She always told your Pops that she felt ugly, and she changed her hair color as often as other people change their underwear. One time she wanted to try platinum blonde, what we used to call 'suicide blonde' —you know, dyed by her own hands. But she used a cheap brand with too much bleach, or she let it stay on too long, and the hair got so brittle that it broke off down to stubble. Your Pops gave her a fuzzy watch cap and made her stay inside until the hair grew back." (So this is my genetic heritage.) "Then when she got the 'big C', the meds they gave her—you know, the chemo—made it all fall out. Good thing she still had that watch cap."

"What was she like as a person, I mean, what kind of things did she like?"

"She liked animals, horses especially—I told you she was a Wyoming girl. Liked to cook. She liked dancing the Texas two-step. But she also liked serious music—the longhair stuff—like you do. She even had a lot of records of symphonies and such. Your Pops cleaned out everything when she died, even threw out all of her music." (A few houses away, some kids are arguing about the rules of some game they are playing, "Take it and read," the kid yells. Someone runs back into their house, intentionally slamming the screen door.) Uncle Dan's gaze swings to the left searching for a memory. "One thing I *do* remember clearly: she absolutely *loved* you."

I guess Uncle Dan felt he needed to say that. I swallow hard, but feel nothing. All this revelation about a world I could never have imagined, yet it still seems hollow. I struggle to restructure my self image. Uncle Dan hands me a kretek. "Last one," he says.

40

A Tour of Duty

A gentle breeze slides through the backyards and lifts a musty, desiccating pong from the whitewashed asbestos shingles that clad Uncle Dan's bungalow. The chalky odor reminds me of old, wet ashes in a neglected fireplace. Momentarily, the few remaining lilac blossoms release a whiff of perfume as an afterthought of protest over the intrusion.

I sling the dregs of my coffee onto the dirt around the lilac bush. Maybe it will help fertilize the pitiful thing—anyway, that sludge gave me a sour stomach and was starting to etch the enamel on my teeth. I return into the house and find Uncle Dan looking out the front picture window.

"Know anybody who drives a black four-door sedan?" he asks without turning around.

"Right now, I don't know anybody."

"Then get me that green toolbox from the closet."

I bring the toolbox to Uncle Dan, and from it he removes a cowboy-style revolver and a box of bullets. Out on the porch, in full view of the black car, he opens the cylinder and slowly and deliberately loads the pistol. In the car, the passenger speaks quickly to the driver then slides down in his seat as the car smoothly pulls away. Uncle Dan removes the bullets and returns the gun and ammunition to the toolbox. "I think it's time for us to move," he says. "This neighborhood ain't what it used to be."

After locking the doors for the first time since Uncle Dan moved in here, we come back to the kitchen table. "I think you should take a vacay from this town, Jonathan. You never chose Cleveland. You're only here because I dragged your ass out of the Wyoming sticks to save you from a life of fatal boredom. Find a place where *you'd* like to live."

"Any suggestions?"

"Who the hell knows. Any change of scenery would be an improvement." Uncle Dan lights his last cigarette and meditates on the curls of smoke rising from the coal. "I still think you would benefit from a tour of duty in South East Asia. Too bad the war is over."

"What's it like, South East Asia?"

"Depends on where you go. It's a big place. People are nice for the most part—as long as there's no shooting going on. Food is tasty, girls pretty, weather hot or rainy most of the time. Anyway, that's Vietnam. I've been to Singapore on R&R—and Taiwan too. All nice places. Definitely a culture shock. You'd like it."

"What do you know about Indonesia?"

"Never been there. But people say the island called Bali is paradise. Why?"

"I met a guy in Toronto. He's over there teaching now."

"It's worth a shot. Besides, we're out of clove cigarettes."

I take Professor McGill's card from my pocket and enter his coordinates into my phone. My simple text reads:

Hi McGill, Jonathan Brendel here. We met at Holst concert in Toronto. Planning a trip to Indonesia. Hope we can get together for dinner or coffee.

"It's 9 at night here. What time is it in Jakarta?"

"It's on the other side of the planet, so it's gotta be twelve hours. Around 9 am, but then there is the international date line, so it is either yesterday or tomorrow, I'm not sure. Can't your phone tell you?"

"Probably. But I'm still learning this new phone you got me. Haven't used it yet—no friends left to call." Feeling like a desperate gambler, I say a weak prayer, roll the dice, and send out the text. To my surprise, I get a reply about two minutes later.

Hello Brendel. Was waiting expectantly for your touch. Synchronicity. Music dept here to hold workshop on contemp composition. Asked if I knew any Western composers. Mentioned you. They want. You. Contact is a local with improbable foreign name: Ann O'Malley. Email her at (etc., etc.).

Then, seconds later:

Coffee? Sure. Get here first.

* * *

For the rest of the evening, we make plans for the short and medium terms—long term plans are entirely up to me but will include composing, and will depend upon whatever wild hare pops out of whichever rabbit hole. Tomorrow, Uncle Dan will pay off the loan on the Audi. Later, he will sell it back to the dealer and repay himself the money he will front me for the trip, then he and I will split the difference of whatever is left. Uncle Dan will also quit his job, sell his bungalow, and move back to Elk Mountain, Wyoming—the order of those events is to be determined. (And he will keep the last cigarette in case of emergency.) Anyway, that's the plan. Whatever I don't need in Jakarta will go with Uncle Dan, or get thrown in the trash. I will buy a one way ticket to my future, and, following Uncle's advice on ancient military strategy, burn all my bridges back to Cleveland.

41

Points, Lines, Planes

From an early age I was taught to work hard to achieve my goals—goals that require a great effort of imagination to create. I don't care much for the work part, but the woolgathering is pleasant enough. Auntie Sadie strongly encouraged that practice, so did Amity. This advice about hard work and diligence seems logical and obvious to the point of being trite—it was a recurring theme in Benjamin Franklin's maxims, and also appears in at least one of Solomon's Proverbs. So it's frustrating to recall that whenever I have experienced real success, it seems to have come out of the blue. For instance, I was looking to teach piano lessons when Timo called with the orchestra commission.

Coincidence? Possibly. But I seem to excel at serendipity—and accidental meetings with just the right people, one of whom has connected me with composers and academics in Indonesia. Whenever I take steps toward a goal, the success comes from someplace unexpected. I have to envision my success and formulate a plan; although, as a rule, nothing happens unless I take actions. Then, the results arrive independent of my efforts and seem to materialize providentially—I polish my objective on the left side, but it shines on the right.

Working on the belief that I actually could effect some success in my life, I spent so many of my present moments fantasizing about my future. As long as the great and wonderful experiences were somewhere off in a distant potentiality, my present could be exciting with imagined possibilities and even pride over dreamed-of successes that had not yet materialized. Because my head was always envisioning the future, or creating a work to be performed later, I was rarely in the moment, rarely enjoying what I had. And why not? Mindfulness may be the remedy in some vexing situations, but how can living completely in the *present* be useful to anyone other than a sequestered monk? To be totally present is to be stagnant. Unless, maybe, we can be present while in the process of envisioning a future course.

So I come to the conclusion that everyone needs to have a vision of the future in order to make living in the present worthwhile; there needs to be a reason. It could be family or a special person you want to make your family. It could be a concept—fighting for liberty, country, democracy, or your brothers-in-arms. People who live solely for pleasure usually come to an early, gnarly, toothless end, and not a pretty one at that. But there *is* a higher purpose to live for—parents with babies know that; scientists, theologians, and artists know that. I have at least one thing to live for, and it's my *one* way to connect to all-that-is, one unique talent that informs every waking moment (and often my dreams) and that is music—*my* music. And where it comes from, I don't know. And where it will take me, I know even less. But today it is taking me away from Sector B and to Jakarta by way of New York, Frankfurt, and Singapore.

* * *

This is the third time I've flown on a plane. The first time was a gift from Amity for my twenty-first birthday—a round-trip to Toronto (I count that as two). I remember how excited I was to board that plane in the middle of a late-winter Cleveland slush storm—walking through which had churned my wet socks into a salty woolen sorbet. We hadn't seen anything but gray skies for three months, so after the plane lifted off and sliced through the thick sleet, I was shocked to find that the sun was shining up there above the clouds. Logical as the meteorological fact may be, that the sun still existed above Cleveland's gray-as-concrete ceiling is one possibility I had not considered.

* * *

The flight from Cleveland Hopkins to JFK is short, and the plane is small. In the seat-back pouch there is an in-case-of-a-crash card that identifies this plane as an E-Jet. I'm not sure what qualifies it for the "E" prefix, it can't be "electric" because the predominant odor confirms that it obviously burns jet fuel, so maybe the E stands for "exhaust"—which smells like somebody's beach flip-flops are burning, and permeates the cabin air and saturates my clothes.

* * *

My scheduled flight connection is very tight, and when I exit (*deplane* is such a vulgar word) at JFK there is a flight attendant at the end of the ramp holding a sign that reads, "Singapore Airlines." I wave to her and she smiles, grabs my arm, hustles me over to a golf cart, and we race off to the appropriate terminal. She drives way too fast for the crowded concourse while frantically yakking on the walkie-talkie and beeping the horn all the way—I am definitely in New York. By the time I get to the gate, it is 30 minutes past the scheduled departure time. As soon as I enter the plane, the flight attendant closes the door and tells me to take my seat and buckle up, while she and her co-workers pantomime the safety announcements to a captive full-house.

I navigate my way to my seat, noticing the many scowls from Europeans onboard. It seems they blame me for the delayed departure. (Sure. I'll play along, why not?) I adjust my countenance as if to say, *"All of you have been inconvenienced because the CEO of Singapore Airlines told the captain to hold this plane so that the world's greatest living composer could get on. So cool your coconuts. Most of you will be getting off in Frankfurt anyway."*

From my window seat on the right side of the plane, I can see the tip of the wing as well as the tarmac below. A cargo door slams below my seat, and a baggage handler wearing a fluorescent yellow reflective vest with matching headphones walks to his train of empty baggage carts and drives off. We back away from the gate. The guy in the middle seat next to me looks like a college student who's way too excited and overly cheerful. I put in my earphones to indicate that I don't want to talk, but he insists.

"Are you an architect?" he asks.

"No. Why do you ask?"

"You don't look like a bloke, but more like an artist of some sort." (Bloke?)

"Close. I'm a composer."

"So do you write music for films or video games?"

"Not yet."

"Has any of your music been performed?"

"A couple of things." Time to get out of this interrogation. "Well, you don't look like a *bloke* either. Are you an artist?"

"Kind of. I'm an *architect*," he says with the panache of someone who identifies with his *raison d'être* before having engaged in it.

"Cool. Has any of your work been built?" Now it is *he* getting itchy.

"A couple of things." (In my mind's eye I see blueprints for a tool shed and a chicken coop in Arkansas.) "I'm taking a semester abroad to study architecture in Frankfurt," he says. (I wasn't aware that Frankfurt was famous for its buildings.) "Aren't you afraid of A.I.?"

"I'm not sure what you mean."

"Artificial Intelligence. There's this new program that can compose music, and they say it's as smart as Beethoven. Maybe soon you won't be able to sell your music."

"If I were writing music to make money, then I would be worried, but that's not why I create. It's a spiritual thing. You're an architect; you must understand."

"Oh yeah. Sure, of course."

At just this moment, a fight attendant approaches and asks if either of us is willing to change seats with an old lady in an exit row since passengers in exit rows need to be strong enough to open the door in case of an emergency. Not wanting to give up my window seat, I flatter my neighbor by nominating him as the younger and stronger of us. He smiles with pride and moves off to the better seat. A moment later he is replaced by an ancient woman wearing a beautiful blue and gold batik jacket.

She speaks to me in Indonesian. "*Apa kabar*," she says with a smile that includes flat teeth and halitosis. I assume it is a greeting, so I repeat the same to her, then put my earphones back in. She's seasoned enough and polite enough to get my message without being offended.

Once we are at altitude, there is a sudden flurry of activity as the flight attendants rush down the aisles passing out the promised meal and tiny cups of water. Due to the delay, the box of noodles is probably not as warm as it should be, but it tastes pretty good and I think it's safe. Still, I add extra hot sauce as a psychological prophylaxis against a fear of food poisoning. As soon as I finish, the efficient women return and whisk away everyone's dishes and cups. Without a beat, there is another interruption as the flight attendants hand out tiny pillows and blankets—I'd better make myself as comfortable as possible—including the pit stop in Germany, it's 23 hours to Singapore.

The long flight gives me time to ponder things. And I've come to realize just how much information I missed in my life up to this point, especially how many clues I missed, and I conclude that a wealth of what I assume to know in my quixotic reality has been distorted through the lens of my romantic assumptions, or communicated through misunderstanding. How I misunderstood the depth and nature of Amity's genius, Timo's references to Baker, and in both Marga *and* Yulia, the complex intertwining of artistic drives and biological urges—two different expressions of the same creative force. But what surprises me most is the revelation, and extent, of Amity's secret life. There is so much that she withheld from me, which I suppose parallels what I kept from her. Apparently the selfish belief that the other didn't have a need to know, was mutual.

* * *

Since the incident at Sector B, I repeatedly have been drawn back into my past. And I've found that when I travel backwards in time, I compress the present like a spring, so that when I return to the present, I leapfrog time, bypassing many of my "nows." In whatever form it's conducted, time travel carries with it the high probability of regret over things lost in the collapsing interstices. Those days lived in memories have been the shortest days of my life. Consequently, just for today, I'm struggling to stay out of the past. But there's not much incentive to live in the present moment either, since the constant routine required to sustain life gets boring, and boredom leads to apathy and ennui—a direct line to the temptation to review the past. Fortunately, my life has never been routine. Still, I think the way to avoid becoming a sad-sack is to borrow that technique from the philosophers and gurus and stay in the present moment. So. At this moment I am in a chilly jumbo jet roaring across the Atlantic ocean, and the flight attendants have just turned off the cabin lights.

I'm glad that I chose a window seat because I have something to look at other than the selected movie—Hollywood's latest version of giant battling robots laying waste to an evacuated megapolis with their collateral damage. Outside the window, the wing tip bounces from minor turbulence, but the sky is mostly clear. Moonlight reflecting off the ocean below gives the waves a sparkle that resembles the texture of a cheese grater. I've never flown at night before, so this is a new experience. Since the incident at Sector B, my sleep has been very irregular and I often have insomnia until just before dawn. But I'm leaving all that behind. Maybe when I get to Jakarta, the jet lag will reset my internal clock. What Amity said about Professor McGill is now true about me: I am traveling to the other side of the world, which is about as far away from my problematic past as I can go without leaving the planet. The dark mood is lifting. I plug my headphones into the armrest and dial up the classical music channel. The music is light and bright and colorful: François Poulenc's *Sextour*.

When the Poulenc ends, I am wrenched out of my nap by a growling bass tuba playing a Ralph Vaughan Williams concerto. After Poulenc's fresh and fruity sextet for winds and piano, this dark and burbly brass feels as tepid as a sonic mud-bath. It's 1 AM back in Cleveland, and inside this plane it's bed time for everyone but me and, I hope, the pilots. My neighbor, Madame Batik, is sitting bolt upright with eyes closed, perfectly quiet and perfectly still, like a mannequin advertising transcendental meditation. I might need to use the water closet, but I don't want to disturb her so will try to hold my water until we get to Germany.

I use the wifi to check my email. Professor McGill has sent me another terse missive that sounds like an afterthought to his previous message: *When people meet you here, they will ask if you are married. Don't be surprised. They're not prying, it's just something they do. Like Americans always asking what you do for a living.*

Great. More impossible explaining to do.

42

The Hand on the Tiller

Dialing through the audio selections, I come across some old techno-pop disco dance music. It's minimalist yet complex and continually building. It turns out to be the intro music to an all-night talk show called *Wall-to-Wall at Night.* The host is a reporter from Las Vegas named George who specializes in paranormal topics. Tonight, George is filling in for the regular host whose name is also George. After giving a rundown of weird news headlines, George introduces his guest.

"Now that the world's governments are finally releasing—slowly releasing—information from their secret vaults of UFO research, we're beginning to get an idea of just what we're up against, and maybe some insight into why they kept it secret for so long. Tonight our first guest is a retired Navy captain and former Naval Attaché to the US embassy in Sweden, who worked in the Office of Naval Intelligence before he moved on to top secret, special projects. He is now a laser-focused investigator on the topic of Unidentified Aerial Phenomenon, also known as UAPs, formerly known as UFOs. His extensive access to classified information—the kind of stuff most ufologists would drool over—has led him to believe that these craft

are solid, three-dimensional objects, and that they pose a real physical threat to the entire human race. In a little while he will give us his analysis of the recent spate of sightings and what it might portend for national and international security, and why we need to be a lot more concerned about these objects than we currently are. With that I welcome for the first time on Wall-to-Wall, Captain Ulrich Baker. Captain Baker, it's a real honor to have you on the show tonight."

Then I hear that voice from the Christmas party.

"Thank you George. I am likewise honored to be here." (My head is swimming.)

"As you probably know, I've been researching and reporting on UFOs for almost five decades, and I have heard all sorts of different stories from witnesses and abductees. And the one thing I've never been able to determine with any certainty is the real intent of the UFO occupants. I've been told that they are saviors come to heal our suffering planet, demons leading us to Hell, and just about everything else in between, including that they are evolved human beings from the future visiting Earth on some kind of archaeological junket. So why don't I just go straight to the big question I'm sure everyone is asking. Why do you think they are a threat to humanity?"

"That's a good question, George. There are any number of reasons to come to that conclusion. One of which is the abduction phenomena you alluded to in your opening remarks. Friendlies don't abduct people against their will, perform unwanted medical tests, insert tracking devices, or impregnate human women to create chimeric offspring. It's bad enough that this kind of thing used to happen to one-in-a-million people worldwide, but these crimes against humanity—and that's truly what they are—are now happening at an alarmingly accelerated pace. There are incidents that your audience has probably read about in the news or seen

on Tucker Carlson's show, of UAPs harassing Navy warships and interfering with our pilots in the course of their aerial maneuvers. And these—we'll call them 'alien invaders' for lack of a better term—these invaders are stepping up their intrusions into our restricted airspace over nuclear silos and nuclear power plants. Any of these infractions, if done by a rival nation, would be a big enough violation that it would be declared an act of war and trigger the appropriate military response."

"Well, realistically Captain Baker, our military—as advanced as it is in human terms—is in no way capable of contending with craft that can pop in and out of dimensional space-time. Unless you have some top secret equipment you're not telling us about." (He chuckles.)

"You're funny, George. But you are also correct. Right now, there is not a military in the world that can face this challenge alone. To save our sacred democracy, in fact our very civilization, we will need total global cooperation among nations, and undoubtedly a unified governing body. All of this will require massive funding for research and development."

"How much funding do you estimate?"

"George, we'll need to develop all-new technologies to fight interstellar or inter-dimensional enemies. The cost is really unknown, but for a start, I'd estimate three to four times the current defense budget."

"So you're talking about four trillion dollars!"

"It may even be north of that number. We may well need to mortgage the gross international product of future generations to fight this war today, though I expect it will be a very long war. And ironically, it's probably the one thing that can unify all of humanity. But what's the alternative? Are we willing to pay the cost of surrendering our children—our children's children—and *their freedoms and way of life, so that gray aliens, giant mantises, or reptilians can use them as slaves, guinea pigs, or steaks on the table?"*

"Wow! On that somewhat-less-than-cheerful note, why don't we take this short break and pick it up in a few minutes with some phone calls. If you want to be a part of the show, and if you have questions or comments for Captain Baker, you can use the instant message app, text, email, or call us at..."

Some spooky and spacey bumper music in a minor key fades in with plenty of echo effect. Perfect.

I should have known that the purpose of his project was to make money—in this case *take* money from tax-payers. When you get to the bottom of most Earth-shattering phenomena, especially wars, there always seems to be somebody with one hand in the till, and the other on the tiller steering for Treasure Island. Of course, Baker can't be alone in a scam this byzantine. It takes a lot of propagandists to create fear-porn on a scale as large as his operation will require. People can be driven half-mad by fear of their imagined destruction. Nor can they turn away from their terrible, hypnotic thoughts any more than they can put down some eldritch book by Edgar Allan Poe or H. P. Lovecraft.

I use the radio show's long commercial break to craft my question, give it an intriguing title, and send it from my phone via email over WiFi. After a few phone calls from people sharing stories of the inexplicable fear they continue to feel after seeing a UFO, George asks his producer about what's come in on the message lines.

We have an interesting email from Jonathan who is listening to us on a trans-Atlantic flight. He writes, "Thank you for your service, Captain Baker. I have two questions. First, would you be able to re-create a system as complex as a UFO if you had only a concept and an excellent group of engineers, with an exceptional scientist—let's say a physicist of Nordic type—in charge? And second, witnesses have seen UFO lights cycle through a number of colors before the craft takes off. We know that cobalt is disruptive, but which hue is the hardest to hold?"

"Good questions," Baker says. "Your listeners are really well-informed, George."

"Aren't they amazing?"

"I think Jonathan may be referring to that flap—a rash of sightings—they had in Cleveland a month or so ago. People there reported seeing a brightly-glowing sphere that rapidly changed color and could travel extremely fast or extremely slow with no visible means of propulsion."

"Yeah, I remember that story. What about the possibility of re-creating a UFO?"

"I think Jonathan has a good idea. With the right people and equipment, anything is possible. Though I have no interest in engineering."

"And what about Jon's question regarding the cycling of colors by UFOs? People say the Cleveland UFO turned gold right before it flew away."

"It probably has to do with frequencies of vibration. But one thing I do know, 'Nothing gold can stay.'"

Baker is communicating directly with me in a code that no one else could possibly know. And I feel he is also connecting with me in a psychic way like that of some practiced adept. I feel ecstatic and frightened at the same time. It's a strange emotional lemonade that I taste in my jaw and stomach muscles. But the more I think about it, the less worried I am. I didn't reveal any of his secrets, I just let him know that I am still here, and for what it's worth, I'm not intimidated.

I unplug the headphones and look out the window at the Atlantic Ocean below. Its sparkle has changed—the moon is at a different angle from what it was before. I follow the wing to its terminus at an amber marking light. Amber? I've never seen amber lights on a plane before. Plane markers should be the same as those of any ship: port is red, and starboard is green. I'm sitting on the right side, so if there is any marker to see, it should be green. I look closer and notice that the light isn't connected, and it's farther away than it appears. It might be a lighthouse off in the distance. But it doesn't move. It just hangs out there pacing our jet at 600 miles per hour.

The instant I squint my eyes to focus on it, the ball of light snaps to just about 20 yards off of the wingtip, still pacing. The color shifts to a deep burgundy red, then the ball seems to disappear. I've seen this gimmick before, so I keep my eyes trained on the spot. When the ball reappears, it changes from red to deep blue, purple, then a dusky, ghostly white with an ultraviolet halo. I'm trying to remember the sequence of colors on Amity's flaming chariot when Madame Batik lets out a brief percussive *eek!* and grips my left arm with her fingernails. "Jinn!" she says in a loud whisper so as not to alert the demon. I punch my reply into translate and it tells her what I mean to say, "*Bukan jin, Hanya manusia.*" "Not a genie, just people." Relieved, she holds my arm with both hands and hides her head slightly behind my shoulder. Outside, the orb has shifted into its misty 24 karat gold color, and accelerates past us leaving behind a trail of sparkling metallic-looking plasma. Less than a minute later, two fighter jets pass us on either side with a thunderous roar causing the plane to buck in their wake. The captain calmly explains that we are experiencing some turbulence and to: "Fasten your seat belts. Please!"

There is a flurry of activity in the front of the plane, and soon a stewardess makes her way to my row. "Sir!" I'm still entranced by the sparkling trail outside, and don't immediately understand that she is addressing me. She looks nice, but looks can be deceiving—this woman is as tough as buffalo gristle.

"Sir you must close that window shade immediately!"

"Why? I'm just..."

"Are you disobeying a direct order from the captain?"

"No ma'am."

"Good." she says, then reaches across us and slams down the sliding plastic window shade.

The incident reminds me of how little control I have over anything, and just how fragile my freedom may be. Then, as the plane dances on the turbulence, I become keenly aware of the absence of *terra firma* beneath my feet, which curiously enough, makes me laugh. I lean my head on the little pillow against the wall and pull the airline blanket over my head and shoulders. I have no alternative but to go along for the ride.

43

The Next Leg

Soon we land in Frankfurt to refuel and swap out some passengers. Everyone is directed to exit the plane with our personal items. Once we pass through metal detectors and our bags through x-ray machines, we are herded into a glass-walled waiting room that is guarded by imperious-looking security guards brandishing automatic rifles. Madam Batik sticks to my side like an old friend. No one speaks. After an hour, we are led single file into the hallway and ordered to wait while a canine team sniffs for contraband. Through the glass walls I see two soldiers with long-handled mirrors looking at the undersides of the seats we just vacated. Nobody is arrested. We are now cleared to leave the country we never officially entered.

* * *

In a few days I will have a cup of coffee with Professor McGill in Jakarta. Although I hardly know him, I wonder if he will act differently when he is away from his betrothed Chiara. I wonder if he will notice a difference in me sans Amity—or any other friends for that matter. I plan to pick his brain regarding that philosopher's concept of epoché and how the suspension of disbelief helps him understand reality, especially when accepting the *unreality* of my experience already requires such a colossal suspension of disbelief.

* * *

Flying with the Earth's rotation—anti-clockwise, as they say— should enable us to travel more quickly, except for the fact that we're still held back by the planet's gravity (something Amity doesn't worry about anymore). This penultimate leg of the trip is the longest part—about 12 hours to Singapore where I'll catch a shorter flight to Jakarta. There's a breakfast of spicy noodles, and a lunch of rice and curry, a snack, and soon some dinner to be offloaded from a rolling cart. I think the reason for all the meals is to break up, for us *and* them, the long and tedious ride on autopilot. There are also movies, magazines, and meditation, but it's really impossible to sleep, even though most passengers seem to manage. I suspect they've taken motion sickness medicine, which evidently is just a sedative and their sleep a mild coma.

Sometime after dinner, and mostly from boredom, I drift off into a dream. I am in a noisy warehouse, a factory that produces a loud droning sound as a byproduct of making whatever it makes. I notice that if I focus on that persistent pink noise, I can isolate every note and chord I've ever written—and some combinations I've never imagined. I also notice that I am hungry, which imme- diately transports me to the factory employees' lounge. There is just one vending machine, and the only thing it dispenses is milk, served at body temperature. I push on the buttons, but all it delivers is change: lots and lots of small change—rare and valuable change—but nothing to eat. I awaken with a sour taste in my mouth.

The cabin is relatively quiet and dark with the exception of a black video screen displaying a regional map with our flight path as a green line over countries' borderlines which are outlined in red. Presently we are flying directly above Iraq. I think of ancient Babylon, Nebuchadnezzar, and Jimmy Strong. I try to calculate the time. It might be noon in Cleveland, but it seems to be about 4 AM on this plane, though it may be only 8 or 9 PM. By factoring in all the variables including delays in arrival and departure times in the different time zones, adjusting for degrees of longitude from Greenwich Mean Time, and employing all the liberal arts math I know—I've given myself a tension headache. I finally give up and accept the fact that in order to calculate exactly where we are in the flow of history, I'd have to be a mathematical savant.

Madame Batik has surrendered to exhaustion and slouches forward with her chin resting against her chest and her arms lying loosely in her lap—looking for all the world like a marionette that's had its strings cut. I put my little blanket over her neck and shoulders. It feels good to have a friend again. I turn up my collar against the airplane's chilly breezes, then fold my arms and settle back into my seat. Slowly and quietly I slide up my window shade. Outside the sky is dark and I can see nothing of the land below us.

* * *

When we arrive in Singapore, Batik and I are the last passengers to leave the plane. There is a two hour wait for the Garuda flight to Jakarta, so we're in no hurry. She lets me know with words I don't understand and hand gestures I do, that she needs help with her bag that is still in the compartment above the seat she traded with the young architect. As she is signifying, I notice that she is wearing a sparkling diamond tennis bracelet, and her bag, which is an expensive job from one of those French clothing designers, is heavy. She leads the way while I waddle behind, somewhat off-kilter from the uneven weight of our bags. The flight crew and attendants who bid us farewell at the door are unable to sustain their forced smiles until we are off the plane. As soon as we exit the plane onto the gangway, they sigh.

In Singapore's Changi airport, anyone making a through connection to another country must stay in the international zone behind a glass wall that separates us from the rest of the city-state. I can only catch glimpses of the airport wonderland that includes flower gardens and a circular waterfall. When we arrive at the waiting area for our next flight, Madame Batik leads the way to two empty seats away from the crowd, then signs for me to hold her place while she goes to the rest room with her bag. She's gone so long that I begin to wonder if, after our short friendship, she too feels comfortable enough to abandon me. Her return a few minutes later proves to me that I cannot trust my own powers of prophecy.

During her time in the ladies' room, Madame Batik managed to wash up, brush her teeth, change her clothes, do her hair and makeup, and in the process, chisel off from her appearance about a generation and a half. She no longer looks like a tired old grandma, but instead, a vibrant business executive with a peppermint smile. I'm stunned. I gesture my approval of her transformation. She shakes her head and waves her hands as if to say that it's not for me. But her appreciation of my compliment is clear: people everywhere like to be told that they are pretty.

44

Who Needs Words?

Madame Batik sits and looks out the window where planes are coming and going, and begins speaking in her native tongue, which to me sounds mostly like rolling 'R's, 'B's' and 'D's'. Occasionally there is a word I understand, like *teknologi* and *politik.* Whatever is on her mind, it's deep. And personal. She is probably grateful that I don't understand her words. Although we've been through a lot these many hours that we've been neighbors, we are still strangers operating with that principle of "intimacy on encounter," so she can be fully honest knowing that her words will not return as fodder for embarrassment or blackmail.

Unlike most women I've listened to in my life, Mme. Batik rarely looks at me while she talks. She mostly stares out the window at all the take-offs and landings of other people's lives. I focus as closely as I can, and try to hear something in the tones and pitches. Her voice is clear and in the range of a lyric contralto. With a few years of training under a good voice coach, she might be able to sing *The Rape of Lucretia.* As she speaks, she adjusts a perfectly fine white silk bow around the collar of her white silk blouse. I can tell that whatever she's saying, it's all true—from her point of view, it's all true.

Never have I focused as closely on anyone's story as I am on Mme. Batik's. She rolls on softly and smoothly with rubbery words. "Brdrburdrd..." is what I hear, but in my mind I see a story. I see parties with glowing iridescent silk gowns, huge fragrant bouquets, and colorful music from a percussion orchestra. I see a little girl who grows up too quickly and abandons her mother to run off to Holland where she remains to this day incommunicado. I see a man whose presence is so distant that he might as well not be there. Are my creative juices concocting this narrative soup, or am I eavesdropping into her thoughts? I don't know. But if it is the latter, I am probably violating some ethical standards for mind-reading. She assumes I cannot understand her, therefore she is speaking freely. So for me to understand by some other means, some extra-sensory perception, likely constitutes a betrayal of her trust.

I refocus my attention in the moment and concentrate on her tones and her facial and physical expressions. When she looks sad, I frown and shake my head slowly. When she smiles, I mirror that. When it sounds like she's asking me a question, I put up my hands and shrug my shoulders as if to say, "Good question. I don't know either." A mental image that I cannot block drifts in from the left, of a man—her lover, or her husband, or both. And a death, with corresponding images and pain so intense that she blocks it from herself. She goes silent. I look at the floor. My mind begins to fill the empty space with a soundtrack I invent without effort. I agree to let my subconscious perform its forlorn concert as long as it records the score for me to write down at a later date. It will make a powerful third movement in a future symphony.

My chain of thoughts is broken when I feel the good lady's hand upon mine. Her skin is soft for her age—she is obviously not one to engage in manual labor like washing dishes or doing yard work. She smiles and nods in my direction as if to say that it's my turn to speak. I begin.

"You wouldn't believe the shit I've been through recently." She nods her head. "Three women have loved me," I tell her, "one a decade on the average. Two are now dead and one has flown off to Waterbury with an impudent bore in a weather balloon full of swamp gas. Anyway, it doesn't matter. As Uncle Dan says, *Che sera, sera* and all that happy horseshit."

"Hmm," Mme. Batik nods. Then softly, "Um hmm."

"But it *does* matter, does it not?" Mme. Batik turns her hands upward and shrugs her shoulders. "People say that everything is relative, but I say that everything is relevant." Batik nods. "Right now, in these two, one-way conversations we're having, you don't have a clue as to what my words mean, but, is that even true?" She shrugs. "I mean, I could talk to you about the things that I think are important and meaningful, but isn't everything? Important and meaningful that is?" She nods and shrugs at the same time. "Here we are sitting in a kind of airport detention center, but we could just as well be riding horses in Wyoming. The fact is, we appreciate each other's company even though we know next to nothing about each other. But it's the *humanity* of our encounter. We both have known death, so we both appreciate life—my life, your life, *our lives*. We are alive Madam Batik. We are alive!" She smiles a full smile and nods with an appreciative understanding—of something.

There is an announcement that I miss, but Mme. Batik hears. Still smiling, she stands and puts her bag over her shoulder.

She holds up her boarding pass and gestures for me to give her mine. I trust her. Why shouldn't I? I give her the pass which she takes with hers to the airline desk. After a brief discussion in Indonesian (and a little gift box from Mme. Batik) the clerk understands, and with a bounty of smiles and pleasantry, leaves her post and leads us to some wide seats in the first section of the plane. (Mme. Batik got me bumped up to first-class so that we could sit together!) Even though this is the last leg of the flight, we will ride the next two hours in comfort.

Now that our time together is nearing the end, and our conversation has virtually dwindled down to silence, I feel a bit sad. Mme. Batik is looking through the air travelers' "dream book," a glossy catalog of overpriced luxury items, and occasionally she shows me a photograph of expensive jewelry and then points to herself. I'm not sure if she is indicating that she wants these pieces or that she already owns them. For a fleeting moment I get the idea that she might be asking me to buy them for her. I shake that thought—not even a shameless gold-digger would be that audacious.

45

On the Red Carpet

When we arrive at Soekarno–Hatta Airport, the crew and passengers are more cheerful and pleasant than at any other segment of this journey. The stewardesses (and yes, they are all very obviously women) hold back the coach passengers while Mme. Batik and I are allowed to disembark. I am first to exit, and I pause just outside the door to wait for my travel companion. The gangway connection is not perfect, which reminds me of leaving Marga's office in the steel mill, so I reach for Mme. Batik's hand to help her across the threshold. This little gesture visibly brings her great joy. Once outside the plane she taps her foot a few times on the gangway floor as if to assess the stability of this not-as-of-yet terra firma. I hold out my elbow to give her something to hang on to, and say, "Grab a wing." She loops her arm through mine and, arm-in-arm, we walk together down the ramp.

Once inside the airport proper, we still have to go through customs. Mme. Batik shows me her passport and signals for me to give her mine. She then leads me by the arm to the head of the line at the customs checkpoint, and after a few friendly words and smiles with the agent, she picks up his rubber stamp and validates both her and my passports. Nearby, uniformed guards with rifles smile and nod to her. (The good lady has juice!)

Following Uncle Dan's advice, I have packed very few clothes—about as much as I could stuff into the maximum-sized carry-on bag—so there is no waiting at a luggage carousel for me. I pantomime a big suitcase and point to Mme. Batik. She shakes her head and pats her carry-on bag. I shake my head as well, and we continue on into the main concourse. We are getting a lot of looks from people who may be surprised to see an elderly Indonesian woman and a young American man walking together, seemingly as a couple. At one point, a paparazzo looking for a story asks if he can take our picture. Mme. Batik snuggles up to me and gives a big cheesy smile. The photographer loves it. The two have a short conversation and the photographer scribbles Batik's answers in his reporter's notebook. I wish I could understand more bahasa than "jinn" and "New York." She returns to my arm, happier than ever, and we continue on to...where? I'm supposed to meet someone from the university near the taxis. So I stop and point to the sign with the picture of a taxi, my friend Batik nods, and we press onward while a hundred people stare, all smiling and some waving.

Just inside the doors near the taxi stand there are dozens of limo drivers holding up signs. Mme. Batik is submerged in her phone and texting someone. I don't know my "point of contact" or what my driver will look like, so I just read the placards. As I examine every face, there is one that looks out-of-place. She is youngish, college age, wearing an ankle-length brown maxi skirt and a white blouse covered by a little batik-print jacket in matching brown that is similar to the blue jacket Madame was wearing when I first met her. The younger woman has long black hair in an old-fashioned classic style, rolled up in a bun on the back of her head and pushed forward so that it frames her face with a shiny black halo. She catches my stare, focuses for a split second, then remembers to hold up her sign:

J Brendel.

* * *

Ann O'Malley is my point of contact, guide, and translator while I am in Jakarta. She is a graduate student from the university's music department. Mme. Batik puts away her phone, and steps up to introduce herself. Ann appears to recognize Mme. Batik, squeals with delight, and puts her hands over her heart. The two women laugh, hold each other's hands, and act as if they are the best of friends. (Why should I be surprised? After all, there are only 280 million people in Indonesia, and coincidence seems to be a major component of my life.) I clear my throat.

"Oh, Mister Brendel, I'm sorry. I am just so surprised to see that you know Soehita," Ann says with a heavy British accent.

"We only just met on the flight from New York. I don't even know her name. I've been calling her Madame Batik because of her pretty jacket that looks a lot like yours."

"Soehita was a movie star when she was young. She is still a star. Only now she is more famous as a jewelry and clothing designer. My jacket is her brand—she designed it."

"Oh that makes sense. She kept showing me jewelry from the airline magazine." Soehita speaks deeply and quietly to Ann. Ann shakes her head and waves her hand to dismiss the comment.

"What is she saying," I ask.

"She thinks that you and I are a couple." Soehita speaks some more. "She says that you are a very kind man who listens attentively to her when she speaks, and that is rare. She also says that you are very brave and that you chased away some kind of ghost or demon that was following the plane."

"Oh yes. The jinn." Ann looks surprised.

"Sounds like you had a very interesting trip. I didn't know that you speak bahasa Indonesia."

"I don't. But her heart speaks through the music of her voice." Ann translates, and Soehita speaks low and close. Ann blushes. "What did she say?"

"She said that when you ask me to marry you, I should accept." I feel my face heat up. I remember what Professor McGill texted me about marriage being a common topic of conversation. So I switch to questioner.

"Is Madame Batik, I mean Soehita, married?"

"She was married," Ann replies, "to a former governor of Java. But he died in a terrible accident."

"Oh, I think I saw that. Tell her I'm sorry."

"Maybe I won't translate that. She doesn't know what we're talking about. It was a very sad time in her life." I nod. Of course, this is what I saw when she spoke to me in Singapore. It confirms that my ESP is working. Ann and Soehita have another lively and rapid interchange that Ann interprets for me.

"Soehita's chauffeur is stuck on the other side of town with a flat tire. She asks if we can drive her home. I told her we'd be honored, and she said she'd like to treat us to lunch. I hope you don't mind." We step through the exit doors into a zone where the frigid airport air mixes with clove cigarette smoke from the taxi drivers. A little farther and the intense tropical heat hits me with a heavy blanket of steam that yields just enough for us to enter into and be enveloped by its dimension. We walk to the car.

Soehita sits next to me in the back of the silver Mercedes, and Ann sits up front with the university's driver, Udin. Soehita is busy talking, making the two laugh, as Udin navigates the rivers of motorcycle traffic through the enormous metropolis. Soon we arrive at a little noodle shop in an open storefront. Ann explains that this is called a *rumah makan*—a restaurant with food service in the front, and the owner's living quarters in the back. Soehita must be a friend or family of the owner, since she goes directly into the back room and distributes gifts (like an Auntie Santa Claus) among the squeals of joyful reunion. Outside, on the curb, an entrepreneurial mechanic is using a toothbrush to clean motorcycle parts in a coffee can half-filled with gasoline. Udin waits in the car.

Ann and I sit at a small table with four red, molded-plastic chairs. The tabletop is white Formica with a pattern of blue and green fireworks or dandelions gone to seed. In several places, from age and frequent use, the hard plastic has been worn down to the wood. If I knew when the restaurant first opened, the abrasive quality of ceramic dishes, and the wear-rate of Formica, I could probably calculate how many meals have been served at this table. But even imagining the level of involvement required for that kind of mathematics scares me. (Not that I am afraid of maths *per se*, but rather, lately, I am afraid of wasting precious time on pointless endeavors.) Instead, I become engrossed in this worn spot and the different layers of color—five, it seems— and the lives that rendezvoused here, grew closer, made plans, and shared experiences here. I recognize with awe that it is a correlate to the chipped layers of paint I saw in my dream of the composers' party in New York. Ann sees that I am staring at the scarred tabletop, and apologizes for subjecting me to an atmosphere that she assumes is beneath my station in life. I tell her that the table reminds me of one from my childhood, and she is visibly relieved. I realize that I am slouching. It must be the onset of jet-lag. When I straighten up to correct my posture, my elbows stick slightly to a dried glaze of cooking oil on the table, and I am faced with another calculation that I will not entertain.

With new spring in her step, Soehita dances out of the kitchen carrying a bag of take-out containers and two iced coffees stuck into a cardboard cup tray. She walks right past us with an impish smile and a wink to deliver lunch to Udin in his car, and a coffee to the motorcycle mechanic who signifies gratitude by placing his greasy hand over his heart. The place has such a homey atmosphere that I feel I am already a completely welcome member of the family.

A middle-aged woman emerges from the back room wearing turquoise clam digger pants, a half-apron with a lemon tree pattern, a blue bandanna around her forehead, and a red tee shirt with the face of an angry steer and the team's name misspelled as "Chicsgo Bsullu." She serves us two bowls of chicken soup with noodles, vegetables, and fish balls. Ann puts a spoonful of fresh chili pepper paste in hers and I follow suit. The pepper is much too spicy, and instantly sears my taste buds and reveals the smarting cracks in my chapped lips. Although nobody notices that I'm in pain since my facial muscles are frozen in a nervous grin.

Soehita reappears just ending a phone call, and through Ann, explains that her chauffeur has fixed the tire and the car is now waiting outside. She hands us each a large business card of thick stock, edged in gold, and makes Ann promise that we will all get together again soon. Joined by the restaurant owner, her family, the mechanic, and now Udin, we walk her to the car—a limousine with long, blacked-out windows. There is a flurry of *bon voyage* conversation that is beyond my ken. I look at the large, colorful business card which reads:

Soehita's Fashion

Shiny & Pretty—Bright & Beautiful

Jakarta Sentral, Indonesia

When the car pulls away, the restaurant owner—who, I now learn, is named Dolly or Dali—leads Ann and me back to our table for some sweet desserts made with coconut milk, palm sugar, and something like small, chewy, bright green noodles over crushed ice. It soothes my torrefied throat and stomach. Our eyes meet and lock for a full measure.

"Isn't Soehita the most fascinating woman you've ever met," Ann asks.

"She's definitely fascinating, though I can't say I've ever met a *boring* woman." Ann looks into her glass and pretends to fish for the best green noodle.

"So," she says, "Are you married?"

"No. I almost was."

"Then she handed you the mitten. Why? What did you do?" (I'm not sure what she means, so I answer what I assume she wants to know.)

"*She* decided to marry a co-worker instead." Of course this is only a single two-dimensional explanation of a series of events that would require volumes to explain and analyze, and Ann must knows it too.

"So you couldn't decide, and she decided for you." (What confidence she has in her own analytical abilities—considering the dearth of facts. I wouldn't have expected such cheekiness from a relative stranger with a British accent. More intimacy-on-encounter, I suppose.) "Were you in love with her?"

"I'm not sure what that means anymore. I thought I knew, once. What does it mean to you?" Ann stares at me while she considers her answer.

"Decision. Love is a decision. People create a fantasy that moves them, then they call it love. But anything worthwhile is the result of a conscious choice. A friend of mine from Lebanon was forced to marry a man her parents chose for her. She didn't even know him. At first she was miserable with the idea of being sold off like chattel to some ugly old man. But then she decided that, whoever he was, she would make the best of it. And so she chose—she decided—to love him and be the best wife and partner she could be."

"How did it work out?"

"Quite well. She has decided to be happy, so nothing much can stop her."

"What about the ugly old man?"

"Turns out he wasn't so old or ugly after all."

"I see. That's helpful." Ann returns to her icy drink, aimlessly stirring the noodles while fishing for something pithy to contribute to our stalled conversation. Outside, a man with a pushcart rings his cowbell and a couple in office attire step up to buy some steamed buns.

"So," I ask. "Are you married?"

"No, of course not."

"Why 'of course not'?"

"I'm different."

"Well, *viva la difference*. Everybody is different. What makes you more so?"

"For one thing, I'm Indo, not Bumi." (I turn my palms upward and screw up my face to indicate incomprehension.) "I'm not 100 percent Indonesian. My father was Irish and my mother

Javanese. That makes me Indo. That genetic reality, over which I had no control, carries a stigma. Many people here don't like Indos."

"I guess it's the same everywhere. Some people will always find reasons to disdain others. My friend Jimmy used to say that no matter what you do in life, somebody will love you for it and somebody else will hate you for it. So stick with the winners."

"Quite." She pauses and looks off at her memories in the space between atoms. "My father was a traveling businessman when he met Mother. She moved to Ireland with him, and I was born in Belfast City. Mother thought it was too cold for children and brought me back to Jakarta where she makes and sells dresses in her own shop. When I was old enough, she sent me away to boarding school in Singapore. She thought it was a finishing school, but academically, it was quite rigorous."

"Is your father still alive?"

"I don't know. But because he is not around, and he is not Indonesian, people accuse me of being born on the wrong side of the blanket. Anyway, that's why I'm not married—permanence is not a condition of my experience." She stops and scrutinizes me with curiosity. I consciously stifle the flirtation I had been building up. "Everything is temporary, Mr. Brendel. We strive to extend the desirable experiences. We hope for, and fantasize about, some person who will save us from the entropy—the collapsing world that we live through moment by moment. We elevate and adorn the other with unrealistic notions of permanency." (Another scientist philosopher—I'm getting much more than I asked for.) "Then there are other people who look at me as something exotic, and they fetishize me because I am different."

"Everyone *should* seem exotic to everyone else—we're all

so different. Still, I don't go in for idol worship; it's a first commandment thing with me."

"Idols, be they made of wood, stone, or flesh and blood will always let you down."

"I agree. Worship is wrongly placed on another human being," I say, pretending to keep up with her logic.

"No human can live up to such veneration and expectation. When the inevitable disappointment occurs, the worshiper feels cheated and trapped as if through some deception. And at the rate that people change, one runs the risk of becoming useless overnight." (Time to bring this back to the concrete.)

"Sounds like you've had some first-hand experience with this."

"I am not a child, Mr. Brendel. Nor am I a victim of social trends—you'll find no tattoos or piercings on me."

As I listen, my gauze-veiled impressions of this woman are peeled, layer-by-layer. I recall that mischievous question asked by adolescent boys: "If you and she were the last two humans alive, and were stranded together on a tropical island, would humanity survive?"

I wonder.

46

The Right Word

During the car ride to the university, Ann asks what I plan to teach the music students about composition. I tell her that I'm not sure what they know about Western music in general and my music in particular, so we may need some time to develop a palette we can work with. She tells me that everyone is familiar with my work, and that they particularly enjoyed my concert of *In Reverentia Temporis* performed by the Cleveland Orchestra at Severance Hall. How is that possible? They downloaded a bootleg video recording of it from a music website in China.

At the university, Ann shows me to my room—a dormitory suite for special faculty—and hands me a canvas shopping bag full of university promotional items, bottled water, instant 3-in-1 coffee, some snack food and a magazine. She lives nearby in the women's dormitory, so I should call her if I need anything.

At any time.

Within reason.

Of course.

When she leaves, I microwave a cup of the bottled water for some instant coffee. A knock at the door precedes the entry of

Udin with a case of instant noodles. He makes an apology I don't understand and carries the box into the kitchen area, then exits with a nervous smile and a nod of the head. I microwave a second cup of water.

At my little desk, I examine the rest of the contents of Ann's gift bag, then change out of my sweaty, wrinkled clothes and into a pair of gray university-branded gym shorts and a university-branded tee shirt in deep gold. I adjust the air conditioning setting down to 65° F and settle in for instant noodles and instant coffee. Last item in the bag is the latest issue of the international new music journal, *Tempo*, bookmarked to an editorial within. The title surprises me: "What Brendel Deserves." I read.

"A guest editorial should not require a disclaimer since it can be assumed that the opinions are the writer's alone and not those of the publication, but there you have it. While I am not in the habit of using my precious column inches to question the opinions of music critics, this is one occasion where the views of a petulant journo at the New York Times are so far removed from the reality I experienced that I have to seriously consider whether the hit-piece was politically or personally motivated. Ordinarily the Gray Lady confines items of 'fake news' to assaults on opinions that vary from her well-established political and social proclivities, but her publishing of the harshly delusional critique of Jonathan Brendel's masterful composition, *In Reverentia Temporis*, shows blatant disregard—if not contempt—for composition and exploration in the musical arts.

"As luck or fate would have it, while visiting friends in Ohio, I was graced with tickets to the glorious Severance Hall where I witnessed a unique moment in musical history with the world premiere of Brendel's composition interpreted by the amazing vocal goddess, Yulia Sophia Pasternak, and the legendary Cleveland Orchestra under the baton of Maestro Franz.

"For those of us who were fortunate enough to have been there—and the house was packed—we beheld a confluence of artistic powers that produced an experience on par with the premiers of Beethoven's *Fifth*, and Stravinsky's *Le Sacre du printemps*. Brendel's work is not an Earth-shattering commencement of a new concept or style; there is nothing in the composition itself that would identify it as avant-garde; this is not Cubism, Dada, or Minimalism; I would not even describe it as breaking new ground; however, just as composers in the Romantic Period shifted their focus to man and man's emotions, so too Brendel shifts the focus back to where it should be—on the cosmic and eternal—and he executes this shift so powerfully, that it moves the listener emotionally. Not one person present that night, including the musicians and Brendel himself, could deny the transcendent effect of *In Reverentia Temporis*. The work is truly sublime.

"How startled and disappointed I was then, a day later, to read a scathing review in the self-proclaimed 'paper of record.' The writer of that review, whose name I shall not elevate by publishing it here, called the work 'derivative.' In fact, this petty criticism seemed to be his major complaint. 'Derivative,' he repeated again and again with a snarl, as if it were possible to write any work that could be wholly detached from music history. Even *if* the task of escaping from precedent were possible, and let's disregard the question of its being desirable, the 'new' work would still be derivative in its conscious avoidance of history's contributions. In fact, the unique work would necessarily be shaped by the spaces and components discarded by previous composers. To attempt such 'originality' would be a fool's errand, and as such, the Times' critic himself is well-qualified to make the attempt. As for Jonathan Brendel, he's too smart to play the *rebel sine causa.*

"Here is a good place to say a few words about originality, and I hope the critic is reading. I suggest that the next time he writes an article, he does so without using recognizable sentence structure, grammar, or parts of speech. In fact, if he uses any words at all, his work should be rejected as being derivative. Clearly, derivation is impossible to avoid. Is there a flute solo that can elude the memory of a birdsong? A violin that never crosses into the realm of human voice? Listen once again, Mr. Critic, to the consecrated voice of Yulia Sophia Pasternak as she interprets the holy scripture that is Jonathan Brendel's score, and then admit the truth: Everyone steals from God.

"Those of you who were fortunate enough to have attended Brendel's premiere definitely agree with me. I know because I heard your applause, and stood with your standing ovation. It was thunderous and unlike any I have heard in any concert hall. I also know that you agree because, like me, you cried tears of transcendence during the performance and tears of sadness when it ended. For a timeless ten minutes, Brendel coaxed the spheres into reaching down and lifting our souls out of the mundane and into the ethereal. A lucky person may have this kind of experience but once in a lifetime. I know for me, it was a first.

"I have never met Jonathan Brendel, though I feel that I know him quite well. I know the quality of soul he contains because it clearly spoke through his music. I wish him only the best. If my praise for his praiseworthy music is any encouragement to him, then I will continue to lavish it. And if an elitist wag wishes to sit in judgment of Brendel's brilliance, I suggest that a little introspection, call it 'self-intercourse', may be in order. Let him read Longinus, *On the Sublime,* then revisit and ponder the pioneering contributions of Beethoven, Stravinsky, *and* Brendel. Classical music needs Brendel, and the listening world needs Brendel's next musical contribution."

"Sublime!" I yell, "Sublime!" then simultaneously laugh and cry out of exhaustion and into sleep.

47

Good Morning, Jakarta

Just before dawn, I am awakened by a riotous chorus of tropical birds competing with the Islamic call to prayer. I listen to the unintentional polyphony until the minarets surrender, then I read and re-read the *Tempo* article. ("Sublime" he wrote!) Around 6 AM someone slips a hard copy of the *Jakarta Post* under my door. There on the front page, with a promise of more in the Culture and Entertainment section, is a picture of Mme Batik and me arm-in-arm at Soekarno-Hatta Airport yesterday under the header: "Lady Soehita Makes Grand Return with 'Bad Boy of Classical Music.'" In the Entertainment section are pictures of Yulia and me on stage at Severance Hall, and more of Soehita and me at the airport. The gossip columnist makes oblique allusions to my herculean virility, and innuendos about how my insatiable drives have taken me from the trendy to the classy in just over one month's time. I chuckle, then pull in a deep breath—I have officially made it into the world of international stardom, and I now have my very own caricature to contend with.

I make a cup of instant 3-in-1 Indocafe. Uncle Dan calls. It's a busy morning.

"Hey Jon, hope I didn't wake you. How's the adventure?"

"So far, enormous. I just arrived yesterday morning."

"No matter how you cut it, that is one long-ass flight."

"Definitely. What are you up to?"

"I sold your car and got more than we expected, so I owe you a couple hundred bucks. Oh, and that friend of yours from the orchestra, the one with the mop-top who's a little light in the loafers…"

"Timo."

"Yeah, that's the guy, or whatever…anyway, Timo said you need to call him right away. Said he lost your number—if you can believe that." (He probably deleted it after the Times article.)

"OK, I wonder what *he* wants. I'll call him."

"Another thing, the mechanic who inspected your Audi at the dealership found an AirTag stuck with a magnet under the bumper."

"But I don't own an AirTag."

"That's what I figured, so I drove to a truckstop on Interstate 71 and slapped that bug onto a trailer headed for Mexico City. The Sherlocks and Pinkertons should rack up some hefty travel expenses chasing *that* wild goose."

I tell Uncle Dan about Madame Batik and Ann O'Malley, and he reminds me that I am supposed to "take a year's furlough from the skirts." I tell him not to worry. One would think that I may still be raw from the events back in Cleveland, but truth be told, as long as I stay focused on things outside myself, I don't feel distraught or sad or brokenhearted. In fact, I'm feeling pretty good right now, and one thing I've learned over the years is that when things are going well, I need to work fast and accomplish as much as possible while the luck or the blessing holds out. As Uncle Dan would say, make hay while the sun shines. I call Timo.

"Well well, if it isn't the creature who crawled out from the wine cellar," he says with flamboyant sass. "Where have you been? I thought you'd fallen off the edge of your flat Earth."

"Almost. I was offered a gig as a guest lecturer at Jakarta University." (That's about the easiest way to explain it.)

"Where is that? In Africa?"

"No. Jakarta. Java. Indonesia."

"Oh. Anyway, I have good news, but you have to thank me before I'll tell you."

"Thank you, Timo."

"You're welcome. So, remember that fusty old donor named Baker?"

"How could I forget?"

"Well, just yesterday he wired the money he promised the orchestra, so I put through the transfer to your bank account. Am I not wonderful?"

"You are indeed wonderful, Timo Van der Hout."

"But wait! That's not all! I'm not finished! Last week I got a call from the Library of Congress; they want a copy of your score from *Dignified Time*, or whatever you call it in Latin, so it seems the Koussevitzky grant is still alive."

I pinch myself to make sure that *I* still am. Timo says he has a date, and signs off with "Toodle-oo." There is a knock at the door—Ann. She apologizes for being "cheeky" yesterday, and invites me to breakfast.

* * *

Udin opens the car door for us in the excellent spirit of one who is getting substantial overtime pay for this jaunt. Our destination, it turns out, is not a restaurant but a wet market—so called because most of the food is still clucking and mooing. Ann gives me a tour of the place, which reminds me in some ways of a county fair, then leads me to a food court inside where the animals have been (pardon the expression) cleaned and dressed for dinner. We eat a rice porridge with chicken and scallions, and for dipping, a long, deep-fried noodle that resembles a baguette. From another stall, we get coffee mixed with a blended raw egg—a concoction that tastes pretty much like coffee with heavy cream. The vendor communicates to me with crude and indelicate sign language that this philter is good for men. Ann ignores his raffishness.

At a picnic table in the shade, we linger over our drinks. Ann asks me what the main thrust of my seminar will be. Frankly, I was hoping to get some guidance from her as to the music department's expectations and how they promoted the course— but I'm coming to understand that it was less of a planned structured series, and more of an inspiration resulting from a music department brainstorming session. Therefore, I believe, I have all the leeway in the world. So I tell her that my focus will be on the ethereal, and for a quarter hour I wax eloquent regarding the spiritual aspects of composition. This type of soliloquy is easy for me to deliver since I am an habitué of the metaphysical realm—which is a nice way of saying that I function mostly in daydreams composed of music—and I think about music incessantly, so I am simply verbalizing the thoughts on which I meditate.

The incongruous sound of a bleating goat breaks my trance which delivers me a brief moment of self-consciousness and a logical jumping-off point—which I take. I know I said a lot, but I'll be darned if I can recall what it was. I shift my focus outwards to Ann. She is wearing a maxi dress again today. This gown is indigo blue with a large lace collar that lays flat across her shoulders and round on her back. It looks like a giant crochet doily of the kind called antimacassar that old ladies used to put over the tops of their wing-back chairs to protect them from grandpa's oily hair tonic. She looks enticing in a puritanical sort of way. And she is smiling at me with misty eyes and radiant admiration as if I were Albert Einstein talking about whatever he might have spoken about if he were I. Hers is the familiar look of infatuation, and it's a pity that I'm on furlough.

48

Captain's Log

We've had a busy semester. Throughout these weeks, I required my students to keep a journal of their thoughts in order to follow the evolution of their creative and intellectual development. I compare it to a captain's log from the days of long sea voyages. At first these books might have been written to absolve the captain of liability with the ship's owners in case of any calamity, but as the journey progressed, the logs recorded more and more of the ship master's thoughts and insights. At any rate, they make interesting reading for later generations. Once upon a time, a composition professor required me to keep a log. I figured that this semester would be a good time to resurrect that habit. Here are a few excerpts:

With a tip of the hat to Kandinsky's little book on art, I have titled my lectures *Concerning the Spiritual in Music.* Teaching this way sometimes feels like cheating, but I'm fleshing out my own ideas on creative theory as I guide these initiates into a world from which they can never return unchanged. I have also been working with the students one-on-one in a peripatetic style *a la* Aristotle's School. This way I can help them with the practical aspects of composition—harmony and the like—without subjecting them to peer pressures of any sort. God knows, the creative has enough pressure from *within* himself.

~

My idea of splitting the time between tutorials on composition (theory and technique) and lectures on the spiritual aspects of music and creativity, has turned out well. The students now take their work very seriously and most treat the process as sacred, no matter what their religious beliefs. In addition, since I've been mostly focused on teaching and motivating the students, I've been enjoying doing things, and have not written much about my own ideas. Maybe Amity was right when she said that happy people just live their lives.

~

Thought: Enlightenment comes not from the idea or even the process of composing, but from the very music itself.

~

Most of these students have a deep understanding of percussion, especially the gongs and xylophones used in their national gamelan music, and they are apt to incorporate those instruments as well as Javanese and Balinese scales as a foundation to whatever Western instruments they might want to showcase. I have decided to utilize their expertise by taking the joyful music I composed for Marga's fateful performance and transcribing it for flute and gamelan. Because of the tuning of these instruments, I had to recast the score in a Javanese scale with its three flats, which to me felt like I was driving a car in reverse while looking only in the mirror. The result is very pretty, but the scale and timbre now add a mysterious strength and gravitas beyond that of the original, and manage to catch those deeper dimensions of Marga's persona. I've renamed it, *Marga's*

Theme, subtitled: *In Amantes Memoria.* I am proud of the fact that I did not make her memorial work sad.In fact, my simple directions to the musicians include *Amoroso* and *Appassionato*.

May she finally rest in peace.

49

Konser

Each student composer, with the exception of those who created works for small ensembles, is also required to conduct or lead their performers. I told them to wear formal dress for the concert, so most of the young men are wearing traditional shirt jackets in brown and gold batik. Ann is wearing a long, form-fitting gown with a high neck in midnight blue, covered in matching sequins. Every little move she makes—including breathing—sets off a shower of sparkles. It reminds me of the Atlantic Ocean in moonlight from thirty thousand feet. My compliments to her mother the seamstress. I am overdressed in a tuxedo borrowed from the drama department's costume closet. I look like a *tipo suave* who gambles on *baccarat* in a French Riviera casino.

Since Ann is a voice *and* piano major, I have scheduled her original solo piano piece first in the lineup, and her vocal piece for the very end. When the concert begins, I watch from the wings off stage left. Ann is playing her *Piano Variations on a Theme by Chopin*. As she negotiates a cascading crescendo, she appears to be in a trance. When she opens her eyes she is looking directly at me. I have a flashback to the Gryphon Theatre in Laramie, Wyoming and another dear musician who wore her hair in a bun.

The sequence then follows based on the number of performers and grows in size up to mine, which requires the full ensemble. For the encore, which I was fully expecting, Ann sings a cheerful traditional song called *Seri Langkat.* I'm not sure how the audience truly feels about the new *Marga's Theme*, but my work was the penultimate, and Ann, now backed up by the full orchestra, does a slinky walk-dance across the stage as she sings, sequins flashing to the beat, leaving the audience exhilarated and on their feet cheering.

50

Green Room

After the concert we retire to a makeshift greenroom—actually it's a yellow classroom with one wall that has been draped with green bunting from a bolt of cloth that Ann borrowed from her mother's dress shop. There is a table set up for me to autograph the audience's programs and the musicians' scores. Another table is stacked with snacks including fresh tropical fruits and fried bitter padi oat crackers with a sticky, sweet and spicy coating. There are also syrupy drinks of impossibly fluorescent pink, smelling and tasting like the perfume of roses and orange blossoms, and adorned with colorful cubes of tapioca jelly. The students, musicians, friends, and family members are all in good spirits. My students are especially ecstatic knowing that their existence and participation in this workshop is a once-in-the-history-of-the-universe experience, and they are struggling to prolong it. It's a shame that Professor McGill did not attend. As a student of the phenomenology of place, he would have discovered in this event a new latitude.

Signs of the inevitable artistic postpartum letdown are beginning to show on the faces of the more sensitive—they will be the last to leave after volunteering to clean up. Some school officials come to thank me, then move off to join their colleagues near the door, and quietly disappear. A few of the more serious students hover around me hoping to get one more tidbit of wisdom with which to fuel the furnace of inspiration. To their delight, I share some sanitized versions of Uncle Dan's more useful maxims.

A familiar figure enters the room wearing a white slacks, a blue blazer and a purple and gold patterned hijab that covers her hair and wraps around her shoulders like an extended turtleneck. When she sees Ann, she calls out and the two rush together and hold hands like they did the first time they met at the airport. So engrossed are they in their excited, joyful chatter that they are unaware of the large circle of smiling fans gathering to see the superstar Soehita and her seemingly best friend. Soehita suddenly pauses as if remembering something she had forgotten, and reaches into her handbag for a small rectangular box. In an unexpected instant she removes a beautiful string of pearls and drapes them around Ann's neck. It is a perfect complement to Ann's outfit, and visibly moves the younger woman to tears. And yes, of course, they are real.

Partially as a diversion from her awkward emotions, Ann directs Soehita's attention toward me. The self-assured woman catches my eye and throws me a gesture that says, "Oh *there* you are!" and heads over to my table. Standing in front of me, Soehita points first at me, then the sky as she looks upward, and finally places both hands over her heart. I take this to mean that she was strongly moved by my divinely inspired work. She is talking seriously and a lot, which makes me regret not having learned enough of her language to get even the basic gist of her narrative. She takes hold of my hand with both of hers, passing me a small box as she does. I try to refuse it, but she closes my fingers and grips tighter, speaking all the while in quiet and deep tones. When she stops talking, she gestures with a nod of her head toward the other side of the room where Ann is chatting lively with her friends. I still refuse to take the box, but Soehita wins the struggle when she puts it into the pocket of my tuxedo jacket. I signal gratitude. Now she is happy. She walks back to Ann and her growing circle of new friends.

Across the room a Mediterranean looking man wearing a red fez is talking to a distracted woman dressed in a floor-length, lilac satin abaya with balloon sleeves and a matching headscarf. They are hard to miss, and I'm not sure how or when the couple entered without my noticing. Several of Ann's friends are working to convince her to go somewhere with them: the party after the party. But Ann, my point of contact, indicates with body language that she has a prior commitment with me.

I'm starting to unwind now. The pressures of teaching a semester-long music workshop and organizing this final concert are subsiding—I have fulfilled my requirements and self-expectations without regret, and without revealing my insecurities. The invisible band of stress that I've worn around my head like an undersized crown for the past months is steadily loosening. In this condition, I may be vulnerable to anything; I had better be careful.

The crowd is thinning out. A few, as I've explained, are hanging on until the bitter end, but most decide to leave before the happy times fully wane. In the end, the last person will probably be alone. That could be me. I autograph a program for a young student and then a second which she says is for her brother. I look back at the man in the fez. He is alone and texting on his phone. My mind blanks out for a few long seconds, and when it returns, I am startled.

Like a specter from a Gothic novel, the woman in lilac materializes from a blind spot just outside my peripheral vision. She lays down a program for me to sign. I click my pen without looking up. "Jonathan," she says, and I feel my head begin to tingle. I cover my eyes with my hands and I get a vision of a leather-bound title on the mantel above a fireplace: *Landed Nobility of Europe.* Tea is being served: little cucumber sandwiches and sweet brown bread smeared with clotted cream.

I open my eyes and look up with a jolt. A lock of red hair has escaped the headscarf. Her makeup is heavy, but it looks like her. I reach out and pull her left hand closer to my eyes—the laceration is now a jagged pink scar. "Doubting Thomas," she says.

"Marga..." I begin.

"Don't call me that anymore. It's not safe. Call me Hafsah. It means lioness."

"What happened to you? I thought you were..."

"Jimmy Strong saved my life."

"Jimmy Strong died for you!" Marga lowers her eyes. "How did you survive? I looked for you."

"I hid inside the pipe that Warner cut open. I stayed there until the sharks left. Then I took Jimmy's motorcycle. I was wounded. Pretty badly. I almost lost a rib. The bullet that killed Jimmy passed into me. We were married with blood."

"But where have you been? Why didn't you call?"

"Daddy took me to a private clinic run by a friend of his, then we flew to Aix-en-Provence so I could recover on Grandma's estate."

"Why didn't you at least call me?"

"I didn't think it was safe. Our maid said strange people were coming around in big black cars and watching the house." There is a long, timeless pause.

"So did you enjoy your stay in the south of France," I ask with sarcasm.

"Don't be mad at me Jonathan. I can't afford that. I did the best I could." (This is such a lame excuse for faking her own death.)

"I see. Well, now that you have a new identity and passport, I'm sure you can resume your globetrotting lifestyle."

"Actually Jonathan, I think *you* should travel more."

"Welcome to Jakarta, Madame X."

Marga covers her face with her hands, and I stare at the table. The words and names on the program, in Indonesian and English, seem ephemeral and yet ancient—now obsolete. My wonderful Indonesia experience has been spoiled, its significance greatly diminished by this surprise visitor. She's like a bad squirrel that sneaks into the garden and digs up the seedlings before they have a chance to take root. I don't know what to say, so I ask her, "Who's the Turk?"

"Oh, he's not Turkish. He's an Italian filmmaker I met in New York. He just likes to wear that fez. It gives him a different character."

"That it does, except when he's in Istanbul." I rest for a full measure. "Why did you come here, Marga?"

"I need to ask you a favor."

"Me? What can I possibly do for you? What can you receive from me?"

"I need you to meet me at the airport in Paris. Tomorrow. And please don't ask any questions." I write on her program and sign it.

"I'm sorry Marga. I can't do that." For the first time since I've known her, Marga displays the real fear and panic of uncertainty.

I hand her the program. She reads my message:

"A.B.C.M.A.Y.—Jonathan."

She covers her face with the program and rushes out of the room. The man in the red fez tries to catch up with her while faking nonchalance. The flurry of activity brings silence to the room. From a construction site outside the window comes the sound of a heavy chain falling to the pavement.

51

Dreamland

Ann approaches my table while the others steadily drift away.

"Do you know that woman," she asks.

"Not really. I thought I did, but I was mistaken."

"Good. You should avoid her."

"Why do you say that?"

"Her abaya—that dress. The style is from Dubai. That means she is either a rich man's wife or a gold digger. Either way, she would be bad for you."

"Thank you, Ann. I appreciate your concern. It means a lot to me." This remark makes her uncomfortable: still too much, too fast. I back off a little. At this moment she is the only friend I have.

"I've asked Udin to take us for something to eat," she says. "It's almost five o'clock, We can get some sammies and drinks and watch the sunset from Ancol."

I haven't been able to look at the night sky since the incident at Sector B.

* * *

Ann takes me to a cute restaurant decorated with colorful anime characters I can't identify and lots of pink everywhere. We buy some Australian style sandwiches wrapped in aluminum foil. Mine is Vegemite, which is like a bitter, beery, instant soup paste, sans water, spread over buttered toast. It is an acquired taste. When nobody's looking, I feed some to the seagulls then wrap the rest in the foil and put it into my pocket where it bumps into the box Soehita gave me. While Ann is focused on the seascape, I take a peek inside the box and see that it is a woman's engagement ring. Clearly, I'm not a jeweler, but I'm familiar with their sales pitches from my visits to the stores with Amity. From what I can guess, there is a two or more carat brilliant diamond in that setting. I quickly close the box and bury it deep beneath the sandwich in my pocket.

At *Ancol Dreamland* we walk under a heart-shaped arch to a promenade that leads to a heart-shaped dock called Love Pier. As a way of dismissing the blatant yet incorrect message implied by our being there as a couple in formal attire, Ann tells me that this is a very popular tourist spot with an excellent view. It *is* a beautiful waterfront park where tourists and lovers watch the sunset and eventually take their wedding pictures. But it's all a little much for me; I prefer more nuance. A pretty face, a sparkling ring, and honeymoon breakfast in Hawaii are no guarantee of a successful lifelong partnership. Besides, it's premature for all that kind of thinking since I still have nine more months of furlough from romance.

A vendor sells us his last fresh coconut with two straws.

52

A Ball of Gold

Evening lies off the northeast coast of Jakarta. On the sunset side, the steamy day is dimming to the orange-redness of a cooling ingot of freshly-poured steel, casting a lambent rose-gold that flickers on rippling waves extending to the horizon. The sun sets quickly and red. Civil twilight dims to nautical twilight and stars slowly fade into the dome above. A sliver of a moon rises in the east, and a cool breeze springs up from over the bay. For the people at Ancol Dreamland tonight, nature is delivering a hundred sensual memories to carry us through the less-luminous days of our lives to come.

As I breathe in the warm salt air and listen to the waves lapping against the pilings, star-like lights appear one by one in a perfect line over the eastern horizon. Ann asks which stars they are. "Elon Musk's," I answer. "They're satellites, not stars."

"They remind me of these pearls," Ann says as she fondles the gift that encircles her neck. "When are you planning to leave?"

"I haven't decided yet, but I probably need to move out of the dorm in the next day or so."

"No, you can stay for another week at least."

"How's that?"

"Our university President Artono wants you to stay until commencement day. Didn't he tell you?"

"No. He just stopped by my table to thank me."

"Oh. I'm sorry. Maybe he wants me to tell you. After the concert, he met briefly with the music faculty and they voted to give you an honorary degree: Doctor of Philosophy in Music."

I'm stunned.

"Ann, I don't know what to say."

"I think at the ceremony, '*terima kasih*' would be appropriate."

Smoke from a nearby kretek wraps us in the heady, holy incense of tobacco laced with cubeb and cloves. I lean against the rail and stare out at the green and red marker lights of fishing boats returning from their labors. Ann moves closer to me until her arm is gently touching mine. This is the first time we've touched since we shook hands at the airport on my arrival. "Will you return to America, or go somewhere else," she asks.

'Well, I'm definitely not going to Dubai." Ann smiles. "I may return to help my Uncle Dan move back to Wyoming. Have you ever been there?" Ann shakes her head. "Have you ever ridden a horse?" Again she shakes her head, this time with a sad mouth. "I can teach you how to ride." Ann smiles and presses closer to me.

"I would like that." She leans her head back and inhales the perfumed night air. "Do you like Ancol?"

"Tonight I do."

"So do I. This is the most beautiful night I've ever seen in Jakarta—so many stars and lights."

A new light appears from the north. It moves erratically—up one second and down the next. Then it begins to change color.

"Is that another satellite?" she asks.

"It's probably a weather balloon. See if you can get a picture of it."

While Ann is focusing her phone's camera, I unwrap my sandwich, drop it into the water, then enclose my phone in the aluminum foil.

The orb hesitates for a moment, wobbles, then splashes into the Java Sea like a golden ball of celestial jetsam.

THE END

Acknowledgments

My deepest gratitude to early readers and reviewers Helmuth Svoboda, PhD, JD, Mario Chioldi, PhD, G. Michael Sewell, Kathleen DeJesus, Virginia Haynes, and Keith Brickhouse.

Many thanks also to Olivia Zugay from Story Flow Solutions for her insights, advice, and guidance throughout the publishing phase.

Some who deserve thanks are no longer with us: John Cage provided his kind encouragement, warm hospitality, and artistic inspiration; Jeanne Moreau shared her insights on the art of performance, her moral support, and her excellent coffee; Paul Bunker whose love and knowledge of classical music and its personalities informed characters and scenes herein; And finally, architect, photographer, and long-time friend, Martin Munter for his kind and constructive commentary on early versions of the manuscript.

Alter ipse amicus.

About the Author

G.H. Karshner studied fine art at Cleveland State University and creative writing at The New School and Writers Studio in Manhattan. He has published in Florida Writers, Whiskey Island Magazine, and Machine Bolt Press. He has also written for film and theater. His latest work, *A Symphony in Blood and Rust* was a semi-finalist in the Royal Palm Literary Award Competition.

You can connect with me on:

🌐 https://ghkarshner.com

www.ingramcontent.com/pod-product-compliance
Lightning Source LLC
Chambersburg PA
CBHW031143160726
47991CB00004B/1544